D0179761

"Seldom does one get a thriller about white-collar crime, with an intelligent, independent lesbian and Asian protagonist. It's also rare to find a book with such interesting and exotic settings... Readers will find great amusement in Ava's unconventional ways and will certainly enjoy accompanying her on her travels." — *Literaturkurier*

## PRAISE FOR *THE DISCIPLE OF LAS VEGAS*
### FINALIST, BARRY AWARD FOR BEST ORIGINAL TRADE PAPERBACK

"I started to read *The Disciple of Las Vegas* at around ten at night. And I did something I have only done with two other books (Cormac McCarthy's *The Road* and Douglas Coupland's *Player One*): I read the novel in one sitting. Ava Lee is too cool. She wonderfully straddles two worlds and two identities. She does some dastardly things and still remains our hero thanks to the charm Ian Hamilton has given her on the printed page. It would take a female George Clooney to portray her in a film. The action and plot move quickly and with power. Wow. A punch to the ear, indeed." — J. J. Lee, author of *The Measure of a Man*

"I loved *The Water Rat of Wanchai*, the first novel featuring Ava Lee. Now, Ava and Uncle make a return that's even better... Simply irresistible." — Margaret Cannon, *Globe and Mail*

"This is slick, fast-moving escapism reminiscent of Ian Fleming, with more to come in what shapes up as a high-energy, high-concept series." — *Booklist*

"Fast paced... Enough personal depth to lift this thriller above solely action-oriented fare." — *Publishers Weekly*

"Lee is a hugely original creation, and Hamilton packs his adventure with interesting facts and plenty of action." — *Irish Independent*

"Hamilton makes each page crackle with the kind of energy that could easily jump to the movie screen... This riveting read will keep you up late at night." — *Penthouse*

"Hamilton gives his reader plenty to think about...Entertaining."
— *Kitchener-Waterloo Record*

## PRAISE FOR *THE WILD BEASTS OF WUHAN*
### LAMBDA LITERARY AWARD FINALIST: LESBIAN MYSTERY

"Smart and savvy Ava Lee returns in this slick mystery set in the rarefied world of high art... [A] great caper tale. Hamilton has great fun chasing villains and tossing clues about. *The Wild Beasts of Wuhan* is the best Ava Lee novel yet, and promises more and better to come."
— Margaret Cannon, *Globe and Mail*

"One of my favourite new mystery series, perfect escapism."
— *National Post*

"As a mystery lover, I'm devouring each book as it comes out... What I love in the novels: The constant travel, the high-stakes negotiation, and Ava's willingness to go into battle against formidable opponents, using only her martial arts skills to defend herself...If you want a great read and an education in high-level business dealings, Ian Hamilton is an author to watch." — *Toronto Star*

"Fast-paced and very entertaining." — *Montreal Gazette*

"Ava Lee is definitely a winner." — *Saskatoon Star Phoenix*

"*The Wild Beasts of Wuhan* is an entertaining dip into potentially fatal worlds of artistic skulduggery." — *Sudbury Star*

"Hamilton uses Ava's investigations as comprehensive and intriguing mechanisms for plot and character development." — *Quill & Quire*

"You haven't seen cold and calculating until you've double-crossed this number cruncher. Another strong entry from Arthur Ellis Award–winner Hamilton." — *Booklist*

"An intelligent kick-ass heroine anchors Canadian author Hamilton's excellent third novel featuring forensic accountant Ava Lee...Clearly conversant with the art world, Hamilton makes the intricacies of forgery as interesting as a Ponzi scheme." — *Publishers Weekly*, *Starred Review*

"A lively series about Ava Lee, a sexy forensic financial investigator." — *Tampa Bay Times*

"This book is miles from the ordinary. The main character, Ava Lee is 'the whole package.'" — *Minneapolis Star Tribune*

"A strong heroine is challenged to discover the details of an intercontinental art scheme. Although Hamilton's star Ava Lee is technically a forensic accountant, she's more badass private investigator than desk jockey." — *Kirkus Reviews*

## PRAISE FOR *THE RED POLE OF MACAU*

"Ava Lee returns as one of crime fiction's most intriguing characters. *The Red Pole of Macau* is the best page-turner of the season from the hottest writer in the business!" — John Lawrence Reynolds, author of *Beach Strip*

"Ava Lee, that wily, wonderful hunter of nasty business brutes, is back in her best adventure ever...If you haven't yet discovered Ava Lee, start here." — *Globe and Mail*

"The best in the series so far." — *London Free Press*

"Ava [Lee] is a character we all could use at one time or another. Failing that, we follow her in her best adventure yet." — *Hamilton Spectator*

"A romp of a story with a terrific heroine." — *Saskatoon Star Phoenix*

PRAISE FOR IAN HAMILTON AND THE AVA LEE SERIES

## PRAISE FOR *THE WATER RAT OF WANCHAI*
### WINNER OF THE ARTHUR ELLIS AWARD FOR BEST FIRST NOVEL

"Ian Hamilton's *The Water Rat of Wanchai* is a smart, action-packed thriller of the first order, and Ava Lee, a gay Asian-Canadian forensics accountant with a razor-sharp mind and highly developed martial arts skills, is a protagonist to be reckoned with. We were impressed by Hamilton's tight plotting; his well-rendered settings, from the glitz of Bangkok to the grit of Guyana; and his ability to portray a wide range of sharply individualized characters in clean but sophisticated prose." — Judges' Citation, Arthur Ellis Award for Best First Novel

"Ava Lee is tough, fearless, quirky, and resourceful, and she has more — well, you know — than a dozen male detectives I can think of... Hamilton has created a true original in Ava Lee." — Linwood Barclay, author of *No Time for Goodbye*

"If the other novels [in the series] are half as good as this debut by Ian Hamilton, then readers are going to celebrate. Hamilton has created a marvellous character in Ava Lee... This is a terrific story that's certain to be on the Arthur Ellis Best First Novel list." — *Globe and Mail*

"[Ava Lee's] lethal knowledge... torques up her sex appeal to the approximate level of a female lead in a Quentin Tarantino film." — *National Post*

"The heroine in *The Water Rat of Wanchai* by Ian Hamilton sounds too good to be true, but the heroics work better that way... formidable... The story breezes along with something close to total clarity... Ava is unbeatable at just about everything. Just wait for her to roll out her bak mei against the bad guys. She's perfect. She's fast." — *Toronto Star*

"Imagine a book about a forensic accountant that has tension, suspense, and action...When the central character looks like Lucy Liu, kicks like Jackie Chan, and has a travel budget like Donald Trump, the story is anything but boring. *The Water Rat of Wanchai* is such a beast...I look forward to the next one, *The Disciple of Las Vegas*."
— *Montreal Gazette*

"[A] tomb-raiding Dragon Lady Lisbeth, *sans* tattoo and face metal."
— *Winnipeg Free Press*

"An enjoyable romp with a feisty, ingenious heroine whose lethal martial arts skills are as formidable as her keen mind." — *Publishers Weekly*

"Readers will discern in Ava undertones of Lisbeth Salander, the ferocious protagonist of the late Stieg Larsson's crime novels...She, too, is essentially a loner, and small, and physically brutal...There are suggestions in *The Water Rat of Wanchai* of deeper complexities waiting to be more fully revealed. Plus there's pleasure, both for Ava and readers, in the puzzle itself: in figuring out where money has gone, how to get it back, and which humans, helpful or malevolent, are to be dealt with where, and in what ways, in the process...Irresistible."
— Joan Barfoot, *London Free Press*

"*The Water Rat of Wanchai* delivers on all fronts...feels like the beginning of a crime-fighting saga...A great story told with colour, energy, and unexpected punch." — *Hamilton Spectator*

"The best series fiction leaves readers immersed in a world that is both familiar and fresh. Seeds planted early bear fruit later on, creating a rich forest that blooms across a number of books...[Hamilton] creates a terrific atmosphere of suspense..." — *Quill & Quire*

"The book is an absolute page-turner...Hamilton's knack for writing snappy dialogue is evident...I recommend getting in on the ground floor with this character, because for Ava Lee, the sky's the limit."
— *Inside Halton*

"Fast-paced... The action unfolds like a well-oiled action-flick."
— *Kitchener-Waterloo Record*

"A change of pace for our girl [Ava Lee]... Suspenseful." — *Toronto Star*

"Hamilton packs tremendous potential in his heroine... A refreshingly relevant series. This reader will happily pay House of Anansi for the fifth instalment." — *Canadian Literature*

## PRAISE FOR *THE SCOTTISH BANKER OF SURABAYA*

"Hamilton deepens Ava's character, and imbues her with greater mettle and emotional fire, to the extent that book five is his best, most memorable, to date." — *National Post*

"In today's crowded mystery market, it's no easy feat coming up with a protagonist who stands out from the pack. But Ian Hamilton has made a great job of it with his Ava Lee books. Young, stylish, Chinese-Canadian, lesbian, and a brilliant forensic accountant, Ava is as complex a character as you could want... [A] highly addictive series... Hamilton knows how to keep the pages turning. He eases us into the seemingly tame world of white-collar crime, then raises the stakes, bringing the action to its peak with an intensity and violence that's stomach-churning. His Ava Lee is a winner and a welcome addition to the world of strong female avengers." — *NOW Magazine*

"Most of the series' success rests in Hamilton's tight plotting, attention to detail, and complex powerhouse of a heroine: strong but vulnerable, capable but not impervious... With their tight plotting and crackerjack heroine, Hamilton's novels are the sort of crowd-pleasing, narrative-focused fiction we find all too rarely in this country."
— *Quill & Quire*

"Ava is such a cool character, intelligent, Chinese-Canadian, unconventional, and original... Irresistible." — *Owen Sound Sun Times*

## PRAISE FOR *THE TWO SISTERS OF BORNEO*
### NATIONAL BESTSELLER

"There are plenty of surprises waiting for Ava, and for the reader, all uncovered with great satisfaction." — *National Post*

"Ian Hamilton's great new Ava Lee mystery has the same wow factor as its five predecessors. The plot is complex and fast-paced, the writing tight, and its protagonist is one of the most interesting female avengers to come along in a while." — *NOW Magazine* (NNNN)

"The appeal of the Ava Lee series owes much to her brand name lifestyle; it stirs pleasantly giddy emotions to encounter such a devotedly elegant heroine. But, better still, the detailing of financial shenanigans is done in such clear language that even readers who have trouble balancing their bank books can appreciate the way conmen set out to fleece unsuspecting victims." — *Toronto Star*

"Hamilton has a unique gift for concocting sizzling thrillers." — *Edmonton Journal*

"Hamilton has this formula down to an art, but he manages to avoid cliché and his ability to evoke a place keeps the series fresh." — *Globe and Mail*

"From her introduction in *The Water Rat of Wanchai*, Ava Lee has stood as a stylish, street-smart leading lady whose resourcefulness and creativity have helped her to uncover criminal activity in everything from illegal online gambling rings to international art heists. In Hamilton's newest installment to the series, readers accompany Ava on great adventures and to interesting locales, roaming from Hong Kong to the Netherlands to Borneo. The pulse-pounding, fast-paced narrative is chocked full of divergent plot twists and intriguing personalities that make it a popular escapist summer read. The captivating female sleuth does not disappoint as she circles the globe on a quest to uncover an unusually intriguing investment fiasco involving fraud, deception and violence." — *ExpressMilwaukee.com*

"Ava may be the most chic figure in crime fiction." — *Hamilton Spectator*

"The series as a whole is as good as the modern thriller genre gets." — *The Cord*

## PRAISE FOR *THE KING OF SHANGHAI*

"The only thing scarier than being ripped off for a few million bucks is being the guy who took it and having Ava Lee on your tail. If Hamilton's kick-ass forensic accountant has your number, it's up." — Linwood Barclay

"One of Ian Hamilton's best." — *Globe and Mail*

"Brilliant, sexy, and formidably martial arts-trained forensic accountant Ava Lee is back in her seventh adventure (after *The Two Sisters of Borneo*)... Ever since his dazzling surprise debut with *The Water Rat of Wanchai*, Hamilton has propelled Ava along through the series with expanded storytelling and nuanced character development: there's always something new to discover about Ava. Fast-paced suspense, exotic locales, and a rich cast of characters (some, like Ava's driver, Sonny, are both dangerous and lovable) make for yet another hugely entertaining hit." — *Publishers Weekly*, *Starred review*

"A luxurious sense of place... Hamilton's knack for creating fascinating detail will keep readers hooked... Good fun for those who like to combine crime fiction with armchair travelling." — *Booklist*

"Ava would be a sure thing to whip everybody, Putin included, at the negotiating table." — *Toronto Star*

"After six novels starring Chinese-Canadian Ava Lee and her perilously thrilling exploits, best-selling Canadian author Ian Hamilton has jolted his creation out of what wasn't even yet a rut and hurled her abruptly into a new circumstance, with fresh ambitions." — *London Free Press*

"It's a measure of Hamilton's quality as a thriller writer that he compels your attention even before he starts ratcheting up the suspense."
— *Regina Leader Post*

"An unputdownable book that I would highly recommend for all."
— *Words of Mystery*

"Ava is as powerful and brilliant as ever." — *Literary Treats*

## PRAISE FOR *THE PRINCELING OF NANJING*
### CANADIAN BESTSELLER
### A KOBO BEST BOOK OF THE YEAR

"The reader is offered plenty of Ava in full flower as the Chinese-Canadian glamour puss who happens to be gay, whip smart, and unafraid of whatever dangers come her way." — *Toronto Star*

"Hamilton's Chinese-Canadian heroine is one of a kind... [An] exotic thriller that also offers a fascinating inside look at fiscal misconduct in China... As a unique series character, Ava Lee's become indispensable." — *Calgary Herald*

"Ava Lee has a new business, a new look, and, most important, a new Triad boss to appreciate her particular financial talents... We know that Ava will come up with a plan and Hamilton will come up with a twist." — *Globe and Mail*

"Like the best series writers — Ian Rankin and Peter Robinson come to mind — Hamilton manages to... keep the Ava Lee books fresh... A compulsive read, a page-turner of the old school... *The Princeling of Nanjing* is a welcome return of an old favourite, and bodes well for future books." — *Quill & Quire*

"Hamilton uses his people and plot to examine Chinese class and power structures that open opportunities for massive depravities and corruptions." — *London Free Press*

"As usual with a Hamilton-Lee novel, matters take a decided twist as the plot unrolls." — *Owen Sound Times*

"One of those grip-tight novels that makes one read 'just one more chapter' and you discover it's 3 a.m. The novel is built on complicated webs artfully woven into clear, magnetic storytelling. Author Ian Hamilton delivers the intrigue within complex and relentless webs in high style and once again proves that everyone, once in their lives, needs an Ava Lee at their backs." — *Canadian Mystery Reviews*

"The best of the Ava Lee series to date...*Princeling* features several chapters of pure, unadulterated financial sleuthing, which both gave me some nerdy feels and tickled my puzzle-loving mind." — *Literary Treats*

"*The Princeling of Nanjing* was another addition to the Ava Lee series that did not disappoint." — *Words of Mystery*

## PRAISE FOR *THE COUTURIER OF MILAN*
### CANADIAN BESTSELLER

"The latest in the excellent series starring Ava Lee, businesswoman extraordinaire, *The Couturier of Milan* is another winner for Ian Hamilton... The novel is a hoot. At a point where most crime series start to run out of steam, Ava Lee just keeps rolling on." — *Globe and Mail*

"In Ava Lee, Ian Hamilton has created a crime fighter who breaks the mould with every new book (and, frankly, with every new chapter)." — *CBC Books*

"The pleasure in following Ava's clever plans for countering the bad guys remains as ever a persuasive attraction." — *Toronto Star*

"Fashionably fierce forensics... But Hamilton has built around Ava Lee an award-winning series that absorbs intriguing aspects of both Asian and Canadian cultures." — *London Free Press*

## PRAISE FOR *THE IMAM OF TAWI-TAWI*

"The best of the series so far." — *Globe and Mail*

"One of his best... Tightly plotted and quick-moving, this is a spare yet terrifically suspenseful novel." — *Publishers Weekly*

"Combines lots of action with Ava's acute intelligence and ability to solve even the most complex problems." — *Literary Hub*

"Fast-paced, smoothly written, and fun." — *London Free Press*

"An engrossing novel." — *Reviewing the Evidence*

"Hamilton's rapid-fire storytelling moves the tale along at breakneck speed, as Ava globe-trots to put clues together. Hamilton has always had a knack for combing Fleming-style descriptors with modern storytelling devices and character beats, and this book is no different." — *The Mind Reels*

"An engaging and compelling mystery." — *Literary Treats*

## PRAISE FOR *THE GODDESS OF YANTAI*
### NATIONAL BESTSELLER

"Ava at her most intimate and vulnerable." — *Toronto Star*

"This time, [Ava's] crusade is personal, and so is her outrage." — *London Free Press*

"In *The Goddess of Yantai*... Ava's personal and professional lives collide in a manner that shakes the usually unflappable character." — *Quill & Quire*

# THE
# MOUNTAIN
# MASTER
## OF
# SHA TIN

# THE
# MOUNTAIN
# MASTER
# OF
# SHA TIN

## AN AVA LEE NOVEL
## THE TRIAD YEARS

# IAN HAMILTON

**SPIDERLINE**

Published in Canada in 2019 and the USA in 2019 by House of Anansi Press Inc.
www.houseofanansi.com

House of Anansi Press is committed to protecting our natural environment.
As part of our efforts, this book is made of material from well-managed
FSC®-certified forests, recycled materials, and other controlled sources.

23 22 21 20 19    1 2 3 4 5

Library and Archives Canada Cataloguing in Publication

Hamilton, Ian, 1946–, author
The mountain master of Sha Tin / Ian Hamilton.

(An Ava Lee novel: the triad years)
Issued in print and electronic formats.
ISBN 978-1-4870-0203-9 (softcover).—ISBN 978-1-4870-0204-6 (EPUB).—
ISBN 978-1-4870-0205-3 (Kindle)

I. Title.

PS8615.A4423M68 2019      C813'.6      C2018-905432-8
C2018-905433-6

Library of Congress Control Number: 2018962110

Book design: Alysia Shewchuk
Typesetting: Sara Loos

*We acknowledge for their financial support of our publishing program
the Canada Council for the Arts, the Ontario Arts Council, and the Government
of Canada.*

Printed and bound in Canada

To Brenda Bowlby and Rick Burgess for their years of friendship, and for lending their names to a law firm in Hong Kong.

**AVA LEE LOOKED OUT OF THE WINDOW OF THE FIRST-**class cabin as the China Eastern Airways jet began its descent into Shanghai. It was a city she normally loved to visit, but on this occasion she was filled with apprehension.

"Are you okay?" a woman's voice asked.

Ava turned towards Pang Fai, her friend and lover. "I'm worried about Xu. If he has bacterial meningitis, we have to hope they caught it in time."

Fai squeezed her hand. "At least he's in a hospital now, and I'm sure he's receiving the best of treatment. You'll see him soon enough and then you can relax."

Xu was Ava's closest male friend. He was also, significantly, the head of the triads in Shanghai, chairman of the Triad Society in Asia, and a silent partner in the investment business that Ava co-owned with May Ling Wong and Amanda Yee.

"I keep telling myself the same thing, but as soon as I manage to convince myself that he's going to recover, my mind jumps to Lop getting shot in Hong Kong, and the mess that might create," Ava said. Lop was one of Xu's key lieutenants, and he had been shot the day before.

"You told me that Hong Kong isn't your problem," said Fai.

"I think I said I don't *want* it to be my problem, but if Xu is incapacitated that could create a situation I might not be able to stay away from."

"Why?"

"It's complicated," Ava said, and then realized immediately that she might have sounded condescending. Fai had known Xu before meeting Ava, and she was well aware of his triad links. Ava, though, had never spoken to her in any detail about the dangers she and Xu had confronted together. *What the hell*, she thought. *Fai has handled everything well up to now and she deserves an explanation.* "By that I mean I played a role in Xu's takeover of the Wanchai triads. I am at least partially responsible for deposing — in fact, if not officially — Sammy Wing as Mountain Master, and for the appointment of Lop as the de facto boss. So, whether I like it or not, I have ties to Wanchai that some people will not forget."

"What will happen if Xu's health improves?"

"He could still find it difficult to deal with a problem that's more than twelve hundred kilometres from his hospital bed in Shanghai, and I can guarantee that the last thing he'll want anyone to know is that he's unwell. Rivals would be quick to pounce — and with triad gang leaders, everyone is a potential rival."

"What if he's well enough to travel?"

"That's very optimistic. But if he can travel, he's the best person to restore equilibrium in Hong Kong. Although there would still be the question of what to do about Sammy Wing, and the fact that Lop has been shot can't be ignored. If Lop dies, it will be almost impossible for Xu to turn the other cheek without appearing weak," Ava said.

"Who is this Sammy Wing?"

"He's a lifelong triad who is in his seventies or eighties. He ran the Wanchai triad gang for years. I first encountered him about five or six years ago, when he accepted a hit contract on me from a conman I'd pissed off — "

"A hit contract?"

"Yes, Sammy was hired to kill me. Not personally, of course. He sent a couple of his men to do the dirty work. Later, through Uncle's intervention, he cancelled the contract, but not until his men had tried to do me in," Ava said. "Then, about a year ago, trouble flared up again when Wing took exception to Xu's growing influence within the triad hierarchy. He decided to kill Xu and I was caught in the crossfire. Obviously he wasn't successful. In the aftermath, Xu took control of Wanchai and put Lop in charge. There are people who think Xu made a mistake when he kept on Wing as a figurehead; they think he should have killed him. If Lop's shooting is connected to Sammy, it will look like they were right and Xu was wrong."

"Do you think there is a connection?"

"There are rumours that Sammy's nephew, Carter Wing, who has just taken over the Sha Tin gang in the New Territories, wants to help his uncle reclaim his turf," Ava said. "If that's true, a lot of blood could be spilled."

Ava saw Fai flinch and decided she'd said enough — maybe even too much. She turned towards the window again. Their flight had originated in Beijing and was going to land at Hongqiao Airport rather than at Pudong International, with which Ava was more familiar. "We'll be on the ground in about ten minutes. I think I've been to Hongqiao only once before."

"Pudong is on the eastern edge of Shanghai and Hongqiao is in the western part. It's only ten kilometres from the centre of the city," Fai said, sounding relieved by the change of subject.

"Suen will be waiting for us with a car. The plan is to go directly to the hospital to see Xu," Ava said. "You've met Suen before, right?"

"I don't know if *met* is the right word. I've seen him, of course, but he was always lurking in the background; he's so large he's impossible to miss. I thought he was just a body-guard until Tsai told me he has another role — although I don't remember exactly what that is."

"He is Xu's Red Pole, which means he's the gang's enforcer and runs all the muscle on the ground. In an ideal world, his job is more preventive than proactive."

"And in this case?"

"I won't know until I talk to Xu."

Fai looked awkwardly at Ava. "It's going to be uncomfort-able for me to meet some of these people. They've only seen me with Tsai, when I was basically his paid mistress. It might be difficult for someone like Suen to understand why I did that, and how I finally came to terms with my sexuality only at this point in my life."

Ava shook her head. Pang Fai, although perhaps China's greatest film actress, wasn't well paid by Western standards and was not financially self-sufficient. In the past she had augmented her income by dating and sometimes sleeping with wealthy men. Tsai Men, the son of the governor of Jiangsu province, had been one of those men, and Ava had first met Fai at a dinner with Tsai and Xu.

"Fai, pay no attention to what others think or say — although I can't imagine that anyone associated with me or Xu would ever be disrespectful. All that matters is that you're happy and at peace with yourself."

"Which I am... but I still need reminding now and then that it's okay for me to feel that way," said Fai. Ava and Fai had been a couple for more than eight months, but because of Ava's business demands and Fai's film commitments, they had spent only about two months of that time together. The reason they were flying from Beijing to Shanghai was that they had spent the previous week in the Chinese capital dealing with a problem Fai was having with the China Film Syndicate. Their intention had been, after those issues were resolved, for Ava to travel with Fai to Yantai to meet her parents. Xu's illness had changed those plans, and now the troubles in Hong Kong were threatening to change them again.

The plane's descent quickened and the pilot announced they were making their final approach to Hongqiao. Ava closed her eyes and said a short prayer to Saint Jude, the patron saint of lost causes. She had given up most of her Roman Catholic faith in reaction to the Church's position on homosexuality, but she still turned to Saint Jude whenever she felt that events in her life were spinning out of control. She didn't know what she would find when she landed in Shanghai, so her prayer simply asked for things to be as normal as possible.

Hongqiao, like most of the newer airports in Asia, was built for efficiency. Within fifteen minutes of landing, Ava and Fai were walking through the doors of the arrivals hall into a crowd of people waiting for travellers.

"Ava," a man's voice called out.

Ava looked to her right and saw Suen. Even amidst the throng he was impossible to miss. At six foot four and with 240 pounds of muscle accentuated by a tight-fitting polo shirt, he was an imposing figure. Ava and Fai walked towards him.

He reached for their bags. "I'm very happy to see you," he said.

"Do you remember Fai?" Ava asked.

"Sure," he said, nodding at her. "Good to see you too."

"How's Xu?" Ava asked. "Have they settled on a diagnosis?"

"They're now quite certain that it's bacterial meningitis," Suen said.

"I was hoping it would be something else," Ava said.

"Don't panic. They've shot him full of antibiotics and the doctor told me he's sure they caught the disease in time."

"Is Xu alert? Is he responsive?"

"Sometimes he's lucid and sometimes his mind wanders off and he starts talking nonsense. And he's still physically weak."

"Have you told Auntie Grace about the diagnosis?" Ava asked, referring to Xu's lifelong housekeeper.

"I thought I'd leave that to you. She'll trust whatever you tell her. With me she always has a hundred questions that I can't answer," Suen said. "I assume you'll be staying with her?"

"We will."

"And I assume you want to see Xu first?"

"Of course."

"We'd better get going. It is already quarter to eight and visiting hours end at nine. He's in the Shanghai East International Medical Centre in Pudong, which is a thirty-minute drive from here. Wen is waiting with the car."

Ava and Fai followed in Suen's wake as he barrelled through the crowd. When he reached the arrival hall's exit doors, he stopped and stood to one side to let Ava and Fai pass. When Ava stepped out onto the sidewalk, she saw Wen directly in front of her, standing next to Xu's silver S-Class Mercedes Benz.

Wen bowed his head when he saw her. "*Xiao lao ban*," he said.

Ava smiled. Wen had been the first person to call her "little boss" to her face, although he had been quick to add that most of Xu's men — and even Xu himself — often referred to her that way when she wasn't around.

"Good to see you, Wen, though I wish the circumstances were better," she said.

"The boss will be okay," he said with determination.

Wen was a small, wiry man, but his size was no indication of his grit. Ava had seen his bravery first-hand the year before, when a special unit attached to the People's Armed Police had come to Xu's house — where she was alone with Auntie Grace — to arrest her. Wen had organized the resistance and had been prepared to exchange fire with the police. It hadn't come to that, but Ava didn't doubt for a second that Wen was prepared to do whatever it took to protect her.

"Yes, I'm sure he will be okay," Ava said.

As Wen put their bags into the trunk of the car, Ava and Fai slid onto the back seat and Suen sat in the front passenger seat. "You haven't mentioned Lop," she said. "How is he?"

Suen turned to face her. "He's still alive."

"And what's happening in Hong Kong?"

"The last I heard, it was quiet. Nothing out of the ordinary."

"Except for Lop getting shot."

"I'm hoping that was an aberration, a mistake of some sort."

"Do you really believe that?" she asked.

"No. I said I *hope* that's the case, not that I believe it."

"Does Xu know about Lop?"

"Not yet. Telling him now didn't seem to be the right thing, given his condition."

Ava shook her head. "He needs to know. Not telling him is usurping his authority. I know your intentions are good, but they could be misconstrued later."

"If we do tell him, it might also be better coming from you," Suen said. "You're the one he told about his concerns there, and it's your man Sonny who's been poking around."

"Speaking of Sonny, have you heard from him?"

"He called me a couple of hours ago. He wanted you to call him when you landed," Suen said. "I'm sorry, I should have told you earlier."

"No need to apologize. I know you've got a lot on your plate," Ava said, reaching for her phone to call Sonny in Hong Kong.

Sonny was Sonny Kwok, a man as large as Suen and probably more vicious. He had been a member of Uncle's triad gang in Fanling before becoming his fanatically loyal bodyguard and driver. When Uncle became ill and knew he was going to die, he had asked Ava to employ Sonny, saying, "A Sonny with nothing to do and no ties will eventually get into trouble, and it is the kind of trouble that you cannot begin to imagine." So Ava had hired him. The fact that she lived in Toronto and Sonny wouldn't fit in anywhere but Hong Kong was a challenge, but they agreed that whenever she was in Asia, she had first call on his services. The rest of the time Sonny drove for Ava's father, Marcus, her half-brother Michael, and Amanda Yee, who in addition to being Ava's business partner was married to Michael. They all lived in Hong Kong, and the arrangement had worked well so far. Ava knew that Sonny was as loyal to her as he had ever been to Uncle.

"*Wei*," he answered.

"It's Ava."

"How is Xu?" he asked immediately.

"I'll know soon; I'm on my way to the hospital now. Suen tells me Xu has bacterial meningitis, but it's treatable. I'll call you after I see him," Ava said. "How are things on your end? How is Lop? Any noise from Sammy Wing?"

"Lop is at Dr. Lui's clinic in Kowloon. Lui thinks he should be moved to a regular hospital, but I talked it over with Ko, Lop's right-hand man, and we decided to leave him where he is. If he's moved to a hospital the cops will get involved, and there'll be a lot of questions that no one wants to answer."

"But if Lop's life is at risk..."

"Lui is a good doctor and he has all the equipment you'd find at most hospitals," Sonny said. "He's just nervous about having someone like Lop at the clinic."

"Then why did he agree to take him in?"

"He didn't, really. We showed up on his doorstep with Lop in tow. He couldn't turn us away."

"Lui is your girlfriend's brother, right?"

"Old girlfriend's brother. That might also be why he's reluctant to help."

"So you think Lop is going to live?"

Sonny paused. "I don't know. He caught three bullets — one in his gut and two in the chest. Lui got them out, but

Lop lost a lot of blood, and Liu isn't sure how much damage was done internally."

"Lop is incredibly fit."

"Bullets do their damage whether you're fit or not."

"How about Ko? Is he strong enough to take over, even temporarily?"

"He's a good number two, but that's what he is — a number two. I can't see him running a gang on his own. Besides, he's a Shanghai man, and that's not the best of references around here right now."

"Shit," Ava said.

"The good news is that nothing else has happened since Lop was shot," Sonny said. "If Sammy and Carter were going to make a play for Wanchai, they would have followed up more aggressively."

"Maybe they're waiting to see how Xu reacts. The last time Sammy tried to take him on, Sammy and his gang were taken apart in less than twenty-four hours."

"But that was with Lop in charge of the troops on the ground."

"Even so, the Wings have reason to be cautious."

"The other reason might be that the shooting doesn't have anything to do with Wanchai. Maybe someone just has a hate-on for Lop."

"Do you believe that?" Ava asked.

"Not really. I trust Andy's judgement. If he heard that Sammy and Carter's Sha Tin gang are going to make a play to take back Wanchai, then I believe it," Sonny said. Andy was an old triad colleague of Sonny and Ava's who was loosely connected to the Sha Tin gang.

"What do you know about Carter Wing?"

"He's young, tough, ambitious, and aggressive. He's only been heading Sha Tin for a couple of months, but already he's making a lot of his neighbours nervous," Sonny said. "One more thing you should know: his father died when he was young and Sammy has always looked out for him, so they're close. Now that he's got some power, he might have decided he'll use it to repay his uncle."

"But you haven't heard anything definite?"

"No, just rumours."

"Well, until something else happens, we have to assume that's what we're dealing with," Ava said.

She saw that Suen was listening to her conversation with Sonny. She didn't blame him. With Xu in hospital and Lop in the Kowloon clinic, it might fall to him and the rest of the Shanghai executive to decide on a course of action if the rumours materialized into something more sinister. "Sonny, I have to go. I'll call you after I see Xu. In the meantime, stay completely on top of things there. Let's try to avoid any more surprises."

"How is Lop?" Suen asked as soon as Ava ended the call.

"He's not dead, but he's in no condition to run anything, let alone a war."

"This couldn't have happened at a worse time."

"How close are we to the hospital?" Ava asked, in no mood to respond to something so obvious.

"Ten minutes," Wen said.

"Then let's have some quiet time. I need to gather myself. Having to be in two hospitals in only a few days is a lot for my system to handle."

( 2 )

AVA HATED HOSPITALS. SHE DIDN'T KNOW WHERE THE aversion had come from, but it was a constant, and it made no difference whether she was a patient or a visitor. Since Uncle had died she hadn't been in one until a few days before, when she was attacked in Beijing by a thug wielding a cleaver. She'd fended him off, but not before he'd made a gash in her upper arm that needed treatment. Now, as Wen stopped the car in front of the modern-looking Shanghai East International Medical Centre, she was making her second hospital visit in less than forty-eight hours.

Ava associated hospitals with death. She knew that was irrational and that hospitals existed to treat, not kill, patients, but the instant she saw the nurses and doctors in their uniforms and smelled the disinfectant they used to clean the corridors and rooms, she would begin to feel anxious.

"Are you going to be okay?" Fai asked as she, Ava, and Suen started up the steps towards the hospital's brightly lit entrance.

"I'll manage," Ava said, and then turned to Suen. "This place looks new."

"It's been here about ten years. It was built to serve the international community, so the staff speak both Chinese and English. It was recommended to Xu a few years ago by a doctor he met at a party. The doctor is attached to the hospital, and he told Xu he thought it would be easier to protect his privacy here."

Suen turned left when they entered the lobby. Ava and Fai followed him to a bank of elevators that were signed in both languages. They rode the elevator to the twelfth floor, and when they exited, Suen led them through the patient reception area to a door with the words INFECTIOUS DISEASES written on it. He opened the door and they stepped into an area that had a large U-shaped nursing station in the middle and a perimeter wall of glass interspersed with closed doors. The blinds of several of the rooms were open and Ava could see that each contained a single unoccupied bed.

Suen approached the nursing station. "Xu's *mei mei* is here now. Can you add her to the visitors list?" Suen said.

A young woman smiled at Ava and Fai. "Which of you is the little sister?" she asked.

"I am," Ava said, not feeling the need to explain that she wasn't actually a blood relative.

"You'll need to fill out this form and then sign a waiver," she said, passing two pieces of paper to Ava. "When that's done, you'll have to put on a gown, mask, gloves, and slippers. And I suggest you hurry if you want to spend any time with him, because visiting hours end in about thirty minutes."

Ava completed the paperwork and handed it back to the nurse. "Where do I find those clothes?"

"The room there in the corner," the woman said, pointing to a red door. "And by the way, you can't use a cellphone anywhere in this unit, so if you have one in your purse, please turn it off."

"She told me I'd be banned forever if I was caught using mine," Suen said.

"The same applies to the sister," the woman said.

"Message received and understood," Ava said, and headed for the change room. A few minutes later she emerged appropriately dressed.

"He's in room number nine," Suen said. "I'll walk you there."

When they reached the door, Suen knocked and then opened it. Ava stepped inside, not knowing quite what to expect. The room was dimly lit and the figure in the bed was in shadows. If she hadn't known it was Xu, she wouldn't have recognized him. He lay flat on his back with his eyes closed. An IV drip was attached to his arm and he was hooked up to several other pieces of expensive-looking equipment. As she neared the bed his face became more distinct; she could see that he was pale and gaunt, almost ashen.

There was a chair by the side of the bed. She sat down, reached out, and gently touched the back of his hand. "*Ge ge*," she said. "Big brother, it's Ava. I've come for a visit."

Xu didn't react immediately and Ava started to think he was sleeping, but then he turned his head towards her and opened his eyes. For a few seconds he didn't seem to be focusing, and Ava wondered if he knew who she was.

"It's Ava," she repeated.

"I see you, but why are you here?" he mumbled.

"I'm here to see you. You're in the hospital and I've come to see how you're doing."

"I'm tired."

"Do you want to talk?"

"No. I'm tired," Xu said, closing his eyes.

Ava sat by the bed for several minutes, unsure of what to do. She stroked the back of his hand, but when she didn't get any reaction, she said, "Xu, I'll leave you alone now, but I'll be back first thing in the morning." When he still didn't respond, she leaned forward and kissed him on the forehead, then stood and left the room.

Suen and Fai were still standing by the nursing station, where they had been joined by a tall, thin, middle-aged Westerner. As she approached, Ava heard the man speaking rudimentary Mandarin. His name tag read DR. MARTIN.

"Ava, you're back quickly," Suen said when he saw her.

"Xu said he was tired. I couldn't get much more out of him, and then he fell asleep."

"Doctor Martin was just explaining what's wrong with him," Fai said.

Ava slipped the mask from her face. "Can you explain it to me as well?" she said to him in English.

The doctor raised an eyebrow. "Your English is excellent. Do I detect an American accent?"

"Canadian actually, and you are obviously from the U.K."

"I am. This is my fifth year here, though you might not think so, given the way I speak Mandarin."

"It's a difficult language to learn, and I'm quite sure you weren't hired because of your linguistic abilities."

"That's true enough. And because of the international nature of this hospital we don't get many patients who speak only Chinese."

"Then please explain to me in English what's going on with Xu. I wasn't expecting him to look so weak and disconnected."

"If I understand correctly, you are his sister?"

"That is correct."

"And your name is?"

"Ava Lee."

"Well, Ms. Lee, your brother has bacterial meningitis, which is a swelling of the protective membrane covering the brain and spinal cord. That swelling is caused by an infection of the fluid that surrounds the brain and cord. It is treatable with antibiotics. We've already given Mr. Xu a full regimen, and while it might not appear that we're making progress, the tests we ran a few hours ago indicate that the swelling has already started to recede. His grogginess may be as attributable to the treatment as it is to the disease."

"When will he be more coherent?"

"It's hard to say. Maybe tomorrow, or perhaps the day after."

"How about regaining his strength?"

"That will take longer. Meningitis is quite debilitating."

"But he is definitely out of danger?"

Dr. Martin hesitated and then said, "One can never be completely sure, but I believe we're past the worst of it."

"What will comprise the treatment?"

"More antibiotics, fluids, and lots of rest. He will need to be closely monitored for some time, so don't count on him going home for at least another three or four more days."

"Thank you," Ava said, and then turned to Suen and Fai. "We can go now. There isn't much more we can do tonight."

They left the infectious diseases ward a few minutes later and walked in silence to the main exit. Ava had been alarmed by Xu's weakened condition, but it wasn't something she wanted to discuss. As if sensing Ava's concern, Fai took her hand and squeezed it.

Wen had parked the Mercedes across the street from the centre. "Where am I taking you now?" he said to Suen when they reached the car.

"Xu's house," Suen said.

The Pudong district was separated from Shanghai by the Huangpu River. Traffic was light and the river soon came into view, glimmering under the light cast by a wall of sky-scrapers that lined its southern bank. When Ava had first started coming to Shanghai, she would stay at the Peninsula Hotel on the Bund — a kilometre-long row of historic build-ings on the northern bank — and had been accustomed to taking the Yangpu Bridge across the river. On this occasion, Wen was driving towards the Lupu Bridge.

"Are we going to the French Concession?" Ava asked.

"The Lupu Bridge is the most direct route," Wen replied

"That's the bridge with the long steel arch?" said Ava.

"It's the second-longest steel arch bridge in the world."

"I didn't know you were also a tour guide," Ava said.

"I know some trivia," he said, and laughed.

When the car had cleared the bridge and was driving through heavier Shanghai traffic, Suen turned to Ava. "I promised Auntie Grace I'd let her know when you were on your way to the house."

"Let me do that," Ava said, reaching for her phone and hitting speed dial.

"*Wei*," Auntie Grace answered.

"It's Ava. We're in Shanghai and should be at the house in about fifteen minutes."

"Good. I'm anxious to see you," she said, and then quickly added, "Did you go to the hospital?"

"Yes. I saw Xu and spoke to the doctor," Ava said.

"How is he?"

Several platitudes popped into Ava's mind and were immediately dismissed. "The bad news is that they've confirmed he has bacterial meningitis. The good news is that the doctor says they caught it in time, and he expects Xu to recover fully," she said. "But he's heavily drugged and right now isn't himself. I think he recognized me, but he couldn't communicate very well. He also seems to have lost some weight, so he's going to need a lot of your cooking when he gets home."

Auntie Grace didn't respond right away, and Ava knew she was weighing every word Ava had said.

"Auntie, he's going to be fine. You know I always tell you the truth," she said.

"I never doubt you. I'm just so worried."

"We're all worried, but he's in good hands."

"I wish he was at home where I could look after him."

"You'll have to make do with Fai and me for the next few days."

"And I can't tell you how pleased I am that you'll be here," she said. "I've made dinner for you. I hope you're hungry."

"I'm always hungry for your food," Ava said. "We'll see you soon."

"How is she?" Suen asked when Ava ended the call.

"Worried, but she's a strong woman," Ava said.

Suen nodded and then turned his attention to the road.

They were in the French Concession now, driving along what Ava recognized as Huaihai Road, once called Avenue

Joffre. The Concession was just west of the Bund and stretched for eight kilometres. It was land that had been granted to the French in the mid-1800s as part of Shanghai's International Settlement. Huaihai Road was its main thoroughfare, lined with apartment buildings, cafés, shops, and — a rarity for a Chinese city — an abundance of trees.

"I love these trees," Fai said.

"The French planted them. The Chinese call them 'French planes,' and they line many of the streets in the Concession. They fit in with the European architecture," Ava said.

"Why are they called planes?"

"I was told it's because of the way the branches spread like umbrellas over the sidewalks."

"I'm amazed they've survived."

"Some of them are as old as the Concession itself, about a hundred and fifty years, and they almost didn't survive," Ava said. "Xu told me that in the 1990s, developers moved into this area and began to tear down buildings and uproot trees. Fortunately there was an uproar from the residents, and for once the local government actually listened to them. Development became more tightly regulated, and on some streets the trees were replanted."

The car turned off Huaihai Road and Ava began to recognize some landmarks. A left turn and a right turn later, the car entered a narrow lane and came to a stop at a fruit cart. Suen rolled down his window. "Everything quiet?" he aked the vendor.

"You're the first car I've seen all night," the man replied.

"There's a cart at the other end of the lane as well," Ava whispered to Fai. "They're here twenty-four hours a day. Xu doesn't like surprise visitors."

The car started to move again, making its way carefully between eight-foot-high brick walls that were only a few feet away on either side. The wall on the right was solid brick; on the left the brick was interrupted by wooden and metal gates of various sizes. Halfway down the lane, Wen hit the car horn three times. A moment later, a large flat-panelled metal gate opened and Wen drove through it into a cobbled courtyard. Ava waved at the men standing by the gate. There were always at least two of them on duty at the house.

Ava, Fai, and Suen got out of the car. Suen went to the trunk to get their bags while Fai examined the house. "It is smaller than I thought it would be," she said.

The house was a large one and a half storey. It was constructed of red brick and had a red tile roof, lead-paned windows, and a brown door with a distinctive arched lintel. It wouldn't have looked out of place in a Parisian suburb.

"It's a bit larger inside than it looks from here, but it's still cozy," Ava said. She pointed to a small round metal table and two chairs that sat by a fishpond to their left. "That's where Xu comes to smoke. Auntie Grace won't let him light up in the house. We've had some of our best conversations here."

As if she'd heard her name mentioned, a small woman opened the front door and emerged, framed by the light.

Ava walked over to her, held out her arms, and Auntie Grace stepped into them. Ava was five foot three, but Auntie Grace's plaited silver hair barely reached the younger woman's chin. They hugged, Auntie's fingers digging into Ava's back.

"So good to see you," Ava said.

"Yes," said Auntie Grace, without letting go.

Ava gently freed herself and stepped back. "This is my friend Pang Fai."

"I know who Pang Fai is," Auntie said.

"What should I do with the bags?" Suen asked from behind Fai.

"Just leave them inside the door," Ava said.

The three women walked into the house with Suen trailing. He put down the bags. "What's the schedule for tomorrow?" he asked.

"I want to go to the hospital first thing in the morning," Ava said.

"Visiting hours begin at ten."

"I'll be ready to leave at nine-thirty."

"I'll see you then," Suen said. "In the meantime..."

"If I hear anything from Sonny about activity in Hong Kong, I'll call you right away," Ava said, anticipating his question.

"I don't care what time it is."

"Neither will Sonny, and neither will I," Ava said. "And I expect the same courtesy If you hear something from your man Ko that impacts us."

"You can count on that."

"Then we're settled for tonight. See you tomorrow," Ava said.

"He seems like a dependable man," Fai said as the door closed behind Suen.

"He's very loyal, but he's a bit slow," Auntie said. "He needs someone like Xu or Ava to give him a prod now and then."

"He wouldn't like to hear something like that, especially about me," Ava said.

"I've told him as much to his face," Auntie said. "He didn't disagree."

Ava closed her eyes and inhaled deeply. "Do I smell dau miao?"

Auntie Grace smiled as she looked up at Fai. "Did you see how Ava just tried to change the subject? She does that every time I pay her a compliment."

"I've noticed the same thing," Fai said.

"But you still haven't answered my question," Ava said. "Is that dau miao?"

"I know it's your favourite, so I made it. Can you also handle fried noodles with shrimp, scallops, and squid in oyster sauce?"

"Of course I can."

"Then why don't you take your bags to the guest bedroom while I finish cooking the seafood. Meet me in the kitchen."

The house had three bedrooms, two upstairs and one on the ground floor. Auntie Grace and Xu slept upstairs, unless he had a female overnight guest. At those times Auntie slept downstairs. Ava had always slept in the guest room, and that's where she led Fai. The room was small, with just enough space for a queen-size bed, a closet, a dresser, and two night tables. Across the hall was a bathroom with a single sink and shower stall.

"It isn't fancy," Ava said as she put down her bags at the foot of the bed.

"It's about the same size as my bedroom in Beijing. Besides, who needs fancy? All we need is a bed," Fai said. "I hope Auntie Grace isn't uncomfortable with us sharing it."

"If she is, she'll let us know," Ava said. "As Xu can attest, she isn't bashful when it comes to sex."

Fai looked at their bags. "Do you want to unpack now?"

"No. I don't want to keep Auntie Grace waiting, and that dau miao is calling to me."

## 3

THE KITCHEN WAS AUNTIE GRACE'S DOMAIN. WHEN SHE wasn't cooking, she was sitting at the kitchen table reading a magazine or newspaper or watching a Chinese soap opera on the small black-and-white television that sat on the counter. On this occasion she was cooking at the gas stove with her back turned to the door. There were two woks on the stove. Ava moved behind Auntie and peeked into them. In one there was the familiar dark green sheen of dau miao — pea shoots that Auntie fried with garlic — and in the other, pink shrimp and plump white scallops mixed with golden yellow noodles.

"Take a chair. I'll be finished in moment," Auntie said. "There's beer and white wine in the fridge, and if you want something stronger, Xu has Scotch in the living room."

Ava opened the fridge. "There's Tsingtao beer or Pinot Grigio," she said.

"I'll have a beer," Fai said.

They sat at the rectangular wooden table, which had two settings of plates and chopsticks. Fai raised her glass. "*Ganbei*," she said.

"Good health to us all, especially Xu," Ava said, and took a large sip of her wine.

Fai looked around. "This reminds me of my family's kitchen in Yantai. It has the same kind of rice cooker and, I swear, the same brand of hot-water Thermos."

"It wouldn't be a Chinese kitchen without a rice cooker or Thermos," Ava said.

"Do you have them in Toronto?" Fai asked.

"Yes, but I hardly use the cooker. I'm not very active in the kitchen."

"As you know, I'm no better."

"Neither of you needs to be," Auntie Grace said loudly.

"Thank goodness we have you," Ava said.

Auntie spooned the wok contents onto platters and carried them to the table.

Ava and Fai dug in, their chopsticks in constant motion until the dau miao was reduced to several shrunken pea shoots and the few noodles that were left sat in a shallow pool of oyster sauce. Fai finished her beer halfway through and Auntie replaced it without her asking. The bottle of Pinot Grigio sat on the table and Ava refilled her glass twice.

"That was a wonderful meal," Fai said.

Auntie had sat at the table while they ate. As they put down their chopsticks, she smiled and looked curiously at Fai, something she'd done several times during the meal.

"I've noticed that you've been staring at Fai," Ava said.

"How can I not?" Auntie Grace said. "When you've seen someone larger than life on a movie screen and then suddenly that same person is sitting at your kitchen table, it takes some getting used to."

"I told you about Fai," Ava said.

"I know, but you telling me and her being here are two different things. And I mean that in a nice way," Auntie said, and then turned to Fai. "I always thought you were beautiful, but you can't help wondering if that's the magic of movies. Now I see it's not. You look exactly like you do on screen. If anything, you are more beautiful in person."

"Thank you, Auntie, for being so kind, in both what you said and the way you've received me as a guest in your house," Fai said. "But I have no doubt that over the next few days you'll see me in many other lights — not all of them favourable."

"You aren't a guest," Auntie Grace said. "You are Ava's partner, and that makes you part of this family."

"Thank you for that as well."

Ava yawned. It caught her by surprise and she said quickly, "Excuse me."

"Ava is bored with our conversation," Fai said, laughing.

"That's not true. What I am is tired," Ava said. "Auntie, Fai and I have had a very stressful week in Beijing, which we're just putting behind us. Xu's illness has been weighing on me as well. If you don't mind, I think I'll head to bed."

"You go. Both of you go," Auntie said.

"Can I help you clean the kitchen?" Fai said.

"No. As Ava knows, it happens to be a chore I enjoy, and one I prefer to do alone."

Ava stood and walked over to Auntie Grace. She bent and wrapped her arms around the older woman. "I do love you, Auntie."

"I know you do. Now off to bed with you."

Ava and Fai left the kitchen and went directly to their bedroom. When they reached it, Fai flopped onto the bed. "I'm so full I can hardly move," she said.

"That's the way it is here. Auntie Grace won't be happy until we're both complaining that we're ready to burst."

"Will you still love me when I'm fat?" Fai laughed.

"I'm the one more likely to get fat," Ava said and began to undress. "Are you going to shower?"

"I'm too tired."

"Me too."

"Two unwashed women together in bed. What could they possibly get up to?" Fai said.

"Let's find out," Ava said, and then froze as her phone rang.

"Leave it," Fai said.

"I can't. It could be Suen or Sonny," said Ava reaching for her device. "*Wei.*"

"It's Sonny. We have trouble here."

"Shit," Ava said, sitting up on the side of the bed. "What's going on?"

"Ko just got a phone call from Carter Wing. The Sha Tin crew has picked up seven of Lop's men off the streets and are holding them hostage. Carter gave Ko twenty-four hours to start vacating Wanchai, or the men will be killed."

"God, that's going to create a mess."

"At least the men aren't dead yet."

"And I guess that confirms who's behind Lop's shooting," Ava said, not ready to grapple with the complexity presented by the abduction of seven men. "Why did Carter call Ko, not Xu or Suen?"

"Maybe he tried and wasn't successful."

Ava paused, knowing Sonny was most likely correct. "What did Ko tell Carter?"

"He said he would have to get back to him, but that if any harm came to the men there would be retaliation."

"Under the circumstances, I guess that's as good a response as we could expect."

"Ko is really stressed out."

"That's understandable," Ava said. "But why did he call you instead of Suen?"

"He called and texted him, but Suen didn't respond, so he called me. He must figure I'm more connected than I actually am."

"Right now you actually are more connected than anyone to both sides of this dispute."

"You know I'm not a decision-maker," Sonny said. "What do you want me to do?"

"Tell Ko to sit tight. We have twenty-four hours. I need to talk to Suen, and hopefully Xu. We'll come up with some kind of plan."

"Okay, boss."

"Then reach out to Andy and ask him what he's heard. He's the only person we have who is even remotely close to the Sha Tin gang."

"I will."

"And keep your phone with you."

"Don't worry. I won't be sleeping tonight until I hear from you again."

"You can sleep. I don't imagine we'll have that quick an answer from this end."

"I couldn't sleep even if I wanted to. My adrenalin is pumping like mad."

"Keep it under control."

"I wouldn't do anything without your go-ahead."

"I didn't mean to suggest otherwise."

"I know."

"I'll talk to you as soon there's some news," Ava said, ending the call.

Fai stared at her. "That didn't sound very good."

"The problem in Hong Kong just got far more complicated."

"I have a feeling you're going to be travelling there."

"It isn't something I want to do," Ava said.

"Is there room for me on the trip, if you do go?"

"Not when I think about the problems I may have to deal with," Ava said. Then she saw she had an incoming call from Suen. "*Wei.*"

"Have you spoken to Sonny?" he said, bypassing his normal polite greeting.

"Yes. And I assume from this call that you've talked to Ko."

"I did. I missed his first call. He told me he reached out to Sonny and that Sonny was going to phone you, so I guess we're both up-to-date."

"What are you going to do about the hostages?" Ava asked.

"I told Ko to try to locate our men without making the situation any worse than it is, but until I talk to Xu that's all I feel comfortable doing," Suen said. "I think you should be part of that conversation."

"We can't talk to him until tomorrow morning."

"I know. And my biggest fear is that he still won't be mentally alert."

"What if that's the case?" Ava asked.

"I've spoken to Feng, the White Paper Fan. I asked him to contact the rest of the executive and have them on standby tomorrow morning for a meeting."

"I know Feng. I worked with him on a project a few years ago. He's a good man."

"I told him you're here. He was pleased to hear it."

Ava's mind returned to the problem in Hong Kong. "Suen, now we know it's Carter Wing and the Sha Tin gang making the move on you, have you had a chance to think about your options?"

"If we were only dealing with the Lop situation it would be easier, but those seven men they're holding are a huge problem."

"Do you really think they'd harm them? Isn't it more logical that they're bargaining chips?"

"I'm not so sure. When we took over Wanchai, we killed far more than six of Sammy's men," said Suen. "This could be payback."

"But those deaths were a reaction to Sammy's attempt on Xu's life."

"I'm sure that's been forgotten by now. Triad memories are notoriously short when it comes to the crap their gangs commit, and awfully long when it comes to remembering things done to them. I imagine Sammy Wing has been stewing and planning to get back at us since the day we displaced him."

"Sonny thinks Xu should have killed Sammy back then."

"Sonny isn't wrong, but it's too late to fix that now."

Suen's response was the closest thing to criticism of Xu she'd ever heard him utter. "Hindsight is always perfect," she said. "At the time, leaving him alive seemed like the best choice."

"I know it was. And if Sammy had any sense he could have spent his final years relaxing as the Mountain Master of Wanchai."

"I guess he doesn't like being a figurehead. He still wants to be the real thing."

"That's stupid."

"Stupid or not, it's a gamble he's evidently decided to take."

Suen hesitated and then said, "I'll be in touch if anything happens tonight. Otherwise, I'll see you at nine-thirty tomorrow morning."

Ava put her phone on the night table. "I have to leave it on, but I'm not expecting any more calls."

"I'm almost jealous. There are so many people who want your time and attention," said Fai.

"There's only one person who's going to get that for the rest of this night."

## 4

**AVA WOKE AT JUST PAST SEVEN A.M., A NAKED FAI** wrapped around her. She gently moved Fai's arm, slid from the bed, put on a T-shirt and underpants, and tiptoed from the room. She closed the door quietly behind her and crossed the hallway to the bathroom. Five minutes later she walked into the kitchen to find Auntie Grace sitting at the table. As soon as the older woman saw her, she got to her feet and walked to the Thermos, which had two mugs and a jar of Nescafé instant coffee sitting next to it. Ava was familiar with the routine, so she sat at the table while Auntie made her a coffee.

"How did you sleep?" Auntie Grace asked as she put the mug in front of Ava.

"Like a log. I was exhausted."

"I've been so worried that I've hardly slept since Xu became ill."

"He's going to recover and he'll be home before you know it."

"Having you here makes it easier."

Ava thought about her phone conversation with Suen and felt a twinge of guilt. "Auntie, there may be a business problem in Hong Kong that I have to attend to."

"You might have to go there?"

"It is possible."

"What kind of problem?"

"It's related to Xu, but I was involved in it."

"It can't be handled by Lop or Suen?"

"Lop has been shot, and Suen is unsure about what to do," Ava said, seeing no reason to hide the truth. "We're hoping Xu will be able to give us some advice when we see him this morning."

"Is Lop dead?" Auntie Grace said, alarmed.

"No."

"Thank goodness. I've known him since he was a little boy. His father was one of Xu's father's best men."

"But he was badly hurt and he isn't in any shape to handle this problem."

"Is it complicated?"

"It could be."

"Then that probably excludes Suen as well. He isn't much good at handling complications."

"If I go, it isn't because Suen isn't capable," Ava said. "It's more that I'm familiar with the history and the people who are involved."

"When will you decide if you're going?"

"After I talk to Xu this morning."

"Does Fai know about this?"

"She knows it's a possibility," Ava said.

"Would she go with you?"

"No."

Auntie Grace pressed her lips together. "Would you come back here after Hong Kong?"

"I imagine I would."

"Then Fai can stay with me until you do."

"Once I know for sure what I'm doing, we can have that conversation."

"Once you know what?" Fai said from the kitchen doorway.

"Whether or not I have to go to Hong Kong," Ava said.

"From the sound of things last night, I'll be surprised if she doesn't go," Fai said to Auntie.

"And I was telling her that if she does, you can stay here with me until she gets back," Auntie said.

"I'd like that," Fai said.

"The two of you sound like you can hardly wait for me to leave," Ava said with a laugh.

"Well, we'd get a chance to know each other better," Auntie said. "I don't see how that could be a bad thing."

Ava started to say something but was interrupted by her phone. "Suen, is everything okay? Are we still on for nine-thirty?" she asked.

"No, that's why I'm calling. I'm going directly to the hospital from our offices. I've spoken to Wen. He'll drive you to the hospital."

"Has something happened?" she asked, detecting stress in his voice.

"Everything is totally fucked up," he blurted.

"You'll need to explain."

"The Wings have threatened to kill one of the hostages by noon today."

"How do you know that?"

"Carter Wing just phoned me. He said he's been trying to reach Xu, and he's convinced Xu is deliberately avoiding him. He said he hopes Xu will start to take them more seriously."

"It was Carter who called you, not Sammy?"

"It was Carter, and the nasty little son of a bitch couldn't have been more insulting."

"How did you respond? What did you say about Xu?"

"I didn't know what to say, so I said hardly anything. I listened, and when he was finished, all I told him was that I'd pass the message along to Xu."

"Under the circumstances, that was wise."

"Except we can't do nothing. We have to react. I've called an executive meeting."

"Suen, it isn't my place to tell you what to do, but I strongly suggest that you not make any drastic decisions before you talk to Xu," Ava said. "There is a chance he'll be more alert this morning, and I think you should hold off doing anything until we confirm his condition. This falling-out with the Wings could have far-reaching implications. Xu needs to be given every opportunity to speak his mind."

Suen was silent for several seconds. "I know you're right," he finally said hesitantly. "It's just that Carter made me so fucking angry."

"I understand why, and god knows you may get a chance to retaliate, but for now why don't you go to the hospital at nine-thirty as we planned. If Xu isn't himself, then you still have time to hold your meeting."

"Yeah, that makes sense."

"Okay then, I'll see you at the hospital," Ava said, ending the call. When she put down her phone, she saw Fai and Auntie Grace looking at her with questions in their eyes. "That was Suen. He has some problems to deal with and wanted to say he won't be driving with me to the hospital."

"Do you want me to come with you?" Fai asked.

"It might be better if you stay here with Auntie Grace. I'm

not sure how our meeting will go, and I might have to have more than one. I hate the idea of you just sitting around waiting."

"Stay with me," Auntie Grace urged. "I'll take you on a tour of the neighbourhood."

"Yes, okay. From what I saw last night it's fascinating."

"I don't know about that, but it is different from the rest of Shanghai."

Ava looked at the kitchen clock. "I need to shower and get dressed."

"Do you want breakfast?" Auntie asked.

"If I have time after I'm put together."

"I have pork dumplings. I'll warm them just in case."

"I love being spoiled," Ava said with a smile, and stood up. "I'll be back."

She walked towards the bedroom and was almost at the door when she noticed that Fai was right behind her.

"I want to talk to you," Fai said, her face clouded.

"Sure," Ava said, immediately concerned. "Is something wrong?"

"Let's sit," Fai said, pointing to the bed.

Ava sat, her mind turning over as she wondered what had upset Fai. "I'm sorry if you think I'll be abandoning you if I have to go to Hong Kong," she guessed.

"I don't feel the least bit abandoned. In fact, I feel completely welcomed into a new family," Fai said, joining her on the bed. "The thing is, I'm scared. I had trouble sleeping last night, thinking about what's going on in Hong Kong and worrying that you'll get dragged into the middle of it. I don't want to lose the love of my life after I've just found her."

Ava closed her eyes and took a deep breath. "You know that I've spent the past thirteen years collecting bad debts with Uncle and then being associated with Xu. I can't deny that I've been exposed to danger. You've seen the scars I got from when danger got too close — including this one," Ava said, lifting the sleeve of her T-shirt to display the bandage on her arm from two days before in Beijing. "But Fai, I'm not rash. I don't take foolish chances. And I've proven over and over again that I'm capable of looking after myself."

"No one is invincible."

"I don't believe for a second that I am."

"But you keep challenging fate, and one day you'll take on more than even you can handle," Fai said. "I've heard the stories about you and I've seen you in action, but that doesn't stop me from worrying."

"Are you trying to say you don't want me to go to Hong Kong?"

"No. I'd never put myself between you and what you think is the right thing to do. That would be like your telling me not to take a film role that I felt strongly about," Fai said. "All I'm trying to say — and I'm doing it badly — is that I want you to be careful. I want you to come back to me."

"If I go, I'll be back. Maybe in bits and pieces, but I'll be back," Ava said. When she saw Fai's face cloud over again, she added, "That last part was a joke."

Fai smiled half-heartedly. "I don't mean to be a pain in the ass," she said as she stood up. "You should start getting ready if you want to be at the hospital when visiting hours begin."

\* \* \*

Half an hour later, Ava walked into the kitchen to find Fai
and Auntie Grace in deep conversation. She watched them
unobserved for a moment, feeling a rush of pleasure as she
saw how well they seemed to have connected. "I'm heading
out now," she interrupted.

"You look so professional," Auntie Grace said.

Ava wore a white button-down Brooks Brothers shirt,
black slacks, and black pumps; her hair was pulled back and
held in place with an ivory chignon pin. There was a hint of
black mascara around her eyes and a light touch of red on
her lips. "I don't want the hospital to think that Xu's *mei mei*
is anything other than professional," she said.

Fai and Auntie Grace stood up and came to Ava with
open arms. She stepped into them and the three women
hugged.

"I should get going," Ava said finally.

Wen was standing by the Mercedes as Ava left the house.
He ran to the car's back door and opened it. "Directly to the
hospital?" he asked.

"Yes, thanks."

Wen drove carefully along the lane, stopped briefly at
the fruit vendor's cart, and then worked his way to Huaihai
Road, where he eased into heavy traffic. "It could be a slow
trip this morning," he said to Ava.

"There's no rush," she said, her mind occupied by the conversation she'd just had with Fai. It wasn't often that she
thought in detail about the life she had led. Uncle used to
say that people who spend too much time looking back are
doomed not to see what's coming at them. But now, as Ava
thought about the twists and turns her life had taken, she
recognized that fate had been incredibly kind to her.

Ava had been educated at York University in Toronto and at Babson College in Wellesley, Massachusetts, graduating with a degree in forensic accounting. She had tried working for a couple of large accounting firms but found it difficult to fit into their constricted environments, so — at her mother's urging — she opened her own small accountancy office. It turned out to be just as boring, and Ava had been contemplating giving up accounting altogether when one of her clients ran into trouble with a customer in Hong Kong who owed money long past due and was refusing to pay. Ava cut a deal with her client to go to Hong Kong to try to collect the funds. In the course of doing so, she had met Andy and Carlo — two triads who worked for a man they called simply "Uncle" and who were chasing the same debtor. Ava was successful in retrieving the money that was owed to both parties, and she met Uncle.

Uncle was a small, thin, elegant man in his seventies who always wore a black suit and a white shirt buttoned to the collar. He had been, Andy hinted, the leader of a triad gang. He had since left that life and was operating his own debt-collection business. When he met Ava after her success, he offered her a job. She told him she didn't want to work for anyone but herself. The next day he asked the twenty-five-year-old Canadian to become his partner. As odd as the offer was — made even odder by their age difference — there was a sincerity and simplicity about Uncle that evoked trust. Ava accepted his offer, and for the next ten years they worked side by side, inseparable and increasingly devoted to each other. In some ways she was the granddaughter he'd never had, and Uncle was the grandfather she'd never had.

Their debt-collection business wasn't for the faint of heart. They only took on large jobs that normally ran into millions of dollars, and they were usually successful. Their standard fee of thirty percent of whatever they recovered quickly made Ava a wealthy young woman. But there was a price to be paid for their success. As talented as Ava was at locating money that had been stolen or scammed, recovering those funds was always a challenge — and often dangerous. Over those ten years Ava had been shot, attacked with knives, machetes, and hammers, kicked, punched, and threatened more times than she could count. She had persevered and prevailed, aided by Uncle and his endless contacts and by her skill in bak mei — a deadly martial art that had helped her take on, and take out, many men.

When Uncle died of cancer a few years before, he had willed her his fortune. Added to her own wealth, it gave her more money than she would ever need, so she closed down the debt-collection business. Uncle, in effect, had also left her Xu. She hadn't known about him while she was working with Uncle, but when Uncle was ill and Ava was in some peril in Borneo, Xu had come to her rescue. A short time later she met him at Uncle's funeral and discovered that Uncle and Xu's father had been colleagues, and that Uncle was Xu's godfather and mentor. Ava never understood why Uncle had kept her in the dark about Xu, but after his death they had bonded. Ava often said she had never trusted anyone in her life more than Uncle, but now she and Xu seemed to share that same fierce mutual loyalty. He was always there for her, and she would do anything for him.

She thought again about how kind fate had been to her during her years with Uncle, and now in her friendship with Xu. Maybe Fai was correct in saying that she ran the risk of challenging it once too often. How could her luck continue indefinitely? She had a large scar from a gunshot wound on her thigh and scars on her hip, knee, and back; and now a machete had left one on her arm. If any of those attacks had hit her a few inches lower or higher, instead of being scarred, she knew she could be dead.

"Ten minutes and we'll be there," Wen said as the car crossed Lupu Bridge and entered Pudong.

"Thanks," Ava said, looking out at the sky. The weather was warmer than it had been in cold, dank Beijing, but it was still late winter and the sun was hidden behind banks of grey cloud. Or was it pollution? In Shanghai, Ava could never be sure. To the north of the city there were still a large number of coal-burning factories, and when the wind blew in the direction of Shanghai, their emissions added to those produced by the cars, trucks, and buses of a city of twenty-five million, making the air so bad that schoolchildren weren't allowed outdoors for recess.

Wen reached the hospital at twenty minutes to ten. He stopped directly in front. "I'll meet you here later," he said. "Suen will give me a heads-up when you're ready to leave."

Ava climbed the steps to the entrance and, once inside, made her way to the twelfth floor. Suen was already there, standing at the nursing station wearing a gown, mask, and slippers. Ava waved at him and went to the change room. When she joined him, he said, "The nurse told me Xu slept well and ate some breakfast."

"That's good to hear," she said. "Let's see if he's a bit peppier than last night."

They went to Xu's room. Suen knocked and opened the door. Xu was flat on his back with his eyes closed. "Boss, it's me and Ava," Suen said.

Xu's eyes opened and he smiled wanly. "I'm glad to see you both."

Suen pushed two visitor's chairs next to the bed and they sat down.

"You look better than you did last night," Ava said.

"You were here?"

"I was."

"Then I must be doing better, because I don't remember seeing you," he said.

"You're on the mend, boss," Suen said.

"I sure hope so. I feel like a punching bag."

"You need rest," Ava said.

"I'm in the right place for it," Xu said.

"Are you up to discussing some business?"

"Of course. In fact, I've been wondering what's been going on."

Suen glanced at Ava.

"Do you remember the concerns you had about Hong Kong, about Wanchai?" she asked.

"Yes."

"Well, they were warranted," Ava said, and then hesitated before adding, "Lop has been shot."

He turned his head quickly so he could look at her. "Is he dead?"

"No, he's in a clinic in Kowloon, the same one that you were in. He took three bullets and isn't in great shape, but Sonny says he'll probably live," Ava said. "It appears that Sammy Wing and his nephew Carter are making a play for Wanchai. Taking out Lop was their first step, and then late last night they grabbed seven of your men off the street, and now they're threatening to kill them unless you pull out of Wanchai immediately."

"They told Ko we have until midnight tonight to start leaving Wanchai or they'll kill the men. Then a couple of hours ago, Carter Wing called me to say they're prepared to kill one at noon today unless we start to play ball. He was pissed off that he couldn't reach you. He thinks you're avoiding him," Suen said.

Xu shook his head and closed his eyes again. "Is Ko running things there, now that Lop is down?"

"Yes," Suen said.

"What has he done? What is he doing?"

"Last night I told him to try locating the men without making a bad situation worse. When I spoke to him earlier this morning, he hadn't found them. Now he's waiting for further instructions."

"I don't want to lose one man, let alone seven," Xu said softly. "But I also can't just cut and run from Wanchai."

"The men could be bargaining chips," Suen said, repeating the point Ava had made the night before. "They may have no intention of killing them."

"We can't take that risk," Xu said. "How many men do we still have in Wanchai who are loyal to us and not Sammy?"

"About thirty of the men are definitely ours. For the rest, I'd have to ask Ko."

"How many more could you mobilize at short notice?"

"We have about a hundred good soldiers in and around Shanghai. If you called on some friendly Mountain Masters for support, we could probably double that," Suen said. "Lam in Guangzhou owes you favours, and he's no more than a few hours by car from Hong Kong."

"We can't involve the other gangs," Xu said. "We took

Wanchai by ourselves and we have to hold on to it the same way."

"Do you really think the Wings are prepared for a full-out war?" Ava asked.

"I don't know..." Xu said, his voice trailing off.

Ava could sense his weakness returning and felt a touch of guilt. "Maybe we should drop this for now and let Xu rest," she said to Suen. "You can take it up with the executive."

Suen looked at her and then at Xu. "You may be right," he said.

"No, I'm okay," Xu said. "I just need a moment to think this through. One thing is certain, we can't ignore them. Sooner or later we'll have to talk. As stupid and stubborn as Sammy can be, I can't believe he'd let things get completely out of control."

"We also have to deal with his nephew," Ava said. "Sonny told me he's very aggressive. The way he spoke to Suen this morning confirms that."

"I don't know Carter that well. He was the gang's Vanguard but I dealt mainly with Ling, when he was Mountain Master."

"Is it a big gang?"

"Big enough to cause us a lot of trouble. They must have close to two hundred of their own men on the street."

"We could handle them if we had to," Suen said.

"I know you could, but at what cost?" Xu said. "And by that I don't mean just the loss of men. It would disrupt business for months, if not longer, and I'd have a lot of pissed-off Mountain Masters to deal with if the Hong Kong police or — god forbid — the PLA got involved."

"So what do we do?" Suen asked.

"We start by talking to the Wings," Xu said. "We need to know their endgame: what it is they really want and what they'll be willing to settle for."

"You'd give up Wanchai?" Suen asked, as if the idea were unthinkable.

"No, although maybe it's time to make an accommodation with Sammy. He's still the Mountain Master, but I know that Lop has kept a very tight check on him. Sammy's ego has to be hurting, and the money we've allowed him is just crumbs compared to what he was making before."

"He shot Lop," Suen said.

"I know, but Lop is still alive, and I have seven other men to worry about right now."

Ava sensed that Suen had only one thing on his mind: revenge. She knew enough about triads to understand that taking revenge would only escalate hostilities. "Sammy has always prided himself on his negotiating skills," she said. "I can't imagine he'll refuse to talk to us."

"Well, let's find out," Xu said. "Ava, you know him better than any of us. Will you reach out to him?"

She hesitated and then said, "I will if you think I'm the right person to do it."

"I'd do it myself, but at this point I'm never sure how coherent I'm going to be from one minute to the next," Xu said. "And you do have a long-standing relationship with Sammy. I'd appreciate it if you would."

"Then I'll be glad to do it."

"Feng has all of Sammy's contact numbers."

"I'll call Feng as soon as we leave you."

"Good," Xu said, and then looked at Suen. "While Ava is trying to get in touch with Wing, I want you to start organizing our men. They need to be ready to go to Hong Kong. I hope it isn't necessary to send them, but we have to be prepared."

( 5 )

**"HE SEEMS BETTER," AVA SAID AS SHE AND SUEN LEFT** Xu's room.

"He does, thank God. I suspect some hard decisions will have to be made, and he's the man who knows how to make them," Suen said. "By the way, thanks for telling him about Lop and Wanchai. I've never been very good at delivering bad news."

"*Momentai*," Ava said. "Now, could you call Feng for me? I need Sammy Wing's contact numbers."

"Once you get them, do you want to call Wing from here or do you want to wait until you have some privacy?"

"We need to act quickly, so I'll do it from the car."

"Okay, I'll call Feng first and then I'll give Wen the heads-up that we're ready to leave," Suen said.

"I expect I'll have to talk to Xu after I talk to Sammy Wing, so I probably won't be leaving just yet. But I do want to make the call from the car."

"I'll find out where he's parked."

Ava stood by the elevators while Suen sat in the waiting room and made his calls. Five minutes later he rejoined her and handed her a slip of paper. "Three phone numbers. The first is Sammy's Wanchai office land line, but I can't imagine he'll be there. The second is his cell and the third is Carter's cell."

"Perfect."

"Wen is parked on the street about fifty metres to the left of the hospital entrance as you leave."

"Also perfect."

"I'll stay here until I hear from you."

Ava left the hospital, turned left, and walked down the street. She had gone less than twenty metres when she saw Wen standing on the sidewalk next to the car. "Did Suen explain that I just want to sit in the car while I make a phone call?" she asked when she reached him.

"He did," Wen said, opening the back door for her. "I'll make sure you aren't disturbed."

Ava settled into the back seat and took her phone from her bag. She sat quietly for a few moments as she thought about the best way to approach Sammy Wing. In the past he'd bragged about his relationship with Uncle — although that hadn't prevented him from accepting the contract to kill her — and he often brought up his name with her as a way of creating some kind of bond. It was completely artificial, but Ava went along with it because, while she didn't believe Uncle would ever be close to a man like Wing, she knew they had been triad colleagues for decades. So, she decided, she would be the one to invoke Uncle's name if the right opportunity presented itself.

Next there was the matter of Sammy's attempts to kill her and Xu. Sammy had denied it at the time and tried to offload the blame on Li, who had been Mountain Master in

Guangzhou before Lam killed him. Ava knew that Li had been involved, but she also knew it was in partnership with Sammy. Xu's response to the attack on his life had been amazingly conciliatory, given the circumstances. Ava hoped that was something she could use in their favour.

Finally, Ava reminded herself that, despite his bluster and a tendency to exaggerate, Sammy was shrewd, and not a man to be taken for granted or condescended to — especially when he had a Mountain Master nephew supporting him with two hundred men on the street. *Be respectful,* she told herself as she dialled his number.

The phone rang three times and then sounded like it had been answered, except no one spoke. "Sammy, this is Ava Lee," she said. She thought she could hear breathing on the other end. "Sammy, it's Ava."

"Why are you calling me?" he said finally.

"Sammy, I'm sure you know why."

He didn't answer right away, and she could hear voices in the background. Finally he said, "Why am I hearing from you, and why isn't Xu taking calls from my nephew?"

"Xu knows you and I have a special rapport. I guess he figures we can work things out."

"What special rapport? The last time I talked to you was in that restaurant at the Kowloon MTR station. As I remember, you told me that Xu and that fucker Lop were taking over Wanchai and you were going to leave me in place for appearance's sake."

"Sammy, at least you're alive. How many men who tried what you did can make that claim?"

"I'm supposed to be grateful for being humiliated like that?"

"Not grateful, but don't exaggerate how badly you were treated. I thought you were given a measure of respect — a respect that everyone involved, including Xu, thought you had earned."

"It would have been more respectful to kill me."

Ava drew a deep breath. "Sammy, it isn't too late for that to be arranged."

"Is that a threat?" he snapped. "The girl is making threats now?"

"The *girl* is trying to remind you of the reality of your situation. Have you forgotten about the forces that Xu can bring to bear if he chooses?"

"The reality is that Lop is out of the picture, which means Wanchai is leaderless, and we're holding seven of Xu's men and we're prepared to kill them and whoever stands in our way."

"Is killing those men really neccosary?" she asked, avoiding further mention of Lop.

"Not if Xu pulls out of Wanchai."

"He won't do that," Ava said.

"That is his only option."

"I don't believe you."

"How the fuck would you know?" Wing said.

"I don't, but I do know that you're too clever to paint yourself into a corner with ultimatums like the one you just delivered."

"Why do you think we did what we did? What is it you think we want?"

"You tell me," said Ava.

"We want Wanchai back. We want those pricks from Shanghai gone."

"That isn't going to happen, especially if you harm Xu's men."

"We'll see about that," Wing said, his voice suddenly more menacing.

*Have I pushed too hard?* Ava thought. "What we need to do, Sammy, is talk — talk about what is actually possible," she said. "Everyone has to save face."

He didn't respond. Again she thought she heard voices in the background and wondered if she was on speaker phone. Finally he said, "This is a waste of time. Tell Xu to call me or Carter. He's the one we want to talk to."

"He won't do that as long as he feels you're pointing a gun at his head, and threatening to kill his men is the same thing to him," she said. "He won't talk to you until those men are released and there's an acceptable offer on the table. Right now he has neither, so as it stands, I'm afraid you're stuck with me."

"And what authority do you have?" a different voice — Ava assumed it was Carter's — asked in a condescending tone.

"What I have is Xu's complete confidence. If you doubt that, ask your uncle. He knows I've spoken for Xu in the past and that whatever I've promised has been delivered."

Once again she heard muffled voices, and then Sammy said, "We won't do this over the phone. Where are you?"

"Shanghai."

"Come to Hong Kong."

"If I come, are you guaranteeing that we'll talk?"

"I am."

"And just talk? I'm not in the mood to be ambushed again."

"We'll talk, nothing more. You have my word."

"I need your guarantee. I want you to swear it in Uncle's memory."

"I gave you my word."

"That's not good enough."

"Then I swear in Uncle's memory," Sammy said harshly.

"And I want the same assurance from your nephew."

"Why?"

"We're not sure who's making the decisions."

"Where Wanchai is concerned, I am," Sammy said.

"But my understanding is that Sha Tin is involved in this as well."

"You have my fucking guarantee!" Carter shouted. "Now come to Hong Kong and let's get this settled."

"Fine. I will get myself onto an airplane but I won't be able to get there until this evening. What will you do with Xu's men in the meantime? Can you promise not to harm them until we've had a chance to meet?"

"Get here. If you're early enough, we'll meet tonight. If not, it will have to be tomorrow. Call me when you arrive and we'll tell you where and when," Sammy said.

"But you still haven't told me about the men. Will they be unharmed?"

"We'll see."

"That isn't reassuring."

"It's the best you're going to get."

"Okay, Sammy, I'm going to keep believing you're as clever as I said you were," Ava said.

"Call me when you arrive," he said, and then the line went dead.

*I think he's going to negotiate,* Ava thought, feeling pleased about the way she'd handled the conversation. She got out of the car and walked towards Wen, who had moved away from the car while she spoke to Wing. "I'm going back inside, but I don't imagine I'll be more than twenty minutes. You'll need to drive me to Xu's and then wait while I pack a bag. I'll be going to the airport."

Suen stood on the front steps of the hospital and watched her approach with a look of curiosity on his face. "Well?" he asked when she reached him.

"Let's wait until we're with Xu. I don't want to repeat myself."

"Okay," Suen said, and then turned and led the way into the hospital.

The nurses seemed surprised to see them when they re-entered the ward. Ava wondered if something had happened. "Is Xu all right?" she asked.

"The doctor was just with him. He said he needs more rest and increased his medication."

"Can we talk to him?"

"I guess so, but don't stay longer than necessary."

Ava and Suen quickly put on gowns, slippers, and masks and headed to Xu's room. The room was darker than it had been earlier, and the light emanating from the equipment by the bed was eerie. "Xu, it's Ava and Suen," she said. "Can you hear me?"

"I can. What happened? Did you reach Sammy?"

"I spoke to him and Carter. They're willing to meet with us. I'll be going to Hong Kong today."

"Good. What about our men?"

"They wouldn't make any commitment, but I don't believe they'll do anything rash. I think we've bought some time."

"What do Sammy and Carter want?"

"Do you mean what do they *really* want?" Ava said.

"Yes."

"I don't know. Sammy told me they want the Shanghai men completely gone from Wanchai. I told him that isn't going to happen. That's as far as we got."

"He was still willing to meet after you told him that?"

"He was."

"Then we have to believe they're willing to negotiate."

"I think they are," she said.

"Well, at least we have a starting point," Xu said, almost in a whisper.

"What are you prepared to give up?" she asked.

"Money rather than control, but I suspect they'll want both."

"How should I respond?"

"Don't argue with them," he said, shaking his head. "The most important thing is to keep those seven men alive. So, no matter how outrageous the Wings' demands, keep asking questions. You need to figure out their real bottom line."

"Okay. I'll be meeting with them tonight or tomorrow. If you are still in isolation, I'll let Suen know when and where and I'll stay in touch with him. He'll keep you updated."

"Don't go to any meeting alone," Xu said.

"Don't worry, I learned my lesson with Sammy. I'll have Sonny with me, and we'll get Ko to support us."

Xu reached for her hand. "Ava, I'm sorry you've been dragged into this."

"Don't be. I can't seem to shake Sammy Wing. He keeps popping up in my life like some rancid piece of unfinished business. Maybe this time I'll manage to put him behind me for good."

## 6

**AVA LEFT THE HOSPITAL AND CALLED XU'S HOUSE FROM**
the car. When there was no answer, she tried Fai's cell.

"Hi," Fai said above the sound of traffic in the background. "We're taking a walk in the Concession."

"And I'm just leaving the hospital."

"How is Xu?"

"He's better this morning, more alert, and he isn't as pale. The doctor just increased his medication, but that's to help him get more sleep. I think he's definitely improving."

"What a relief. I'll tell Auntie Grace."

"You can also tell her that I'll be home in about half an hour, but I'm staying just long enough to pack. I do have to go to Hong Kong."

"I was expecting that. We'll head back to the house in time to see you. Is there anything you want me to do for you before you leave?"

"No, but thanks. I'll pack when I get home."

"Where will you stay in Hong Kong?"

"I haven't thought about it yet. I normally stay at the Mandarin Oriental, but I have stayed at Uncle's old apartment in Kowloon. I'll talk to Sonny before I decide."

"How long will you be gone?"

"If things go well, I can't imagine it will be more than a day or two."

"And if they don't?"

"You shouldn't think like that."

"I'm still going to worry."

"I know," Ava said. "Listen, I have some other calls to make. I'll see you soon."

Ava was accustomed to people worrying about her. Her mother, her father, Uncle, Xu, May Ling, and Amanda had all taken their turns, but Ava had never felt accountable for being the source of those worries. They all knew who she was and what she did. It was different with Fai. She was simply looking for love and wasn't bound by blood or business. Ava's history was of no importance to her; when it intruded negatively on their lives, it seemed to Ava that it threw off the balance they had achieved. *I'll get Sammy resolved, spend a few more days in Shanghai, and then go with Fai to Yantai,* she thought.

She opened her phone and called a familiar Hong Kong number.

"*Wei,*" Sonny answered.

"It's Ava. I'll be flying into Hong Kong later today. I'll text you the flight details when I have them."

"I'm guessing that Sammy Wing is the reason."

"Yes. We'll be meeting with him. I won't be surprised if his nephew comes as well."

"When's the meeting?"

"We haven't fixed a time or place. There's no point doing that until I know when I'm arriving."

"You'll want me at the meeting?"

"Oh yes, and Carlo and Andy, and maybe a few of Ko's men. We're not taking any chances this time."

"I'll make sure Carlo and Andy are available," Sonny said.

"When you talk to Andy, you should also ask him if he's heard any more scuttlebutt about the Wings, including anything about Xu's seven men."

"What's going to happen to them?"

"I think they're okay for now."

"Does Ko know that?"

"I imagine Suen has called him, but if you want to make sure, call him yourself when we're finished."

"I will," Sonny said. "Where will you be staying?"

"I don't know. If Lourdes is still in the Philippines, I was thinking about Uncle's apartment," Ava said, referring to Lourdes Bentulan, the Filipina who had been Uncle's housekeeper for close to thirty years and who had inherited the apartment when he died.

"She's back in Hong Kong."

"Then I'll stay at the Mandarin Oriental in Central."

"I actually think that's a better choice from a security viewpoint."

"Do you have any other commitments for the next couple of days?"

"When you're in Hong Kong, you're the only commitment I have. I was supposed to drive your brother and his partner to Shenzhen, but I'll cancel."

"Don't tell Michael that I'm in Hong Kong, though. He'd tell my father and I'd be expected to meet him for dinner or lunch. This isn't that kind of trip."

"Will Amanda know?"

"Yes, I always let her and May Ling know where I am, but both of them are very good at keeping it to themselves."

Sonny was familiar with the complications surrounding Ava's family life, and he never questioned how she handled them. She was the second daughter of the second wife of Marcus Lee. Marcus had four sons — including Michael, the oldest — with his first wife, Elizabeth. He had never divorced Elizabeth and still lived with her in Hong Kong. His marriage to Jennie, and later to a third wife who now lived in Australia, was traditional rather than strictly legal. When Ava and her sister Marian were still of preschool age, a rift had developed between Marcus and Jennie and he had dispatched the family to Canada. He did not abandon them, though. He supported them financially, spoke to Jennie every day on the phone, visited with her for two weeks every year, and deeply cared about and monitored the lives of his daughters. Among Ava's Chinese friends in Toronto, being the child of a second or third wife was common. In fact, it was so common that Jennie Lee claimed — with some justification — that without those children as students, many of the most expensive private schools in the city would be struggling.

Where Ava's life differed from those of most of her friends, and even her sister's, was that she had developed a relationship with her half-brothers from Marcus's first marriage and had even come to know Elizabeth Lee. The impetus had been a business problem of Michael's that needed the kind of help Ava was uniquely equipped to provide. At Marcus's request she had flown to Hong Kong, met Michael and his partner, Simon To, and agreed to assist them. The assistance became messy and violent, but in the end she prevailed, saving their business and Simon To's life.

Michael had been engaged at the time to a young woman named Amanda Yee. Ava took an immediate liking to her and only later discovered that she and Uncle had twice done jobs for her father, Jack Yee. By the time the Michael-and-Simon fiasco was resolved, Ava and Amanda were firm friends, so much so that Amanda asked Ava to be maid of honour at her wedding. Given Ava's status as the daughter of a second wife, that had the potential to be incredibly awkward, until Elizabeth Lee graciously acknowledged Ava at the wedding and thanked her for everything she'd done for the family.

Amanda and Ava's relationship became more entangled when Ava and her friend May Ling Wong decided to start an investment business together. Neither Ava nor May Ling — who lived in Wuhan and owned a business there that she ran with her husband — were able to commit to the new business full-time, so they brought Amanda onboard as a full-time partner. The company became Three Sisters Investments, and it now owned entirely or had a majority stake in businesses involved in fashion, furniture manufacturing, trading, and warehousing and distribution.

"I see Amanda quite often. She's an impressive young woman," Sonny said. "But I can't remember the last time I saw Madam Wong."

"May would hate you calling her that," Ava said, laughing. "And I hope you don't refer to me as Madam Lee behind my back."

"Never," Sonny replied in a very serious tone.

"I'm just teasing," Ava said, reminded again of how literally Sonny took every word she uttered.

"I know that, boss."

She wasn't sure he did but let it pass. "Anyway, stay close to your phone. I'll make my travel arrangements within the hour."

"It will be good to have you back in Hong Kong, even if the reason sucks and it's only for a little while."

"I'm looking forward to seeing you as well," she said, ending the conversation.

Ava looked out the car window. When she saw they were already in the Concession, she decided to wait until she got to the house to book her flight and hotel. Wen drove past a florist, a bakery advertising baguettes, and an outdoor café — all familiar landmarks. Just past the café he turned into the laneway. A quick stop at the fruit cart was followed by a careful drive, three beeps from the car horn, and a left-hand turn into the courtyard.

"Auntie Grace and the other woman aren't home," one of the men at the gate informed Ava when she slid out of the car.

Ava took out her phone and hit speed dial.

"Hey," Fai answered.

"I'm at the house," Ava said.

"We're two minutes away. See you soon."

Ava walked into the house and immediately felt the silence. It was the first time she could remember not being met by Xu or Auntie Grace. Xu had a computer on a desk in the living room and she went to it. She logged on, went to the Cathay Pacific website, and booked a business-class seat on the two p.m. flight to Hong Kong. She then reserved a suite for three nights at the Mandarin Oriental. As she pushed the chair back from the desk, the front door opened and Fai and Auntie Grace entered.

"You look flushed," Ava said to Fai.

"It's warm out there, and Auntie Grace walks very quickly."

"You mean 'walks very quickly for an old woman,'" Auntie said.

"I didn't mean that at all."

Auntie smiled at Ava. "You'll never guess what happened," she said. "When we were buying a cake at the bakery, another customer approached Fai and asked if she's ever been told she looks exactly like Pang Fai."

"What did you say?" Ava asked Fai.

"I told her I've heard that before, but then Auntie Grace let the cat out the bag by announcing that I was the one and only Pang Fai."

"I couldn't help myself. Besides, there were only a few customers in the store, and they're all lovely women. Fai was kind enough to let them take photos with her."

"Then the store owner didn't want us to pay for the cake, but we insisted."

"You mean, you insisted," Auntie said.

"I can see that you two are going to get along very well while I'm gone," Ava said. "I've just made by bookings and now I have to pack. My flight is at two, so I'd better get moving."

Fai and Auntie were in the kitchen when Ava left the bedroom with her Shanghai Tang Double Happiness carry-on bag in one hand and her Louis Vuitton handbag in the other. "I'm ready to leave," she said.

Fai sighed. "I'll miss you.

"I'll miss you too, but I'll be in touch. My flight lands

around five. I'll call as soon as I can. And I'm staying at the Mandarin Oriental, so you can reach me there or on my cell if you want to talk."

"I'll try not to be a pest."

"You could never be that," Ava said. "But take advantage of the time here to relax and do some exploring."

Fai leaned towards Ava and kissed her gently on the lips. "You be careful."

"I will."

Fai nodded. "I'll say goodbye here. I won't walk you to the door because I don't want to watch you driving away."

Ava left the house, closing the door behind her. Wen ran towards her and reached for the Shanghai Tang bag. "Which airport?" he asked.

"Pudong International, Terminal 2. I'm flying Cathay Pacific."

"When is your flight?"

"Two o'clock."

"Good. That gives us plenty of time."

As the car edged along the laneway, Ava sent a text to Sonny with her flight and hotel details. Then she found May Ling's cell number and hit speed dial again. May's phone rang four times and went to voicemail. "It's Ava. Call me," she said.

Traffic was worse than it had been earlier. Ava checked her watch and wondered if Wen was being overly optimistic. Before she could ask him, her phone sounded and she saw May's number. "How are things in Wuhan?" Ava answered.

"They're just fine. How are things...wherever you are?"

"I'm in Shanghai."

"I thought you were in Beijing."

"I left yesterday. Xu hasn't been feeling well and Auntie Grace wanted me to visit."

"Is he okay?" May asked, her voice filled with concern.

"He's in hospital with bacterial meningitis, which means he's not exactly okay. The good news is that it was diagnosed early and is being treated. He's already feeling better."

"Which hospital?"

"Shanghai East International Medical Centre. But May, he's in isolation, so don't think about sending flowers or anything like that."

"How long will he be there?"

Although there was nothing particularly nosy about May's question, Ava felt slightly uncomfortable. Maybe it was in her head and had no basis in reality, but ever since May and Xu had met, Ava had suspected that the two of them were attracted to each other. Nothing had happened that she knew of, and neither of them had spoken directly to her about their feelings, but that didn't change Ava's suspicions. Neither did the fact that May maintained she was happily married to Changxing and Xu had a steady stream of girlfriends. That she adored them both made her suspicions all the more difficult to bear. They were family to her; she didn't want their relationships to change in any way. And nothing changed things more, she thought, than sex. So at times she was careful when speaking to May about Xu or to Xu about May. However, this wasn't one of those times. "At least a few more days," she said.

"Will you be staying in Shanghai until he's home?"

"No, I have to go to Hong Kong. In fact, I'm on my way to the airport right now."

"What's going on in Hong Kong?"

"Xu has a problem there with Sammy Wing and his nephew," Ava said. "Do you remember Sammy?"

"How can I forget him? He tried to kill both of you."

"Now he's trying to retake Wanchai."

"Can't Lop deal with that? I thought he was running Wanchai."

"Lop has been shot. He's alive, but not functioning so well."

"That sounds like a real mess. Are you sure you want to get into the middle of it?" May asked, with the calmness of someone who had gone through many crises with Ava.

Ava didn't have many secrets where May was concerned. May knew Ava from her debt-collecting days with Uncle, and in fact had been a client. Ava had successfully recovered the money that May and Changxing were owed, but the job ended badly when May arranged to kill the person she thought had stolen from them. She did it behind Ava's back, and it took a lot of apologizing from May and convincing by Uncle for Ava to forgive her. But since then, the two women had forged a partnership that was wide open and — Ava thought — unbreakable.

"It is a mess, but I spoke to Sammy this morning and I think there's room for negotiation."

"Do you trust him?"

"No, and that's why I'll have Sonny and a handful of other men, including — I hope — Carlo and Andy, with me."

"Say hello to them for me," May said.

"I will, and I'm sure they'll say hello right back, because they do admire you," Ava said.

"Where will you be staying?"

"The Mandarin Oriental. You can tell Amanda where I'll be, and the two of you can reach me there or on my cell," Ava said. "But please tell Amanda not to mention it to Michael. I don't have time for family this trip. All I want to do is resolve this problem and get back to Shanghai as fast as possible."

"Is Auntie Grace alone in the house?"

"No, Fai is there with her. We were supposed to go to Yantai to meet her parents after we resolved that problem in Beijing, but then Xu's illness changed our plans."

"Is Auntie Grace okay with the two of you under the same roof and in the same bed?"

"She's thrilled to have a film star in the house. In fact, she was showing off Fai to some friends at the pastry shop this morning."

"I really like Fai. I'm so glad you found each other," May said.

"That reminds me of something," Ava said. "Do you remember Lau Lau?"

"The movie director?"

"Yes, Fai's ex-husband."

"Of course I do. He made some terrific films."

"*Made* is the operative word. I met him in Beijing and he's an absolute shell of a man. Between the booze and the drugs, trying to hide the fact that he's gay, and a film system that will only allow him to make kung-fu shlock or stupid historical war epics, he's pretty well been destroyed."

"Where is this leading?" May asked, with more than a hint of interest in her voice.

"Well, after I met him, I rewatched some of his old films, like *The Air We Breathe* and *City Girls*. They were as powerful and touching as I remembered. No other director has made films that depict the horrors of the Great Leap Forward and the Cultural Revolution as brilliantly as he did."

"And?"

"He told me he still has movies like those in his head, movies he wants to make," Ava said. "I began to think that maybe he should be given the chance."

"You just told me the man is wasted."

"But maybe he's not beyond redemption. What if we arranged to have him cleaned up? What if we paid him to write a script?"

"How would we ever be able to do anything like that?"

"I don't mean we'd do it directly. We'd put up the money but we'd work through Chen, Fai's agent and Lau Lau's old agent."

May paused and then said, "Okay, let's assume you get him cleaned up and you get a script, then what? If his script resembles any of the films you mentioned, it would never get made. The film syndicate would never finance it. Even if they did, it would never get past the censors."

"If the script is good — and I would trust Chen's judgement in that regard — then I'm thinking we could consider financing the film ourselves."

"Ava, how much money are you talking about? Ten, twenty, thirty million U.S. dollars?" May said. "And if we did finance it, where would the market be? The government would never allow it to be shown in China."

"Lau Lau has an international reputation."

"Yes, but people overseas don't exactly break down the doors to see Chinese films, especially the depressing type that you've mentioned."

"I prefer to describe them as realistic."

"Whatever — realistic or depressing, they still aren't going to make people laugh, and people like to laugh when they go to a film."

"Can we back up for just a minute?" Ava said.

"Sure."

"A lot of things have to happen before we get to the point where we'd have to decide to finance a movie. All I want is to try to get to that point," Ava said. "I mean, I can't imagine it would cost that much to send Lau Lau to a good rehab facility, and I'm sure his script fee would be reasonable."

"Assuming Lau Lau would go to rehab."

"If he wants a chance to make movies again, he'll have to," Ava said. "Why would he say no?"

"I know there are a lot of ifs and buts connected to what you're proposing, but I can't help feeling hesitant. We know nothing about film making."

"I get that, but we took the same kind of chance when we invested in PÖ. The fashion business wasn't one of our areas of expertise, but we gambled on Clark Po because we saw how creative he was. I'm prepared to take a chance on another person who's proven he can create. I'd like you to be in on it with me."

"I find it hard to say no to you," May said.

"Then don't. What's the point of us having all this money if we don't take a chance every once in a while? Helping Lau Lau get back on his feet could be a really good thing, even if a film never gets made."

"Okay, I'm in," May said.

"Thank you. I'll call Chen in a day or two and try to get things started," Ava said. "And May, thank you. I really appreciate your support."

"You always have my support."

"Who knows, this could work out really well or it might come to nothing. Regardless, I think we'll end up being pleased that we made the effort."

"Lau Lau did make some wonderful films," May said.

"And he can't have lost all of his skill."

"But one reason his films were so good was that Fai was in them. Have you mentioned your idea to her?"

"I did in passing. She thinks I'm crazy to try to resurrect him. She isn't opposed to the idea; she just doesn't think it's going to work."

"If by some miracle it does work, would you envision a role for her in the film?"

"I'd never make that a condition. I want Lau Lau to write whatever he wants. And even if there is a role for her, it would be up to him to decide if he wanted her and up to her to decide if she wanted to do it," Ava said.

"That's wise," May said.

The car horn sounded and Ava looked out the front window. Wen had come to a halt behind a long line of traffic leading to the airport. "I'll be getting out of the car in a minute," Ava said. "I'll call you tomorrow and let you know what's going on."

"Be careful."

"I always am."

"I sometimes worry that you aren't careful enough. I don't want to lose you."

*First Fai and now May telling me to be careful,* Ava thought. Was it a coincidence, or was fate warning her?

## 7

**THE FLIGHT TO HONG KONG TOOK ALMOST THREE** hours. Ava managed to occupy nearly all of that time watching *Our Time Will Come,* one of the most highly regarded Chinese films of the previous year. Given the Chinese government's control over film content and distribution, it didn't surprise her that the picture didn't deal with contemporary issues; it was a fictionalized history of the resistance movement in Hong Kong during the Japanese occupation in the Second World War. Interestingly, the director was a woman, Ann Hui, and the star was also a woman — Zhou Xun, who played a heroic character called Fang Gu. Xun reminded Ava of a young Pang Fai, although that wasn't something she'd mention to Fai. The film ended just as the plane began its descent.

Hong Kong International Airport had been built in 1998 on a manmade island, Chek Lap Kok, adjacent to Lantau Island, and it was still one of the most modern and functional in Asia. It handled sixty-five million travellers a year with almost brutal efficiency, and Ava fully expected to be walking into the sprawling, cavernous arrivals hall within fifteen minutes of landing. She was one minute quicker than that.

Ava didn't see Sonny until he stepped out from the crowd and started to walk towards her, a self-conscious smile spreading across his face. He wore a black suit, a white shirt, and a black tie. The suit jacket was buttoned and it seemed to strain across his belly. He had started to put on weight in recent years but still looked very light on his feet; Ava guessed he was as agile as ever.

"Hey, boss, right on time," he said, respectfully lowering his head just a touch.

"Good to see you," Ava said, handing him her Shanghai Tang bag and then reaching up to kiss him gently on the cheek.

The kiss, as always, embarrassed him. "The car is in the usual place," he said quickly.

They wove their way through the crowd towards the exit. As they did so, they passed the Kit Kat Koffee House, and Ava paused for a few seconds to look. During the years Uncle was alive, he would always come to meet her at the airport, sitting in that bar to wait with a cup of coffee, the racing form open on a table and an unlit cigarette dangling between his lips — the airport was one of the few places in Hong Kong where non-smoking regulations were actually enforced.

"I look in there every time too," Sonny said. "I still expect to see him."

Ava took Sonny's arm. "It's a nice memory."

Sonny bypassed the first exit doors they reached and went to a set discreetly signed VIP. They stepped through those doors onto the sidewalk. Like Xu, Uncle had favoured the Mercedes-Benz S-Class, and he had updated his car every three years. Sonny had been willed the last one. It was silver, also like Xu's. Ava wondered what Sonny was going to do when it hit its three-year anniversary.

"They still let you park here?" Ava asked as they walked to the car.

"Uncle's sticker expired last year, but the airport cops remember this was his car. I think they leave me alone out of respect for him."

He opened the back door for her, put her bag in the trunk, and slid into the driver's seat. "We're going to be in the middle of rush hour," he said.

"We get there when we get there," Ava said. "I'm not going to call Sammy until I get to the hotel. As long as those seven men are safe for tonight, I'll try to have our meeting scheduled for tomorrow morning."

"The more time we have to prepare, the better," Sonny said. "I have Carlo and Andy on standby, and Ko can give us as many men as we want. He's really bent out of shape about Lop. Ko worships him."

"How is Lop?"

"I called the clinic while I was waiting for you at the airport and managed to talk to Doctor Liu. He thinks Lop is out of danger but he still wants to keep a close eye on him for the next few days."

"Lop's surviving the attack does make things a bit less tense," Ava said. "What about Andy? Was he able to find out anything that might help us?"

"No. Word has spread about his connection to you. They've shut him out."

"And there's nothing being said on the street?"

"Right now it's as tight as a drum."

"That might not be a bad thing," Ava said. "The fewer people involved, even on the margins, the easier it might be to come to some kind of arrangement."

"Is Xu really prepared to deal with Sammy? Ko doesn't think that will ever happen. He's primed to fight."

"Then it's a good thing Ko isn't making those decisions."

"But boss, we're not going to the meeting unarmed, are we?"

"No."

"Good. I fired my Cobray M11 last week. It's ready to go."

"Do you still have that nine-millimetre Beretta I used when we went to Macau?"

"I do."

"I'm going to take it to the meeting. It will fit nicely into my bag."

"I'll clean and load it tonight."

They drove onto the Tsing Ma Bridge, which connected the airport to Hong Kong. The bridge spanned the Ma Wan Channel some two hundred metres below. Ava looked down at the armada of ships of all types coming and going from Hong Kong harbour — one of the busiest in the world. It was a sight she never tired of. It always made her feel like she was returning home, or at least returning to her second home.

"I have some idea of what I'm dealing with when it comes to Sammy, but I don't know anything about Carter Wing other than what you told me on the phone," Ava said. "How old is he?"

"Mid-thirties, I'd guess."

"That's young for a Mountain Master."

"Uncle was as young or younger when he took over Fanling," Sonny said, and then quickly added, "But I'm not comparing them."

"I know you're not," Ava said. "You told me Carter is aggressive. What did you mean by that?"

"I've seen him but I've never met him, so everything I'm telling you is second-hand."

"I understand. Go ahead."

"Well, he's always been very pushy, the kind of guy who does more than he's asked and more than he's expected to do. He was a Blue Lantern — a trainee — for about half the normal time before taking the Thirty-Six Oaths and becoming a forty-niner, a sworn triad. He worked for the Red Pole for a few years, and I was told he collected more protection money than any other two forty-niners put together. But he wasn't just tough; he was also smart, and he knew how to get along with the bosses. It didn't hurt that Sammy was his uncle. I'm sure Sammy kept an eye on him and helped him whenever he could. That wouldn't have gone unnoticed among the senior guys in the Sha Tin gang."

"Why was he in the Sha Tin gang? Sammy's turf was always Wanchai. Why didn't Carter join him there?"

"Carter's father was part of the Sha Tin gang. He never made it to the top, but he was assistant Vanguard when he died."

"How did he die?"

"He was shot."

"By whom?"

"One of the Kowloon gangs tried to muscle in on the bookmaking operations around Sha Tin Racecourse. When the Sha Tin guys tried to run them off, there was a firestorm. This was at least fifteen years ago. As I remember it, at least four or five guys died. Carter's father was one of them."

"Uncle was never attached to Kowloon, was he?" Ava asked.

"No, he operated strictly in and around Fanling. Xu's father was in Fanling as well, until he went back to Shanghai."

"So there shouldn't be any personal animosity towards Xu or his family in that regard."

"Only as it relates to Sammy getting dumped."

"Technically, Sammy didn't get dumped. Xu left him in place as Mountain Master."

"That's not how Sammy sees it. And for that matter, Ava, that's not how the majority of the Hong Kong triads see it. Carter for sure doesn't."

"I guess that's understandable, if regrettable," Ava said. "When did Carter rise beyond being a forty-niner?"

"About seven or eight years ago he became assistant Red Pole, and then Straw Sandal. Andy told me that people were surprised when he became the Sandal, because it's a job with a lot of talking attached to it and not much action. But he must have done it well enough, because he was eventually named Vanguard, and that's only one step away from Mountain Master."

"And he became Mountain Master about six months ago?"

"Yep."

"What happened to the old one?"

"He retired, supposedly, but I was told that Carter — with the support of the rest of the executive — shoved him out the door."

"Does that happen often?"

"Not that much, but it was better than the guy getting shot — which has happened more often than anyone wants to admit."

"That speaks well for Carter, I guess," Ava said. "But you said he's been really aggressive since taking over. How so?"

"I've heard that he's fanatical about getting a cut from all the action generated by Sha Tin Racecourse. I mean, the track is obviously in Sha Tin, but it's normal for other gangs to make book on the Happy Valley and Sha Tin races. Carter is demanding a piece of every dollar bet on the Sha Tin races. It's a crazy request, but I've been told some of the smaller gangs are sending him money," Sonny said. "And Ko told me that Carter has been trying to bypass the normal supply lines for all kinds of goods. He wants to deal directly with the sources. That's a problem, because over the years individual gangs have developed expertise and contacts in certain areas and act as the main supplier to other gangs."

"Like Xu does with his mobile devices and software?"

"Exactly, but now Carter wants to deal directly. What's worse is that he's going behind the backs of the other gangs, directly to their factories, and either offering the factories a little more money or threatening them."

"The gangs are tolerating this?"

"For now," Sonny said. "There's a reluctance to start anything that would draw attention to the fact that gangs are squabbling. These days the cops deal roughly with anyone who steps out of line. Carter, I think, is taking advantage of that. He acts like he doesn't give a shit, and as long as the others aren't willing to take him on, he'll keep doing what he's doing."

"It sounds to me like that's the strategy he and Sammy are using against Xu. They're banking on the fact that he won't retaliate."

"I think you're right," Sonny said.

They had crossed the Tsing Ma Bridge and were now on Route 8, headed in the direction of Tsim Sha Tsui, on the Kowloon side of Victoria Harbour. Sonny was a superb driver. Even as he was explaining the workings of Carter Wing's Sha Tin gang, he never seemed distracted and the car was always under perfect control. Traffic bunched up as they neared the Western Harbour Crossing, one of the tunnels that ran under the harbour to Hong Kong Island.

As Sonny brought the car to a momentary halt, Ava asked, "What does Carter look like?"

"Like a young Sammy."

"Really? I've only known a short, fat, old Sammy, and in the years I've known him he's gotten progressively fatter."

"Physically, Carter isn't exactly impressive either. He's about five foot six, and while he isn't as round as Sammy, he's definitely headed in that direction."

The car kept inching forward and finally reached the tunnel toll booths. Sonny paid the HK$65 fee and started into the tunnel, which was a bit longer than a kilometre. A few minutes later they were on Hong Kong Island, and five minutes after that, Sonny pulled up in front of the Mandarin Oriental.

"Welcome back, Ms. Lee," the doorman said as she stepped out of the car.

Ava wasn't surprised to be remembered. She had stayed at the hotel countless times over the years, including three months when Uncle was ill and several times with May Ling, who was an extravagant tipper. She had always tipped well herself, but May put her to shame. "Thanks," she said to the doorman, and then turned to Sonny. "I'll call Sammy as soon as I'm settled. I'll let you know right away what the arrangements are, and then you can pass on the word to Andy, Carlo, and Ko."

Sonny smiled and said, "It's kind of like the old days."

"Sonny, those are the days I've been trying to get away from," she said.

## 8

**AVA'S SUITE ON THE TWENTY-SECOND FLOOR GAVE HER** a clear view of Victoria Harbour and part of the spectacular Hong Kong skyline. The view was one of the reasons she liked the hotel; another was the selection of first-class restaurants on the top floor, three floors above her. The one thing Ava never did when she was at the Mandarin was stay on the twenty-fourth floor, because it was from there that Leslie Cheung, a Cantopop superstar, had jumped to the sidewalk below. His suicide was tragic, and it hit Ava particularly hard. Cheung was homosexual, and whether that contributed to the depression that triggered his jump or not, the twenty-fourth floor was completely off-limits for Ava; she even closed her eyes in the elevator as she passed it.

As always, the first thing she did when she reached the room was unpack her bag and freshen up in the bathroom. The previous week in Beijing had been stressful, and no sooner had she resolved the problem there than Xu's illness and Sammy Wing's power play had landed at her feet. She needed at least one night to herself, she thought as she looked into the bathroom mirror, one night free from carrying the weight of other people's problems. But before she could get to that, there were still things to do.

Ava took a black Moleskine notebook from her Louis Vuitton bag and sat at the desk. It was an old habit. During her years working with Uncle, she had kept a record of every job in an identical notebook. When the case was concluded, the notebook went into a safety deposit box at her bank in Toronto. Her friends found it amusing that she still used pen and paper rather than a digital device to store valuable information, but for her there was more involved than storage. The act of writing something down secured it in her memory in a way that a device couldn't, and she also used it to assist her thought process. Her observations about people and situations filled the pages of the Moleskines, and inevitably, as the jobs progressed, there were also lists of options and the pros and cons that came with them.

She opened the new Moleskine and wrote across the top of the first page: *Sammy and Carter Wing, Sha Tin and Wanchai.* She then proceeded to summarize the events of the past few days and concluded by recording Sonny's observations about Carter Wing. When that was done, she sat back and muttered, "Fai, Suen, Sammy, and Sonny." Those were the calls she had to make, in the order she was going to make them. When those were done, the only thing she wanted to worry about was where to have dinner.

"Hi, babe. How was your flight?" Fai answered.

"It was uneventful, just the way I like them. I'm at the hotel for the evening. I'll have dinner upstairs but I'll be in my room for the rest of the night after that," Ava said. "I hope things are going okay for you there."

"Auntie Grace and I went for another walk this afternoon, and we've just finished dinner. She's insisting that we watch one of my old movies. She has most of them on DVD."

"She is a difficult woman to say no to."

"I know, so I'll give in. I just don't want to watch one of the depressing ones."

"*City Girls* is good."

"Ava, my character dies at the end!"

"Yes, but until she does it isn't too much of a tear-jerker."

"I'll sort it out with Auntie Grace," Fai said. "How is Hong Kong? How is Lop?"

"It sounds like he's going to survive, but for the rest of it, I don't know yet. We'll have some kind of a meeting tomorrow and I'll have a better idea of what's what when it's over. I'm obviously hoping that it goes well enough that I can get back to Shanghai tomorrow night, or perhaps the day after."

"Do what you have to do and don't worry about us."

"Speaking of worrying, has Suen been in touch with Auntie Grace about Xu?"

"He phoned early this afternoon, and then again an hour ago. According to him, Xu has recovered sufficiently and could be out of isolation by tomorrow. The doctor said even if he is, though, they'll want to keep him under observation for a few days after that."

"Auntie Grace must be happy."

"Oh yes. She's been grinning for the last hour."

"Give her a hug for me," Ava said. "Now I've got to make some other calls before I can eat."

"Phone me later if you have a chance. It's going to feel strange climbing into an empty bed."

"That makes two of us. Love you."

"Love you too."

Ava ended the call with a sigh and realized — almost with surprise — that she already missed Fai. The intensity of the week they'd spent together in Beijing had left an emotional mark. She shook her head to clear it. *Let's get on with things,* she thought as she called Suen.

His phone rang five times and then prompted her to leave a message. She hesitated and then said in a rush. "I spoke to Fai, so I know about Xu's condition. Lop seems to be doing okay. I won't be meeting with Sammy tonight, so I'll call you in the morning once things are set."

She sat back in the desk chair. Sammy was next on her mental list. Ava glanced at the Moleskine and the notes she'd made earlier. She had underlined a sentence that read, *We can't let them believe for even an instant that they can push us around.* With that in mind, she called him.

"Are you in Hong Kong?" Sammy asked before the second ring.

"I am," she said, not bothered by his abruptness.

"Are you ready to meet?"

"Tomorrow morning. Mid-morning suits me best."

"Tonight is better for us."

"We're not prepared, and there's no point in meeting until we are. So that means tomorrow morning."

"You aren't worried about Xu's men?"

"There's nothing I can do about those men. They're under your control," Ava said. "All I can tell you is that we're not prepared to meet tonight and suggest that you don't do anything stupid in the interim."

"Fuck off, Ava."

"There's no reason to be abusive, Sammy. You know I'm always honest with you."

He didn't respond right away, and Ava braced herself for more cursing. Instead Sammy eventually said, "Give me a minute."

Ava waited, unable to hear anything on the other end of the connection. Then she heard someone breathing hard.

"We can make tomorrow morning work," Sammy said.

"Who were you talking to? Your nephew Carter?"

"What does it matter?"

"I assumed you were but I wasn't sure — and I'm still not sure — which of you is pulling the strings."

"You're starting to push my limits," Sammy said.

"Sorry, Sammy, I couldn't help myself," Ava said. "I'll be more polite tomorrow. And thanks, by the way, for agreeing to meet then."

"We want to meet in Sha Tin."

"I have no objections to Sha Tin, but it's a big city, so don't expect me to go to some out-of-the-way hole-in-the-wall."

"Is a restaurant in New Town Plaza public enough for you?"

"I know the Plaza, but there have to be at least fifty restaurants in it."

"We'll meet you at Maxim's Palace; it's on the eighth level," Sammy said. "It seats about six hundred people, so you don't have to worry about being alone with us. We'll see you there at eleven, the start of the dim sum rush. But don't worry, we'll book a table."

"I won't be by myself."

"I didn't think you would be."

"Sonny will be with me, and most likely Ko."

"Sonny Kwok?"

"Do you know any other Sonny?"

"No, but I'd forgotten how close you were," Sammy Wing said. "I'm surprised Suen won't be there."

"Xu doesn't think he needs to involve him yet."

"That man has a lot of faith in you."

A sarcastic retort crossed Ava's mind, but she let it go. "Tomorrow morning, Maxim's Palace, eighth level, New Town Plaza, at eleven. See you then," she said.

She finished the call with a sense of satisfaction. If anyone had been uncomfortable, it was Sammy. Her intention hadn't been to rattle him, only to make him realize things wouldn't be one-sided, and she thought she had accomplished that. She phoned Sonny next.

"Boss," he said.

"I just spoke with Sammy. We're on for tomorrow morning at eleven, at Maxim's Palace in New Town Plaza in Sha Tin. He claims it can seat six hundred people."

"I have heard of the place. I don't know how large it is, but a restaurant in the Plaza is certain to be public."

"I still don't want us to go unarmed."

"We won't."

"I told Sammy you'd be with me, and I think we should bring Ko as well. He is the man in charge of Wanchai right now, so it makes sense that he should be there."

"You aren't worried that he might act like he actually is in charge?"

"I'll get Suen to talk to him. We can't be speaking with two voices. Suen will make sure Ko understands how the meeting should be conducted."

"How about Andy and Carlo? Do you want them there as well?"

"I do. They should set up near the restaurant entrance and keep track of who's coming and going," Ava said.

"What time do you want to leave for Sha Tin?"

"Should we drive or take the train?"

"I'd prefer to drive. I don't like the idea of carrying fire-arms on the train, even if they are in a gym bag. And it's an easy enough drive. It's less than twenty kilometres."

"Okay. And I think you should have Ko travel with us so we arrive together," Ava said. "It will also give me a chance to meet him and make sure Suen has briefed him."

"That makes sense. I'll call Ko and let him know. I'll pick him up before I come to get you. I suggest we leave the Mandarin around ten-fifteen," Sonny said. "Andy and Carlo can get to Sha Tin by themselves. I'll ask them to be at the Plaza by ten so they can scout the location. If they see anything odd going on, that will give them time to give us a heads-up."

"It sounds like we have a plan," Ava said. "If anything changes on my end, I'll let you know. Otherwise I'll see you here tomorrow morning."

"It's good to be doing real work again," Sonny said.

His comment caught Ava off guard. It was easy to forget Sonny's past and to take for granted that he was satisfied with driving her father and half-brother around Hong Kong. She knew his loyalty to her held him back from voicing whatever dissatisfaction he felt. She had told him several times that Xu had offered to take him into the gang, but he had declined even to consider it. She wondered if perhaps she should be more forceful, although this wasn't the time to pursue it. Instead she said, "Sonny, I want to tell you how useful our conversation in the car was on the way from the airport. The background information you gave me about the Wings really helped me frame my talk with Sammy, and I'm sure it will be equally helpful tomorrow. So, a big thank-you."

"That's why I'm here, boss," he said, and then paused. "I'll see you in the morning."

Ava checked the time, saw it was almost eight o'clock, and wondered if she could still get a table at Man Wah, the restaurant on the twenty-fifth floor. She dialled its extension on the room phone and a host answered.

"This is Ave Lee; I'm a hotel guest. Is there a table for one available if I arrive in the next few minutes?"

"Ms. Lee, welcome back to the Mandarin. I'm certain we can find something suitable for you," the host said.

She smiled. Both Jennie Lee and May Ling put great store in cultivating relationships with staff at their favourite restaurants and shops. It often resulted in special treatment such as bypassing lines or getting a premium table. It was a talent Ava was trying to cultivate but hadn't quite mastered — though she was getting better at it.

"Is this Mister Chung?" she said.

"It is."

"I'm so pleased you remember me."

"You and Ms. Wong are two of our favourite customers."

"That's very kind of you," Ava said. "Do you think you could extend that kindness by finding me a table near a window? I haven't been in Hong Kong for a while, and I've really missed the evening view of the harbour."

"Come right up," he said. "I have something exactly like that in mind."

\* \* \*

Five minutes later, Ava was met by Mr. Chung at the restaurant entrance and personally led to a table with an unimpeded view of the harbour through one of the large windows in the north wall. The harbour view was spectacular, but it wasn't the only thing worth looking at in Man Wah. The other walls were decorated with an array of paintings on silk, and overhead were rows of exquisite ceiling lamps in gold-plated and lacquered metal, fashioned to look like birdcages.

She ordered a bottle of Cabernet Sauvignon and then sipped jasmine tea while she read the menu and waited for her wine. When the wine was poured and approved, she ordered marinated abalone with jellyfish, hot and sour soup with fish maw, and pan-fried wagyu beef, and then debated between a wok-fried Dover sole with bean sauce and fried noodles with shrimp and roast duck. Her server gently suggested the Dover sole, and she went along with it.

She had eaten dim sum at Man Wah more times than she could count, but dinner less often. Some of those dinners had been memorable, though. Front of mind was a meal she'd had with May Ling. Ava was still nursing a grudge then and didn't really trust May, but over the course of the meal May had opened up to her and the two women began to bond. May was a Taoist; she confessed that night that the very first time she had met Ava, she felt what Taoists call *qi* — life force — pass between them. Taoists, May explained, believe in kindred spirits, in soulmates. They embrace the concept of yin and yang, but the two symbols don't necessarily represent man and woman. Everyone lacks something in their lives, and most people never find the missing piece. When May had met Ava, she told her, she thought she'd found her missing piece, her kindred spirit, her soulmate. At the time Ava didn't completely understand or accept everything May said, but in the years since she had come to share some of May's beliefs.

The abalone and jellyfish were served first, and from there the meal progressed — as it always did at Man Wah — in a measured and well-paced manner. Ava sipped her wine carefully but still managed to finish most of the bottle by the time she'd eaten the last sliver of wagyu. She charged the bill to her room, leaving a large tip, and left the restaurant feeling sated. Sammy and Carter Wing had been completely put aside until morning.

Ava hadn't taken her cell to the restaurant, so she checked it as soon as she got back to her room. There hadn't been any calls or texts, which pleasantly surprised her. She thought about showering, decided to wait until morning, and simply washed her face, brushed her teeth, and unpinned her hair. She took a bottle of cognac from the hospitality bar and carried it into the bedroom, where she stripped, put on a black Giordano T-shirt, and climbed into bed. It was too early to sleep, so she turned on the television. Nothing on the English channels grabbed her interest, so she switched to the Chinese. Her mother watched several soap operas set in the times of ancient emperors that had become guilty pleasures for Ava, but she couldn't find them. What she did find was a channel showing classic Chinese films. Among them was *The Story of Jin Zhi Ruo*.

*The Story of Jin Zhi Ruo* had been the third collaboration between Lau Lau and Fai. It was set during the Cultural

Revolution and detailed the life of a young female doctor in a small country town. Part of Mao's revolution had been the debasement of academics and professionals, doctors among them. Lau Lau's film detailed Zhi Ruo's struggle to serve her community in the face of Party officials who, aided by roving gangs, threatened, terrorized, abused, and ultimately killed her. It was more melodramatic than most of Lau Lau's work — crammed with emotion — and a tear-jerker to an extraordinary degree. Ava debated whether she was up to watching it. Finally she rolled over, picked up her phone from the night table, and called Shanghai.

"Hi. I was just thinking about you," Fai said.

"Where are you?"

"I'm in bed."

"Me too. I was just trying to decide if I wanted to watch *The Story of Jin Zhi Ruo* on television."

"Goodness me, Ava, even I can't bring myself to watch that anymore," Fai said. "Lau Lau was going through a bad time when he made it, and he took it all out on poor Zhi Ruo. What he did to that woman was terrible. I've always thought she was my surrogate."

"That settles it. I'll find a comedy instead."

"A better choice."

"How was your evening with Auntie Grace?"

"It was wonderful. We sat in the kitchen and talked, or rather, we sat in the kitchen and she grilled me about making movies and various actors. She does like to gossip."

"How personal did you get?"

"About me and us, I managed to avoid being indiscreet, except for telling her how much I love you," Fai said. "When it came to my colleagues, I was more forthcoming."

"I had a conversation with May Ling earlier this evening about one of your former colleagues."

"Lau Lau?"

"Yes."

"Are you still thinking about trying to do something with him?"

"I am."

"I wish you wouldn't."

"I know, but I find it very difficult to accept that someone with that much talent is unredeemable."

"Many have tried to redeem him. All have failed."

"That may be true, but I spoke to May anyway about putting up some money to get him into rehab, and if he can negotiate that, then we might put up more money for a script," Ava said. "Fai, it isn't like we can't afford it, and if we go into it with our eyes open then the potential downside is minimal, while the upside could be... what? A great film?"

"I doubt you'll get to the point where you can get an adequate script out of him," Fai said, then paused. "Ava, what is it that you see in Lau Lau that's making you so stubborn about this?"

"I guess I'm having a problem reconciling the wreck of a man I saw in Beijing with the wonderful things he was able to put on film. And I keep thinking that he's too young for those movies to be his final legacy. Surely there's more in him; surely he has more to contribute."

"Ava, Lau Lau is a drunk, and there isn't a drug he won't use. Maybe those are his crutches, his excuses, because there's nothing more he has to give creatively," Fai said. "And even if you manage to dry him out, his sexuality is practically out in the open. How could you expect him to function in a system — in a culture — that would despise him because of it?"

"I think he was crushed by the system. If we can get him away from it, maybe he'll rediscover at least part of what made him so great."

"You're not going to give up on this, are you," Fai sighed.

"Not yet, but I do hear what you're saying, and I won't leap into anything," Ava said. "I'm thinking I should speak to Chen. If we're going to do anything, it would have to be through him. For all I know, he might tell me he has no interest."

"I'm willing to wager that's exactly what he will tell you."

"That may be the case, but I want to talk to him anyway. Could you give me his contact information?"

"I'll text it to you. I'm not keen to, but I will."

"Fai, I'm not going to pursue this anymore tonight. You've made some valid points that I want to think about," Ava said. "But the thing is, my memories of Lau Lau keep nagging at me. He's the last piece of unfinished business from our Beijing adventure, and I'm never completely at ease when I have unfinished business."

## 9

## AVA DREAMT OF UNCLE.

Before Chow Tung's death, her father had dominated her dreams in repetitive, frustrating scenarios that saw her trying to meet up with him in hotels, airports, or restaurants. She was never successful and woke more than once with tears in her eyes. The dreams were so frequent that there were times she dreaded going to sleep, but now she never gave it a thought, because it was Uncle who was now her usual nocturnal visitor.

This night, Uncle was sitting in the Kit Kat Koffee House. He called to her as she passed, and Ava went inside to sit with him. They were the only people in the place. His racing form was open and spread across the table. He was smoking, his face wreathed in the haze, and an ashtray full of cigarette butts sat on the form.

*Are you coming or going?* he asked.

*I'm not sure.*

*That does not matter. I am just pleased that I caught you.*

*Were you waiting for me?*

*Yes. I was told you were in Hong Kong.*

*Do you know why?* Ava asked.

*You have a meeting with Sammy Wing and his nephew Carter.*

*Do you know Carter?*

*I do. He is an easy man to dislike, and an easy man to underestimate.*

*That sounds like Sammy.*

*There are similarities. They both think they are smarter than they are, but I found them to be sly rather than intelligent. Neither of them hesitates to lie, and the only needs that concern them are their own.*

*So I can't trust them?*

*Not at all.*

Ava wanted a coffee but there were no servers, and no one behind the counter. *Are we completely alone?* she asked.

*I thought our conversation should be private,* Uncle said, his eyes fixed on her.

*Why?*

*I have known Sammy for more than forty years. He has ears everywhere. He is a sneak, and he has never been any different.*

*What is it you want to tell me that you don't want him to hear?*

Uncle shifted in his chair and leaned slightly towards Ava. *When you meet with the Wings, Sammy will do most of the talking. I do not want you to be fooled by that,* he said slowly. *Carter is the one making the decisions. He is the true enemy, and he is vicious.*

*Vicious how?*

*Sammy talks and acts tough, but in all the years I have known him, he has never personally fired a gun or put a knife into someone. Carter has done both many times. I think he enjoys doing it.*

*I've handled tough men before.*

*I know, and I do not doubt your abilities, but Carter is unpredictable. He likes to attack when his target least expects it. With him, you have to be particularly careful.*

*Be careful.* There were those words again, Ava thought as she woke. She opened her eyes to see daylight flickering around the edges of the drawn curtains. She lay quietly for a few minutes, gathering her thoughts. She had managed to put Sammy and Carter to one side the night before, but now they filled her head.

She slid out of bed and went to the bathroom. When she came back, she made a cup of black coffee and found her cell. As soon as she picked it up, it rang. She saw Suen's number and felt a rush of fear that something had happened to Xu.

"Good morning," she said. "How is Xu?"

"He keeps improving, but that's not why I'm calling," Suen said. "Our problem in Hong Kong just became more complicated."

"What's happened now?"

"Sometime during the night, someone deposited the body of one of our men at the entrance to a bar we own in Wanchai. His throat had been slit."

"When you say one of your men, was it one of the seven?"

"It was."

"My god, how terrible," Ava said, collapsing into a chair. "Who told you this?"

"Ko."

"Does Xu know?"

"I haven't been at the hospital since last night. I saw that you called and I listened to your message, but I spent the entire evening there, which is why you couldn't reach me."

"When will you see him again?"

"I'm not sure," Suen said. "I've been thinking about it, and it seems to me I should wait until things are clearer at your end. I mean, one of our men is dead, but I'm hoping the other six are still alive. I don't want to give the boss incomplete information."

"How is the boss?"

"He's getting better by the hour, but this kind of news might set him back."

"Then don't say anything just yet."

"How long should I wait?" Suen asked.

"I have a meeting scheduled at eleven o'clock this morning with the Wings — or maybe I should say I *had* a meeting scheduled," she said. "I have to call Sammy to find out if it's still on or if the body was their way of telling us it's been cancelled."

"If the meeting is still on, I'm going to wait until you've spoken to them. If it isn't, I'm heading directly to the hospital to talk to Xu."

"I'll phone Sammy right now."

"Tell that son of a bitch that if I have to come to Hong Kong again, I'll bring enough men and firepower to wipe him, his nephew, and all of their men off the face of the earth."

"I understand how you feel, but you know there's no point in aggravating an already bad situation, and threats aren't going to save those six other men."

"I'm still going to be organizing my men."

"I wouldn't expect you to do anything less."

Suen paused. "Call me as soon as you've spoken to the Wings."

Ava ended the call and cursed silently. She had tried to keep her emotions in check as she was speaking to Suen, but the death of Xu's man alternately enraged and depressed her. *Why is excessive violence so often the way these people communicate?* It made the thought of calling Sammy repugnant, but Ava knew she had no other option. With resignation she punched in his number.

"*Wei*," he answered.

"This is Ava."

"I know who it is and I know why you are calling," he said calmly.

"Then you should be ready to tell me why you killed Xu's man."

"He tried to run," Sammy said.

"What?"

"He punched one of our guards and was halfway out the door when we stopped him," Sammy said. "Carter was livid and decided to make an example of him."

"The other six men are still alive?"

"They are, and instead of complaining about the one who's dead, I think you should be grateful that we let the others live past the midnight deadline. As I remember, we left that up in the air."

"I'm not going to thank you for using common sense."

"From that remark I take it that you're still prepared to meet with us this morning."

"I was more concerned about your willingness."

"Truthfully, Carter isn't convinced it's worth his time, but we'll still be at Maxim's at eleven," he said.

"Sammy, there can't be any more nasty surprises between now and then."

"The dead man brought it on himself. Make sure that Xu and Suen understand that."

"I think you should assume they're at the limit of what they're willing to understand," she said.

Sammy paused and Ava braced herself for an insult. Instead he said, "We'll be there at eleven. The rest is up to you."

The line went dead. Ava threw her head back and took deep breaths until she felt herself start to calm down. When she felt under control, she called Suen.

"Ava?" he answered.

"I spoke to Sammy. The other six men are still alive and the meeting is going ahead as scheduled," she said. "Sammy said the man they killed tried to escape."

"Do you believe that?"

"Whether I do or not doesn't change reality. The fact that they still want to meet has to be viewed positively."

"Can you trust them enough to go to the meeting?"

"If we weren't meeting in such a public place I'd have more concern, but Maxim's is about as public as you can get. There will be hundreds of people around us," Ava said. "Besides, Sonny and I will be armed, and Andy and Carlo will be with us as well."

"Is there anything Ko and his men can do?"

"Ah, I'm glad you mentioned that," she said. "I want Ko to come to the meeting, but I don't want him to say anything. I want to handle this my own way."

"Do you want him to be armed?"

"Of course."

"I'll tell him," Suen said. "He'll probably be relieved that he's not expected to talk."

"Does he know about Xu being hospitalized?"

"I don't think so, although he might be wondering why Xu didn't call him directly after Lop went down."

"Is he the type of person to overreact if you tell him the truth?"

"No, he's solid."

"Then I don't see any reason not to tell him, especially since Xu is on the mend. As long as he keeps it to himself until Xu is out of isolation, there shouldn't be a problem."

"I'll fill him in."

"And have you decided what to tell Xu?"

"Now that the meeting is going ahead, I don't think I'm going to tell him anything until after."

"I think that's wise," Ava said. "But don't stop making your preparations. If things go badly, how soon can you get to Hong Kong with enough men to make an impression?"

"Ko has been gathering weapons and we're holding more than a hundred flight reservations for tomorrow and the day after. If we have to move faster, I can get some men on planes tonight."

"Hopefully you won't have to do that."

"Xu has high hopes for your meeting. He wants this resolved as peacefully as possible."

"I know he does, but it takes both parties to agree before that will happen."

"You sound doubtful about the outcome. That isn't like you."

"Sammy is acting confident, almost cocky, so I can't help thinking they've got something else up their sleeve. But maybe I'm overthinking this," Ava said. "Call Ko right away, will you? Sonny is picking me up around ten. We all need to be on the same page by then."

She ended the call, instantly regretting that she'd voiced her concerns about the Wings to Suen. It was more typical of her to keep her feelings secret, and she chided herself for being so candid. Ava made another coffee and put it on a table near the window. She drew the curtains and looked out at mist and rain covering the skyline like a giant grey shroud. It was typical late winter weather for Hong Kong, and it suited her mood.

Ava sat and stared at the harbour until she'd emptied her cup. She thought about making one more and then decided she'd better start getting ready. She pushed herself up from the chair and gasped as pain shot through her upper arm, a reminder of the wound left by the machete attack in Beijing. The hospital in Beijing had treated it well, so she wasn't expecting complications, but there was still a constant dull ache that painkillers couldn't completely eradicate.

She went into the bathroom, slipped off her T-shirt, and looked at the tightly bandaged arm. There wasn't any swelling. The bandage would need to be changed in a few days, and she hoped she would be back in Shanghai and have help when the time came. She turned on the shower, changed the setting to a fine spray, and stepped in. Her bandage was waterproof and had already survived several showers, but she didn't want to risk water hitting it at full blast.

Half an hour later, dressed for business in her black slacks and button-down shirt, she sat at the work desk and opened her Moleskine notebook again. Before she could finish reviewing her notes, her cell rang.

"'Boss, it's Sonny. I'm on my way to get Ko. We should be at the hotel right on time."

"Has Suen spoken to him?"

"Yes. It was the first thing Ko mentioned to me."

"That's good. Have you been in touch with Andy and Carlo?"

"They left for Sha Tin an hour ago. They'll position themselves near the entrance to the restaurant and keep an eye on who goes in and out. Ko wanted to send some men as well, but I told him not to bother. If Andy and Carlo don't know them, they might mistake them for Wing's men. We don't need that kind of confusion."

"Carlo and Andy are armed?"

"Yes, and so is Ko. I have our guns with me."

"Hopefully they're an unnecessary precaution," Ava said.

"I can't imagine they'd start something in a public place, but I've seen dumber things happen."

"Even if it's only a one percent possibility, I don't want to risk it," Ava said. "Has Ko heard anything about the six men?"

"No, and he thinks that's positive."

"And did he update you on Lop's condition?"

"There hasn't been any change, and again he thinks that's positive."

"Ko is quite upbeat for a man in his position."

"His mood shifted when he found out you were in charge. If things go sideways now, he knows he won't be blamed."

"But is he reliable?"

"I'm sure he is. He just doesn't seem cut out to make decisions at this level."

Ava looked at her Cartier Tank Française. "Sonny, I have time for breakfast. I'm going downstairs to the Clipper

Lounge. If you get here early, either wait outside or come and get me — it's your choice."

"I'll be outside. See you soon."

Ava picked up her Louis Vuitton bag and removed her wallet so she'd have ample space for the gun. She put the wallet, along with her passport and Moleskine notebook, into the room safe. After one last look in the mirror, she was ready for the morning.

She had debated between a skirt and slacks and opted for the freer movement the slacks could provide. Similarly, she decided on a pair of flat shoes rather than pumps. Not wanting to look completely drab, she wore a pale pink shirt with the two top buttons undone. Around her neck was a plain silver crucifix, but the watch, her ivory chignon pin, and a pair of green jade cufflinks added an element of luxury that would be perfectly appropriate for Maxim's Palace.

Ava rode the elevator to the lounge on the mezzanine level and was quickly seated. She opted for the the Clipper's specialty, a breakfast buffet. She started with a bowl of congee — plain rice porridge — with salted eggs and preserved bean curd as side dishes. Uncle had eaten congee nearly every morning, and Ava had joined him most days during his last months, amazed that he never seemed to tire of its blandness. The Clipper's congee was good, but she had finished only half the bowl before she went looking for more sustenance. The buffet had a variety of typical Western breakfast foods, but Ava couldn't be in Hong Kong and not eat Chinese. She piled a plate with har gow, cha siu bao — barbecued pork buns — and pan-fried turnip cake. She slathered the steamed shrimp dumplings and the turnip cake with chili sauce and proceeded to devour them. She wasn't normally a hearty eater at breakfast, but stress spiked her appetite. Despite a calm exterior, Ava was anxious about the upcoming meeting.

Shortly before ten she took the stairs down to the lobby. Not to her surprise, the Mercedes was already at the entrance. Sonny was chatting with the doorman while Ko looked on. She recognized Ko when she saw him, although she hadn't connected his face to the name. He was one of Suen's senior men, and she had often seen him lingering in the background in Shanghai; he had also been up front and centre with Lop when the Shanghai men invaded Wanchai. Like most of Xu's men, he had no tattoos, visible scars, or jewellery. He was clean-shaven and his hair was buzz-cut. In brown chinos and a white polo shirt, he looked more like the manager of a convenience store than a triad.

"Ko, it's good to see you again," she said as she approached them.

"*Xiao lao ban,*" he said, bowing his head slightly.

Ava saw Sonny glance at Ko in surprise, and she realized he hadn't heard her addressed as such. "Sonny, that's how some of the men refer to me in Shanghai. I think it started as a bit of a joke, but it seems to have stuck," she said, and then turned to Ko. "You mustn't call me that in front of the Wings."

"I won't," he said earnestly.

Sonny smiled as he opened the rear door. "*Xiao lao ban,*" he said as she slid into the back seat.

"I thought Ko would be armed," she said softly, ignoring his teasing.

"He has a gun and jacket in the trunk. My gym bag is in there as well, with what we need."

Ko sat up front with Sonny. As the car pulled onto Connaught Road to begin the trip, Ava saw him pull out his phone and check it for messages.

"Is everything okay?" she asked.

"As much as it can be," Ko said. "The wife of one of our men who was captured keeps texting me. I don't know what to tell her."

"Nothing for now," Ava said.

Sonny drove the Mercedes through the harbour tunnel, emerged in Tsim Sha Tsui, and then headed northeast through the New Territories to the district of Sha Tin. Ava had been in and around Sha Tin many times without actually spending much time there. It had a population of about 600,000, but without New Town Plaza and especially Sha Tin Racecourse, it wouldn't be a prime destination for anyone who wasn't living there.

Ava's first trips to Sha Tin had been with Uncle during horse-racing season, and despite her lack of interest in the sport, she had been genuinely impressed by the track and its atmosphere. Horse racing had been a Hong Kong passion — and the only form of legal gambling — for more than 150 years. For the first hundred years or so, Happy Valley on Hong Kong Island was the only racing venue, but in 1978 the Hong Kong Jockey Club had completed construction of the Sha Tin course. It could accommodate 85,000 people, and the grandstands were nearly always full during the one-day-a-week, nine-months-a-year racing program.

The mood in the car was tense. Ava tried to lighten things by asking, "Do either of you go to the races in Sha Tin?"

"Given that our business is on Hong Kong Island, I don't get into the New Territories that often," Ko said tersely.

"I prefer Happy Valley," Sonny said.

*So much for small talk*, Ava thought. There was no more conversation until Sonny turned the Mercedes into the parking garage at New Town Plaza. Ava looked at her watch. "We have ten minutes to spare."

"It will take us that long to walk to the restaurant. This mall is enormous," Sonny said.

"Do you know where we're going?"

"I scouted it out last night," Sonny said.

"Is Maxim's as big as Sammy claims?" Ava asked, pleased he had taken the initiative but embarrassed that she hadn't thought to ask him.

"It is."

"Good. At least he wasn't lying about that."

They all got out of the car and walked to the trunk, which Sonny had opened. Ko took out a blue windbreaker and put it on. "Where's your gun?" Ava asked.

"In the jacket. I had a special inside pocket made to hold it."

Sonny unzipped his gym bag and pulled out Ava's gun, wrapped in newspaper. She removed the papers and put the gun in her bag.

"I have to take the gym bag," he said. "The Cobray is too big to conceal any other way."

"They'll figure you have something like that in the bag," Ko said.

"That isn't a bad thing," Ava said. "It could be a deterrent."

"Are you really expecting trouble?" Ko asked.

"With Sammy Wing, I never know what to expect," Ava said. "Now let's get going. I don't want to be late."

They entered the mall, Sonny leading them past store after store until they finally reached a bank of elevators that Ava doubted she would have found on her own. They took an elevator to the eighth level, where Ava saw the sign for Maxim's about twenty metres ahead of them. Andy was standing nearby in front of a herbalist's store. He stepped back into the store's doorway and they joined him there.

"What have you seen?" Sonny asked.

"Sammy, Carter, and four of their men are inside. Two of the men arrived half an hour ago. The rest of them arrived together five minutes ago."

"Where's Carlo?"

"He's standing on the other side of the restaurant. We've been texting. He saw what I saw."

"They don't have more men in the vicinity?"

"Not that we've seen, and we've been here for a couple of hours."

"Stay here and keep your eyes open. If you see anything suspicious, text me. If you see anything that really alarms you, don't be afraid to come into the restaurant and find us," Sonny said.

"Got it," Andy said.

Ava had been hovering in the background as Sonny and Andy spoke. Now she stepped forward. "Hey, Andy, good to see you, and thanks for the help," she said.

"Hi, boss. Good to see you too. You know Carlo and I would do anything for you."

"Well, let's hope all you have to do today is hang around for another hour and then go home."

"Sammy is a lot of things, but he's not crazy enough to try anything here."

"I thought the same thing when we were supposed to meet with him in Shenzhen, and that didn't turn out so well."

Andy shook his head. "Sorry, boss. I shouldn't be giving an opinion."

Ava looked at the man, who was barely taller than her, weighed maybe thirty pounds more, and on at least three occasions had risked his life for her. "You've earned the right to say anything you want to me, Andy. Always remember that, and never hesitate to do it."

Sonny interrupted. "Ava, we should be going into the restaurant."

"Bye, Andy. And if I don't see Carlo, give him my best wishes as well."

"I will, Ava."

Sonny, Ko, and Ava left Andy and walked to Maxim's entrance. It was busier than Ava had expected for that time of day, and when she looked into the restaurant she saw that a lot of tables were occupied.

"We're meeting Sammy and Carter Wing," Ava said to the host.

The host looked down at a sheaf of papers. "Are you the Lee party?"

"Yes," Ava said.

"Follow me."

He led them past a seemingly endless number of tables towards the far end of the restaurant. Ava saw Sammy at a distant table, sitting with a man who looked like a younger version of himself. She tried to locate the other men Andy had mentioned. Two men were standing against a wall behind the table and two were sitting at a nearby table, showing an inordinate amount of interest in their approach. She assumed the four were Wing's men.

Neither Sammy nor the man Ava was sure was Carter

rose to greet them. "Have a seat," Sammy said when they reached the table.

There were six chairs at the round table. Sammy and Carter sat together on the right side. The remaining chairs were positioned so that whoever sat in them would have their backs to Wing's four men.

"We haven't met," Ava said, stepping towards Carter with her hand extended. "My name is Ava Lee."

He looked at her in disgust. "I'm Carter Wing," he said finally, not taking her hand.

"Do you know Sonny and Ko?"

"I know Ko. I've heard of Sonny."

"Who hasn't heard of Sonny?" Sammy said, and then pointed to the chairs. "It's good to see you again, Ava. Have a seat."

"I'd like to be able to say the same, Sammy, but the circumstances aren't ideal," Ava said, reaching for a chair and moving it so she had a clear view of the men against the wall. She turned to Sonny. "Position those other chairs so you can keep an eye on the two men at that table."

"You are so mistrustful," Sammy said.

"Well, we have a very complicated relationship, so a girl can't be too careful," Ava said. "And I'm sure you can understand that the body you dropped in front of the bar in Wanchai didn't exactly engender trust."

"Did she explain to you why we had to kill him?" Carter interrupted, directing the question at Ko.

"She told me, but it isn't something I want to discuss," Ko said. "You should also know that Ava is handling this meeting on our behalf, so I won't be answering any more of your questions."

"I can't say that's a shock," Sammy said. "That's a typical Uncle strategy. He taught Ava well."

"I was wondering how long it would take for you to drop his name into our conversation. It was much faster than I expected."

Sammy turned to Carter. "Ava was Uncle's pride and joy. She could do nothing wrong where he was concerned."

Carter nodded as he stared across the table at her. Ava looked back at him. He was about forty, she guessed. He had a round, fleshy face but not the jowls that cascaded under Sammy's chin. He had a small nose and thin pink lips, but what really caught her attention was his eyes; they weren't much more than dark slits. If his intent was to convey malice, he did it well. She couldn't tell how tall he was sitting down, but Sammy was three or four inches taller than Ava, and she imagined Carter would be about the same. He was certainly built like Sammy, although he hadn't yet attained the girth that the years had piled onto his uncle. Still, his short-sleeved blue sports shirt strained across his chest, exposing a tattoo.

"We're drinking tea," Carter said, motioning to the two pots and the nest of cups that sat on table.

"Tea is all there's going to be. We're not here to eat," Sammy said. "We're here strictly for business, and I'm sure you feel the same way."

"We do, and I don't need the tea," Ava said.

Sammy smiled, sat back in the chair, put his hands together, and placed them on top of his protruding belly.

*The fatter he gets, the more he looks like a malevolent Buddha,* Ava thought.

"Why don't you start?" Sammy said.

"Start how? Start with what? We're still waiting for you to explain what you think you're doing and what you hope to gain by it," she said.

"The answer to what I'm doing and what I hope to gain is the same. I'm reclaiming Wanchai."

"Reclaiming Wanchai from whom? You're already the Mountain Master."

"Ava, don't play games with me. Lop is dead or out of commission and that rat pack army of his is lost without him. You know we're holding six of Xu's men. I have men in Wanchai who are still loyal to me, and I have the considerable backing of my nephew," Sammy said. "So Xu should abandon whatever illusions he has about still having any kind of control. If he's as smart as he's supposed to be, what he should be doing right now is finding a way to leave Wanchai while keeping as much face and business intact as possible."

"You and Xu made an agreement," Ava said. "He's honoured his end of it. I know he's expecting you to do the same."

"The only reason there was an agreement in the first place was because I had a gun pointed at my head. And, as I remember it, you were the one holding that fucking gun."

"And if you'd been dealing with any Mountain Master other than Xu, you would have been dead," Ava said. "He spared your life and then helped you save face. You should thank him every night at bedtime, Sammy, instead of attempting to pull shit like this."

"He humiliated me."

"He gave you a chance to retire gracefully. Why do you need all this tension and violence? You've earned the right to live out the rest of your years in peace."

"You aren't listening to me — I have no interest in retirement. I'm going to get Wanchai back and I'm going to run it the way I see fit."

"Does that mean eventually turning it over to your nephew to add to his new empire?"

"That is none of Xu's fucking business."

"Speaking of Xu, why isn't he here? Why are we talking to you?" Carter Wing snarled. "I still don't get it."

"I've explained about Xu already. I'm not going to do it again," Ava said. "And this isn't the first time that Sammy and I have negotiated on behalf of other parties."

"They're partners," Sammy said to Carter. "She and Xu are partners in some business. I found that out before my last go-round with them. She's probably got a stake in Wanchai, and if she has, he'd never want anyone to know about that."

"So, first Uncle and now Xu. You get around, don't you," Carter said to Ava. "At least he's closer to your age."

Ava felt Sonny stiffen and gently tapped him on the knee. "Insulting me won't help us get closer to resolving our problem," she said.

"You're the only one with a problem, and the resolution is simple. Xu and his men must leave Wanchai," Sammy said.

"That isn't going to happen. But there is, perhaps, room for compromise."

"I'm not interested in compromise."

"Xu understands that you may have suffered financially from the changes made in Wanchai," Ava continued, as if Sammy had never spoken. "He is prepared to increase the amount of money you're getting as long as the number is reasonable."

"This isn't about money," Sammy said.

"He also understands that you may feel left out of some of the important decisions, and he's prepared to talk about expanding your role."

"I don't need his permission to expand my role. I'll look after that myself."

"We're trying to find a middle ground," Ava said. "Won't you help?"

"There's none to be found."

"I think I'll have some tea now," Ava said, reaching for a cup.

Sonny took one as well and then picked up a pot and poured for both of them.

She took several sips, put the cup down, and leaned towards Sammy. "You tested Xu before and you came up short. If you challenge him again, what makes you think it will be any different?"

"I'm ready for him this time."

"Ready how?"

"There's no Lop. And there's the not insignificant fact that we're holding six of his men."

"Sammy also has my full support," Carter Wing said. "Make sure Xu understands that."

"Oh, I will. But I think he knows that already, and it doesn't seem to bother him," Ava said. "If you don't mind my being blunt, you're putting an awful lot at risk on the assumption that Xu will capitulate in order to save his men, and on the assumption that he doesn't have someone as capable as Lop prepared to step in."

"He won't sacrifice six men," Sammy said.

"You don't know that. In fact, *I* don't even know that. What I'm saying is that it's careless and dangerous of you to make that assumption."

"Our message is clear. Leave Wanchai and we turn the men loose. Don't leave and we'll kill them. I want an answer today," said Sammy.

"Do you have a specific deadline?"

"Midnight."

"I have a lot of calls to make. There will need to be discussion. Can you make it midnight tomorrow?"

"When we extended the deadline to tonight, we were already giving you an extra twenty-four hours," Carter said. "I would have killed all the men last night, but my uncle is a kinder man than me and persuaded me to hold off."

"But you must understand that even if Xu did agree to leave Wanchai, it would take days, if not weeks, to disentangle his interests," Ava said, ignoring Carter's remark.

"I'd accept a commitment from him. I'd want it sworn, of course, with some other Mountain Masters as witnesses. If he did that, we'd work out a schedule. But it would be days, not weeks, and we'd hold on to the men until he fulfilled his commitment," Sammy said.

"Okay, I think I know where you stand. But just to make things perfectly clear, you are asking Xu to turn over Wanchai in exchange for the lives of his men," Ava said. "You have absolutely nothing else to offer?"

Sammy paused. "We'd keep buying those knock-off devices from him, some software, and those perfumes he's making. There — I've given him a bone. There's nothing else I'll offer."

"You've offered enough," Carter said to Sammy. He looked at Ava. "My uncle is also more generous than me."

"If you say so," Ava said.

"When will you talk to Xu?" Sammy asked.

"After I leave here."

"When will I hear from you?"

"That's another assumption you've just made," Ava said. "You may not hear from me. Xu may decide to call you himself, or he might decide he doesn't need to tell you what he's going to do."

Carter suddenly looked angry and turned to Sammy. "Let's go. We've made ourselves clear. These idiots can do whatever they want."

Sammy nodded at the men standing against the wall, and they started to move in their direction. Ava saw Ko's hand reach inside his jacket, but he withdrew it when the men came to a stop next to Sammy and Carter.

"Bring the box here," Carter said to the men seated at the other table.

One of the men stood and walked over to them, carrying a box the same size as the ones Xu used to pack his cellphones. The man put it in front of Carter.

Carter and Sammy stood up. "We brought you a gift, but don't open it until we leave," Carter said, pushing the box across the table to Ava. "And don't worry, it isn't a bomb."

The six men left, with Carter and Sammy leading the way. Ava waited until they were at the exit before looking at the box.

"I'm not sure I'd open that," Sonny said.

"It is a bit small for a bomb," Ava said, sliding the inner box from the sleeve. She opened it and stared into it, then passed it to Sonny and Ko.

"Holy shit," Ko said.

"Fingers. Six of them," Sonny said.

"Well, if we didn't know what kind of man we were dealing with before, we sure do now," Ava said.

( 10 )

AVA WASN'T OVERLY SURPRISED BY THE OUTCOME OF the meeting. Despite her reservations going in, she had hoped there would be room for compromise until the Wings slammed that door shut. She was, however, shocked by the box of fingers. She had been around triads long enough to know they had a penchant for removing body parts as a means of persuasion or punishment, but what Carter had done was beyond the pale. Putting one finger in the box would have delivered the same message as six. Carter Wing was obviously as malicious as described.

"What are we going to do?" Ko asked, still visibly shaken.

"We need to find Xu's men, and we need to find them tonight."

"Do you believe what they said about killing them?" Ko asked.

"We can't afford not to, which is why we don't have any time to waste."

"We don't have any real links to Carter's organization, and we know very little about Sha Tin."

"Did you offer money in exchange for information?"

"No."

"It's time we did," Ava said. "How many Hong Kong dollars do you think it will take to get potential snitches interested?"

"I have no idea," Ko said.

"It would take a lot," said Sonny.

"How much is a lot?"

"Half a million might do it."

"Hong Kong dollars?"

"Yeah."

"We need to move quickly, so let's pay for speed. We'll put up a million," Ava said. "I'll tell Andy and Carlo to spread the word among their contacts here in the Territories. Sonny, you can do the same. And Ko, will you let your men know what we're offering?"

"The money won't make a difference to my men. They care about their brothers."

"I wasn't thinking about the Shanghai men. Your Wanchai men are more likely to have contacts in the Territories... And that leads to a question I was going to ask: how loyal are those men? Sammy told me last night that part of the Wanchai gang is still loyal to him. Could that be true?"

"We have a hundred and sixty men on the ground, thirty of whom came here with Lop and me from Shanghai. Those thirty are completely loyal. The rest we inherited, but they seemed happy enough. We pay well and we treat them with respect. I haven't seen any signs of discontent."

"Which doesn't mean they don't exist," Sonny said. "Hong Kongers are proud people. It doesn't matter how well you run the gang — you're still mainlanders, and there will always be some level of resentment."

"I can understand that, but am I wrong in thinking that the right amount of reward money will take priority over resentment?" Ava asked.

"Not everyone can be bought, but there are brothers who would sell their mother for a lot less than a million," Sonny said.

"Those brothers are the ones who need to hear about our reward. Let's get the word out as quickly and widely as we can. We need to get it to the ears of the right snitch today." Turning to Sonny, she said, "Andy and Carlo should still be outside in the mall. Would you mind getting them?"

As she watched Sonny leave, Ava said to Ko, "You and I should call Suen now. He's waiting to hear about the meeting."

"He isn't going to be pleased."

"Who *is* pleased?" Ava said, as she found Suen's number and pressed it.

"Hi, Ava," Suen said.

"Can you hear me okay? There's a lot of noise coming from your end."

"I'm outside the hospital. I was waiting for you to call before going inside," he said. "Give me a minute and I'll get into the car."

Ava put the phone on speaker mode and set it on the table between her and Ko.

"What's up?" Suen said, his voice clear.

"I'm with Ko. The phone is on speaker. We're at the restaurant in Sha Tin and the meeting is over."

"So soon?"

"Sammy and his nephew were direct and they're not interested in finding common ground. There was no point in dragging things out. We know where they stand."

"And from the sound of things, they haven't changed their position."

"They have not. They want all the Shanghai men gone from Wanchai and Sammy back in charge," Ava said. "I floated the idea of giving Sammy more money and even restoring some of his former authority, but they weren't interested."

"They had no interest at all?"

"Nope."

"That's stupid of them."

"They don't see it that way. They seem confident that, with Lop incapacitated, you won't be as effective on the ground. They're also convinced that Xu will cut a deal rather than let his men die. The only deal they say they're prepared to cut is the one they've put on the table," Ava said.

"How did you respond?"

"I told them they were making some risky assumptions."

"Is that how the meeting ended?"

"No. They've given us until midnight tonight to decide how to proceed."

"What happens if they're not satisfied when midnight arrives?"

"They said they'll kill the six men," Ava said. "And Suen, I believe them."

Suen paused and then said, "Ko, have you organized the weapons I asked for?"

"We're still working on it. Right now we could equip between forty and fifty of your men."

"And how many of your men can you count on for support?"

"Our thirty men from Shanghai. Until we met with the Wings, I assumed we could count on most of the others, but now I'm not so sure. Sammy Wing was boasting about having a lot of men in Wanchai who are still loyal to him."

"I wouldn't use those men unless you have to," Ava said. "You don't know how much you can trust them in a fight, and the last thing you need is Sammy Wing and Carter Wing knowing what your plans are."

"I agree, but if I don't use them I'll have to bring more men from Shanghai, and I'm worried that will take too long."

"There are no easy choices."

"Were they firm about the midnight deadline?"

"It would be foolish to assume they aren't, but we're going to be doing everything we can to locate the men before midnight. If we can find them, we'll go in after them. The way I see it, they are the Wings' main leverage. If we can get the men back, they'll be forced to back off."

"Or just go toe to toe with us," Suen said.

"But at least the playing field would be more level," Ava said. "Right now it seems to me they're banking on Xu's basic decency. They're convinced he won't sit back and let his men die. That's why they've set such a tight deadline. They don't want to give us time to think or to get properly organized."

"They could be bluffing about killing our men."

"That's possible, but when our meeting ended, Carter left us with a gift — a box containing six severed fingers," Ava said. "So, while it's possible they are bluffing, it's also possible that they might continue to send us body parts from the men for the next week. They're obviously cruel enough to do it. Suen, in all honesty, I think we should believe them."

"That fucking Sammy Wing," Suen said.

"Don't leave out Carter. He deserves to be cursed just as much, if not more than Sammy," said Ava.

"Fuck them both. We'll fuck them both."

Ko reached towards Ava and touched her gently on the arm. "Sonny is coming with Andy and Carlo," he whispered.

Ava saw the three men weaving their way through the tables. "Suen, why don't you go talk to Xu. We'll start organizing our hunt for the men, and I need to brief Sonny and two friends of mine. Call me back as soon as you've finished with Xu."

"If he's out of isolation he might be able to speak to you himself."

"As unpleasant as the subject is, it will be good to know that he's well enough to do that," she said, ending the conversation.

"I haven't heard Suen that angry in quite some time," Ko said.

"He has every reason to be. We all do," Ava said, standing to greet Andy and Carlo.

"Hey, Ava, good to see you," Carlo said.

He and Andy had worked for Uncle in the collection business before Ava joined him. Once she did, they had returned to their triad gangs and only did odd jobs when she or Uncle needed them. Carlo was about five foot six, skinny like Andy, and heavily tattooed. He had a thin, scraggly beard and was now wearing his hair in a modified mohawk. Despite appearances, he considered himself to be a ladies' man. Most of the women he propositioned turned him down, but he was never upset about being rejected and, to Ava's amusement, kept trying. Ava had a lot of time for both men. Carlo had been working for Sammy Wing when Xu took over Wanchai, and he had almost been caught up in the violence. Ava had bailed him out, and though Carlo was still with the Wanchai gang, she was sure his first loyalty lay with her and his second with Xu.

"Sammy and Carter and their men left the mall?"

"We saw them leave the restaurant and followed them to their cars. They're gone," Carlo said.

"Good. I wouldn't want to get ambushed on the way out of here."

"Sonny said you want to talk to us about the men the Wings are holding," he said.

"Yes. We need to find them. We need to find them today," she said. "I'm willing to pay a million Hong Kong dollars for any information that leads us to them. And if either of you comes up with a connection who has the information, I'll pay you two hundred thousand."

"That's a lot of money."

"It isn't that much when you divide it by six."

Carlo turned to Andy. "We have a lot of contacts in Sha Tin. Do you want to partner on the two hundred thousand?"

"Right now, no one in Sha Tin seems interested in talking to me."

"A million dollars might change some minds," Carlo said.

"It just might," Andy agreed with a nod.

"Before you start calling people, I want to remind you that time is not our friend. You need to be aggressive but there's a danger that word you are poking around could get back to the Wings. You could be added to their enemies list. Are you okay with that?"

"Sammy hates me already," Carlo said. "One more reason isn't going to make any difference."

"The same goes for me," Andy said.

"Then go to it. Try to find those men. I'll have my cell on, but if you can't reach me, call Sonny."

Carlo turned to leave but Andy lingered.

"Is there something you want to ask me?" Ava said.

"What do we do if we find someone with hard information and he wants more than a million?"

"We'll pay whatever we have to pay. If a million isn't enough, then agree to whatever they want."

"One more thing. I expect that whoever we find will want to deal in cash. I can't imagine them turning information over to us without getting paid first."

"I'll make sure I have a couple of million in cash available by early this afternoon," Ava said. "But Andy, what happens if we pay them and they stiff us? What if the information is bogus?"

"Carlo and I know all these guys, and Sonny will know most of them as well. No one will pull that kind of stunt when they know we'll come after them."

"No one is going to stiff us and get away with it," Sonny added.

"Then I won't worry about that possibility," she said to Andy. "Now you and Carlo get going, please."

"Where are you going to get that much cash at such short notice?" Sonny asked as Carlo and Andy left.

"Do you have a million or two readily available?" she asked Ko.

"No. We try not to keep too much cash on hand in case we're raided, and all our banking is funnelled through Shanghai. We could ask them to do a wire transfer or something."

"Don't bother. I'll look after it myself," she said, picking up her cell.

"Hi, Ava. I was wondering if I'd hear from you," Amanda Yee said as she answered Ava's call.

"You would have eventually. This is a bit sooner than I expected, but I need some help."

"What can I do?" Amanda asked without hesitation.

"I need two million dollars in cash within the next two hours or so."

"American dollars?"

"Hong Kong."

"That should be easier. Let me call the bank and get back to you. I don't think it should be a problem," Amanda said. "How do you want me to get the money to you?"

"I'm not sure where I'll be, so call me when you have it and we'll figure out a plan then," Ava said.

"Okay, I'll get right on it."

Ava put down her phone, delighted with her partner's reaction to a request that begged for questions. "Amanda will get the money," she said to Sonny. "I'll probably meet her in Central. Where do you think you'll be?"

"Andy and Carlo can handle Sha Tin. I'll ask around in Fanling and Tai Po. There's a lot of interaction between those gangs and Sha Tin."

"How about you?" she said to Ko.

"I think my time will be best spent finding more firepower for Suen. I have a list of Mountain Masters I haven't spoken to yet. I think I'll stay here and do that."

"What kind of reception are you getting from the ones you've spoken to?"

"They're reluctant to get involved but they don't want to piss off Xu entirely, so they throw just enough weapons my way to make it look like they're co-operating."

"Have you talked to Lam in Guangzhou?"

"No."

"He's been a good friend and ally to Xu. If you like, I can make that call for you," Ava said.

"I'd appreciate it."

Ava nodded. "I think that wraps things up for now. If you're going to Tai Po, you'll need the car," she said to Sonny. "I'll take a taxi back to Central. Both of you keep yourselves completely available."

"We haven't heard back from Suen or Xu," Ko said. "Should we wait here until we do?"

"Whatever decisions they're making won't affect what we're trying to do over the next few hours," Ava said. "We don't have time to sit and wait — even for Xu."

## 11

AVA CAUGHT ONE OF THE DISTINCTIVE GREEN AND white New Territories taxis at the mall exit and told the driver to take her to the Star Ferry terminal in Tsim Sha Tsui. She considered calling Lam, the Mountain Master in Guangzhou, but decided to wait until she'd heard from Suen or Xu. She hoped it would be Xu, but it was Suen who reached her as the taxi was leaving Sha Tin and entering Tai Wai.

"They're keeping Xu in isolation for another day," he said the instant he heard Ava's voice.

"Has there been a setback?" she asked, trying to hide her disappointment.

"No, he seems stronger, and he was certainly more alert and talkative," Suen said. "I think they're just being very cautious."

"I'll be so glad when he's back home."

"No more than him. He's really frustrated about not being able to speak to you. He tried to convince the doctor to let him use a phone, but there's no flexibility in the cellphone rule."

"Did you tell him about the man killed by the Wings?"

"No, I decided it wouldn't serve any useful purpose. If he were stronger I wouldn't have hesitated, but —"

"I understand. I think you made a smart decision," Ava said. "What did he have to say about our meeting and the Wings' ultimatum?"

"He was disappointed but not surprised. He said that taking out Lop showed the Wings' level of commitment. He doesn't expect them to back off until we give them no other choice."

"Does that mean you're coming to Hong Kong?"

"I have a flight booked for tomorrow morning. I don't want to leave until Xu is out of isolation. Can you and Ko handle things until I get there?"

"There isn't much to handle right now beyond trying to find your men."

"Xu asked what you think your chances are of being successful."

"I have no idea, but we might have increased our odds by offering to pay for information that leads us to them. Sonny, Andy, and Carlo are spreading the word now. I told them to offer one million Hong Kong dollars, but I'll go higher if I have to. In fact, I'm on my way right now to pick up two million in cash. If the boys can find a snitch, I want to have the cash in hand to pay him."

"Where did you get the cash?"

"From my company. You can count on my billing you for whatever amount I have to pay."

"You know that won't be a problem," Suen said.

"What did Xu say about the hostages?"

"Unless you can find them, there's nothing to be done. He won't do a deal with the Wings just because they're threatening to kill six of our men. If he did, we'd look weak and we'd be opening the door for other gangs to pull the same stunt. We can't let the Wings establish a precedent by giving in to extortion."

"I can't abide the thought of letting those six men die," Ava said, and knew the statement was unfair the second she voiced it.

"Ava, you know that's the last thing Xu wants, but whether they live or die will be decided by the Wings, not us," Suen said carefully. "And I have to tell you, despite how real you think their threats are, Xu and I both think they could be bluffing."

"We'll know soon enough. Midnight isn't that far off."

"Speaking of which, Xu asked if you could try one more time to get an extension from them," Suen said.

"Using what reason?"

"Whatever you think will work."

"I don't think anything will work."

"It was just a thought..."

Ava realized she might have sounded dismissive and said, "I'll tell you what, if we haven't located the men by early evening, I'll call Sammy. I don't think it will accomplish anything, but I'll try anyway."

"I'll let Xu know, and I'll tell him about the money you're putting up," Suen said. "An amount that size might just entice someone."

"That's our hope."

"And if it does?"

"Then that's when we'll talk about what to do next," she said. "Obviously we'll make every effort to free the men, but who knows what that would entail."

"I'm going to call Ko when we finish our conversation," Suen said. "Xu wants him to follow your directions until I can get to Hong Kong."

"Suen, I'm more comfortable with him reporting directly to you."

"I'll stay in touch with him, but you're there on the ground. Xu is just worried that Ko might get motivated to try something on his own. He wants to make sure that someone he trusts is keeping Ko in check."

"From what I've seen of Ko, I don't think it's likely he'll strike out on his own."

"Maybe not, but it's what the boss wants."

"Okay, tell the boss I'll keep an eye on Ko," Ava said, knowing it was pointless to argue with Suen.

"I'm going back into the hospital in a few minutes, but I should be available by phone in an hour or so."

"I won't call unless I have something concrete to tell you," she said, and ended the call. As she did, she noticed the taxi driver looking at her suspiciously in the rear-view mirror. He had obviously overheard her conversation with Suen, and she could only imagine how strange he must have found it.

"We're making a movie," she told him. "That was my partner on the phone, and we were discussing different plot ideas."

"Sounds like an exciting movie," he said.

Ava put the cell in her bag next to the gun and then sat back as the cab wound its way through Kowloon to Tsim Sha Tsui. She got out at the ferry terminal just as a boat was leaving the dock. That was no concern, since she knew there was a ferry every eight minutes at that time of day. She paid the

HK$2.70 fare — about thirty US cents — and walked over to the waiting area. There she found a quiet corner and phoned Mountain Master Lam in Guangzhou.

"Ava Lee. To what do I owe this honour?" he answered.

"How are you, Lam?"

"I'm well enough. But then, you haven't told me what you want yet." He laughed. "That may change things."

"It is a bit serious, I'm afraid."

"As serious as what we've done in the past?"

"It could be headed in that direction," she said. The memory of Lam putting a bullet into the head of Li, his Mountain Master and a co-conspirator with Sammy Wing against Xu, was still vivid.

"Oh. Then I'll just listen."

"Sammy Wing is trying to reclaim control of Wanchai, with the assistance of his nephew Carter. They shot and wounded Lop and they've also killed one of Xu's men and are holding six more as hostages. They've threatened to kill them tonight at midnight unless Xu agrees to their demands. He won't agree," she said.

"I've heard rumours about the Wings but I didn't give them any credence," Lam said calmly, which was his usual state. "But why are you calling to tell me this? Why haven't I heard from Xu?"

"Xu is in hospital in Shanghai. He has meningitis and he's in an isolation ward, with no means of communication except through visitors," she said, feeling comfortable about sharing the information with a man Xu trusted. "He's going to be okay and should be home in a few days, but in the interim we have this problem with the Wings."

"You certainly do."

"It's already a mess and has the potential to get much worse. Suen is flying from Shanghai with fifty to a hundred men, but he needs weapons for them. With Lop out of action, it's fallen to his man Ko to supply them. Ko has come up with enough for about fifty men. I was hoping you could supply enough for another fifty."

"Does Xu know you're calling me?"

"No. Do I need his permission?"

"What I meant, Ava, was did this request originate with him?"

"I didn't mean to snap," she said, realizing she might have offended him.

"You can snap at me anytime."

"Thank you, I'll remember that. And in reply to your question, no. I'm the one who thought you might be able to help."

"We have trucks leaving here every day for Hong Kong. I'll see what I can do about getting one loaded by tonight with what you need. I assume, since a war might be in the offing, that you'll want semi-automatics and automatics."

"I don't know how imminent a war might be, but your weapon options sound right."

"Ava, I will send the weapons, but I hope they won't need to be used," Lam said. "When we fight among ourselves, no one wins. All that happens is we attract unwelcome attention that the cops and the army use as an excuse to hammer us."

"Xu knows that, and he'll do everything he can to avoid conflict. But Lam, you can't expect him to roll over because Sammy Wing demands it."

"Sammy Wing is nothing but a fat, useless fuck, but his nephew is a different animal. Tell Xu to take care when dealing with him."

"He knows."

Lam paused. "Who do I inform about the shipment?"

"You can call me."

"You will hear from me or my Red Pole, Wa, before the end of the day."

"Thank you, Lam. I'll let Xu know how helpful you've been. He values your friendship."

Lam paused again. "Ava, is he really going to get well? Meningitis is a tricky disease. I don't want to lose him — our brotherhood can't afford it."

"The doctors expect him to be going home in a day or two. They caught and treated the disease in time."

"Thank God for that."

"I'll wait for your call," Ava said as a ferry pulled into the dock.

She went to stand in line as the ferry emptied and then filed on. She went to the front of the boat so she was facing the Hong Kong skyline. It was a fifteen-minute crossing, and her favourite time to make the journey was in the evening, when the skyline was a wall of almost magical light. Ava loved the design of the seventy-two-storey Bank of China building and of the International Finance Centre, with its auspicious eighty-eight storeys. But her favourite building was Jardine House; every time she saw it, she smiled. At fifty-two storeys it wasn't as imposing as many others, but it had a distinctive feature: 1,700 identical circular windows. Those windows had prompted the local population to nickname the building "the House of a Thousand Arseholes." That name came to Ava's mind every time she saw the building, and it did so again, prompting yet another smile.

Ava waited until they had docked at the Star Ferry pier in Central before making more phone calls. She hit Sonny's number as she started walking up Pedder Street towards the Mandarin. The hotel was less than a kilometre from the pier, and with normal foot traffic it usually took her about ten minutes to get there.

"Ava," Sonny answered. "Is everything okay?"

"Yes. I spoke to Lam. He'll send enough guns for fifty men by truck later today. I don't have any details yet, but could you let Ko know he'll have the weapons he needs for Suen? Also, when you have a chance, text me Ko's number."

"That's great news. It's funny how things turn out. When I first met Lam, I had no time for him and didn't trust him at all — he was just so slick," Sonny said. "How wrong I was. He's been a great friend to you and Xu."

Lam, like Xu, was the furthest thing possible from the typical public image of a triad. Tall and slim, with long grey hair that he wore in a ponytail, Lam usually dressed in designer jeans and silk shirts and looked at the world through small, round red-tinted glasses. "Now I'm going to owe him another favour. I'm losing track of how many that will make," Ava said. "I hope he never decides to cash them in all at once."

"Are you in Central yet?"

"I just arrived on the ferry and I'm walking to the hotel. I'll call Amanda in a minute and arrange to meet her and get the money."

"I'm in Tai Po. While I don't want to sound overly optimistic, I'm getting some interesting reactions to our offer. A couple of the guys I talked to said they don't know anything but thought they might know someone who does. They're trying to get hold of them now."

"Fingers crossed," Ava said. "Stay in touch."

Walking in Central was often a stop-and-go affair with the human equivalent of traffic jams at street corners, but Ava was able to move unimpeded for most of the way to the Mandarin. She called Amanda when she'd entered the lobby.

"Any problem with the money?" Ava asked.

"No. The bank is organizing it for me. I'm heading over there to get it in a few minutes."

"Could you bring it to the Mandarin Oriental?"

"Of course."

"And will you stay for dim sum?"

"I'd love to."

"Good. Call me when you get to the hotel."


The morning had been a blur, and Ava was pleased to get back to the calmness of the Mandarin for an hour or two. She went to her suite, put her gun in the safe, and then sat at the desk. She checked her cell for texts and saw that Sonny had sent her Ko's number and Fai had sent her Chen's contact information. She had nothing definite to say to Ko until she'd heard from Lam, and there was no urgent need to call Chen. She tried his office number anyway.

A receptionist answered, asked who was calling, and put Ava on hold. Chen was Fai's agent. Until the week before he had been completely opposed to Fai's relationship with Ava and had been openly hostile towards Ava. His fear — and it was justified — was that public knowledge of her sexuality would destroy Fai's career in China. Although that fear hadn't dissipated, he had decided that Fai's happiness was also a priority, and that meant accepting Ava. His acceptance was now buttressed by his admiration for Ava's handling of the crisis in Beijing, which had saved both a film and Fai's career.

"How is Shanghai?" he asked when he came on the line.

"My plans changed since the last time we talked. I had to make a side trip to Hong Kong on business. But Fai is in Shanghai and I'll be joining her again in a day or two."

"You're hard to keep track of," he said. "What can I do for you?"

"Do you remember my asking you about Lau Lau and a film script?"

"I do, and I told you I'm no longer his agent," Chen interrupted. "I also told you that I think paying him to write a script is a bad idea."

"I've spoken to my business partner, and despite your opinion we've decided we want to do it ... assuming, of course, that Lau Lau is in good enough physical and mental shape to undertake it," she said. "It means he'd have to be clean and sober, and I don't think he'll make that happen on his own, so he would have to go into rehab. Would you talk to him and see if he's prepared to do that?"

"Ava, I'm not his agent anymore."

"But surely you're still his friend."

"Even so, he might not want to talk to me. We parted rather acrimoniously."

"I'm sure if you went to him with a serious offer he wouldn't refuse to listen."

"What kind of offer?"

"If he will agree to go into a rehab facility that you choose, and if he finishes the treatment, then my partner and I will commit to financing a script."

"You want me to choose a rehab facility?"

"Given your business, I thought you would know which ones are best."

"Unfortunately, I actually do know a lot about rehab facilities," he said. "What kind of script are you thinking about?"

"He told me he's been making movies in his head. Tell him to put down the best one on paper."

"I know what kind of movies he's been imagining. No one is going to put up money to have them made."

"Why not?"

"For one thing, they're political poison. For another, they are seriously depressing."

"Depressing, or dealing with real life in an honest, emotional way?" Ava asked.

"I know you're a fan of his old work, but there aren't enough of you fans out there to make this worthwhile."

"Let me be the judge of that," she said. "What I'd like you to do — as an old friend of his and, hopefully, a new friend of mine — is to take this one step at a time. And that starts by getting him to agree to go to rehab."

"I don't think he'll go without a commitment that you'll pay for a script."

"We'll commit. You can write up the agreement."

"And what's the point in writing a script if there's no chance of the film being made?"

"I know this sounds a bit naive from our side," Ava said carefully, "but if he finishes a script and you like it, we'll find a way to finance it, even if we have to do it all ourselves. Chen, we have enough money to make this happen."

"What do you mean if *I* like the script?"

"Fai has told me you have tremendous taste. We'll trust whatever you and she have to say about the script's quality."

"In the unlikely event that we ever get to the point where we have a great script, would hiring Fai be part of the deal?"

"No."

"But you'd want Lau Lau to direct."

"Of course."

"You'd also need a producer."

"Do you know enough to fill that role?"

"I'm an agent, not a producer."

"Still, I'm sure you know enough to do it."

Chen laughed — a loud, roaring laugh, not the chuckle of someone slightly amused.

"What's so funny?" Ava asked.

"Despite what I know about this business, and despite everything I know about Lau Lau, I just realized that you're pulling me into this thing. Maybe I'm the one who's naive."

"So you'll talk to Lau Lau about rehab?"

"I don't even know where to find him."

"He's living in an artists' commune about ten minutes from Fai's house. I'll get her to text you the exact address."

Chen sighed. "I can't believe you're talking me into this."

"So you'll go to the commune and talk to him?"

"I'll go, but I have no idea what will come of it."

"As long as you give it your best shot, we can't ask for more than that."

"I promise you I'll give it my best shot."

"Thank you so much, Chen."

"I don't want any thanks. And I don't want any blame if this doesn't work, either with rehab or at any point further down the road."

"It's entirely on me," Ava said.

"I don't often hear those words in my business," Chen said. "Have Fai send me Lau Lau's address."

Ava ended the call, thought about sending a text to Fai, and instead called her. Her cell jumped directly to voicemail. "Hey, it's me. Do me a favour and send Lau Lau's address to Chen. He's agreed to see him," she said. "Things are progressing here. I'll call you tonight and give you a more complete update. Love you."

She left the desk, walked to the window, and stared out at the harbour. Talking to Chen had been a pleasant distraction. She knew it was possible that nothing might come of trying to resurrect Lau Lau's career, but she felt a strong obligation to try. What was strange was that she wasn't quite sure why she felt that way. Despite what she had said to Chen and May Ling, there was more to it than simply giving Lau Lau a chance to make films again. In some ways Fai and Lau Lau were so deeply entangled that Ava had trouble separating them. She had helped rescue Fai from her confusion, and maybe even from despair. Was she feeling guilty about leaving Lau Lau behind? Was her attempt to help him just another way of expressing her love for Fai? Could Fai have real closure in terms of her failed relationship with Lau Lau while he was in such desperate need? *I'm overanalyzing this,* Ava thought.

Just then her cell sounded and she saw an incoming call from Amanda. "Are you in the lobby?" she asked.

"I've just left the bank. I'll be at the hotel in five minutes. Do you want to meet at Man Wah?"

"How are you bringing the cash?"

"I have it in a tote bag."

"I think it's better if you come to my suite first," Ava said, giving her the number.

"See you soon," Amanda said.

Ava returned to the desk, her conversation with Chen again coming to mind. She had anticipated his initial reluctance but not the burst of enthusiasm, however brief, that he'd displayed later. He had given her a touch of hope that her idea wasn't completely crazy. Still, she had to rein in her expectations. *If Lau Lau can get through rehab and write a script of any kind, I will have done enough,* she thought. Then she looked down at her notebook and saw the names of Sammy and Carter Wing. *This is what I need to be concentrating on,* she reminded herself.

A few minutes later there was a knock at the door, and she went to greet Amanda.

Amanda was an only child whose parents had the money to spoil her — and they had. From the time she was a child she had eaten in the best restaurants in Hong Kong and wherever they travelled in the world. She wore only designer clothing and had a jewellery collection that needed its own safety deposit box at the bank. Amanda was five feet tall, thin, and elegant. On their first meeting she had matched Ava's image of the stereotypical spoiled Hong Kong princess. But as Ava got to know her that image had disappeared. Amanda was smart, well-educated — she had a degree in international business from Brandeis University — and mentally tough. She had been engaged to Ava's half-brother Michael when they first met and had stood by Ava's side to help rescue Michael's business and his partner from the grasp of a

Macau-based triad gang. Her strengths were emotional and intellectual rather than physical, and she was someone Ava had come to rely on.

Amanda was wearing black skinny jeans and a pink cashmere sweater. Her hair hung loose around her shoulders, framing her fine features. Since meeting Ava she had abandoned her former excessive use of makeup and wore only a touch of lipstick and mascara. A long scar above her right eye provided her face with a touch of drama. She had received that scar in Borneo, when she was attacked by two thugs while trying to resolve a business dispute.

Ava held out her arms and Amanda rushed into them. "I've missed you. I'm so glad you called," she said.

Ava stepped back into the room. "Did May explain to you why I'm here?"

"She said you're dealing with a 'Xu problem,'" Amanda said. She was aware of the connection and the complications it sometimes produced.

"I am," Ava said, and then pointed at the black tote bag. "I'm hoping this money will help me with it. Thanks for getting it for me."

Amanda carried the bag to the desk. "I wasn't sure what denominations you wanted, but I got thousand-dollar notes. There are a hundred in each stack. If I'd gotten anything smaller I'm not sure they would have fit into the one bag."

"I don't think the people I'll be dealing with will object to thousand-dollar notes," Ava said. "Did the bank ask any questions about why you wanted this much cash?"

"No. When my father ran the trading business, he used to carry cash to China all the time. That's how business was done back then, and from time to time it still is." Three

Sisters now owned the trading business. Ava and May Ling had bought it to give Jack Yee a secure retirement and to make sure Amanda joined forces with them.

"I remember that one of the jobs Uncle and I did for your father was to recover a large amount of cash that had gone missing in China."

"When he reminisces about the business, that's always one of the stories he tells," Amanda said. "It's funny, whenever he does talk about the old days, he usually tells stories about things that didn't go well."

"Well, that one turned out okay, but I understand why it sticks out in his mind. I'm the same when I think about my time working with Uncle. The jobs that went sideways are the ones I remember most clearly."

"I can't believe too many did."

"Don't get me started," Ava said, and then opened the Saint Laurent tote to look inside. There were twenty stacks of bills. "Are you going to leave the bag with me?"

"Of course."

"I'll get it back to you," Ava said. "Are you hungry?"

"I'm ravenous."

"I'll put this money in the safe and then we can head upstairs."

They took the elevator to the twenty-fifth floor. The restaurant was busy but the host found them a table near the window. A moment later the server brought a pot of jasmine tea and menus.

"We can order dim sum or something off the lunch menu. It makes no difference to me," Ava said.

"Dim sum, please."

"Beef puffs with black pepper sauce, prawn dumplings, abalone and chicken buns, dumplings with cuttlefish and scallops?"

"Oh yes. The beef puffs are especially good — order two servings."

Ava placed their order and then poured the tea. "I had dinner here last night. I've eaten here more times than I can count and I've never had a bad meal."

"My father preferred the Mandarin Grill. He liked to have a steak with beer for lunch."

"Is he enjoying his retirement?" Ava asked.

"Not especially. He complains that my mother sticks to him like glue. After all those years of doing his own thing, he finds that hard to take."

"My father normally spends two weeks a year with my mother. A few years ago he spent a month, and by the end of it he couldn't wait to get back to Hong Kong — and she couldn't wait for him to go."

"May said you don't want me to mention to Marcus or Michael that you're in the city. Naturally I haven't."

"Thanks. This is a business trip that I don't want to extend even for an hour. I just want to get things resolved and get back to Fai in Shanghai."

"So things are going well with Fai?"

"Very well. In fact, sometimes so well that it scares me."

"We're all so happy for you."

"We?"

Amanda looked slightly uncomfortable and then said, "I told Michael about Fai. He told Marcus and his brothers."

"Does Elizabeth know?"

"Of course she does, and she's probably the happiest of anyone. Whenever I see her, she asks about you. She really cares for you — not a typical first wife's attitude towards children from a second wife."

"She's a kind woman. I'd like to get to know her better, but I can't help feeling that would be disloyal to my mother."

"What a complicated family," Amanda said. "I told Michael a few weeks ago that if he ever has thoughts about taking a second wife he should expect me to cut his balls off before I kill him."

"Michael is part of a different generation," Ava said, laughing.

The prawn dumplings and beef puffs arrived at their table and they ate quietly for several minutes. Then Ava asked, "Did May mention what I want to do with Lau Lau?"

"She did, and she sounded excited about it."

"I know it hardly fits with our business model, so you don't have to agree to participate. May and I can handle it ourselves if you want."

"We're partners," Amanda said. "And in my mind that means we're partners in everything. You supported me when I wanted to invest in the Borneo furniture-manufacturing business, and you bought my father's trading company. You can count me in on anything you and May want to do."

"Thanks. It may amount to nothing anyway."

"I hope not. It could be fun, and a nice change from dealing with Suki Chan and the nuts and bolts of that warehouse and logistics empire she's intent on building for us."

Ava smiled. Suki Chan was a widow, about sixty years old, who was a long-time friend and business acquaintance of May's. When Suki's husband died, she was finally free to grow the business as she'd always wanted. Three Sisters had bought into the business and was financing its expansion. Suki, who always dressed in a grey or blue Mao suit, was a dynamo. Ava and May dealt with her on the strategic big-picture level, but it was left to Amanda and her team to cope with the day-to-day details of a very complicated business.

"Suki is going to make us a lot of money," Ava said.

"I know. I just hope I'm left with enough energy to enjoy it."

The rest of their order arrived. As Ava's chopsticks were plucking a gleaming, translucent scallop dumpling from its steamer basket, her cell sounded. It was Andy. Her pulse quickened.

"Andy, where are you?" she said.

"I'm with Carlo in a restaurant near the Sha Tin MTR station," he said softly. "We think we've found our man."

"Is he triad?"

"Yeah."

"Sha Tin?"

"Yeah. He was close to the old Mountain Master. From what I can gather, Carter Wing has treated him like dirt since he took over."

"How did you find him?" Ava asked.

"Sonny called me from Tai Po and gave me his name and number. Sonny had spoken to a friend of his, and the guy told him that anything we can do to shit on Carter would go over well with his buddy in Sha Tin."

"Have you actually spoken to this buddy?"

"We have. He's sitting in the restaurant here, waiting for me to finish this call."

"And he knows the location of our six men?"

"He says he has a good idea but he won't give us any specifics until he's paid."

"A million?"

"Yeah. And Sonny says you're going to have to pay the guy in Tai Po something as well."

"I'll pay ten men as long as we get the information we need."

"How do you want to handle this?"

"I want to meet him."

"I told him you would, but he won't do it in Sha Tin. He's nervous as hell just sitting here with us, even though there isn't a triad in sight."

"Did you tell him who I am?"

"No, I said you're an interested party, that's all. And when you meet with him, you don't have to give him your name. He doesn't need to know. All he wants is the cash."

"And if he gives us the wrong information?"

"We'll find him, and he already knows Sonny is involved. That's usually enough to keep people in line. No one wants to mess with Sonny."

Ava knew Sonny hadn't been an active triad in ten years, but it seemed that his fearsome reputation had survived. In fact, she thought, maybe it was because of his absence that his reputation kept growing. He was like a mythical character, an urban legend. "Where do you want to meet?"

"It might be safer if it's somewhere outside the New Territories."

"Central?"

"That would work."

"Would you and Carlo come with him?"

"Yeah, and I think Sonny and the guy from Tai Po should be there as well."

"Why the guy from Tai Po?"

"He recommended this other guy to us, and he wants to get paid. Also, he needs to know there are consequences if he's bullshitting us or if he ever thinks about playing both sides."

"Okay, then let's do it that way," Ava said. "There's a noodle shop about four blocks from the Mandarin Oriental where Uncle used to go all the time."

"I know it. I was there a couple of weeks ago."

"How long will it take you and Sonny to get there with those guys in tow?"

"An hour or so."

Ava checked the time. "That would be just after two. The lunch rush should be over by then."

"Who's going to call Sonny?"

"You do it. If there's a problem, get back to me. Otherwise, I'll expect to see the five of you at the noodle shop," Ava said. She put down her phone to find Amanda staring at her. "That probably sounded stranger than it is."

"The opposite is more likely true, but you know I don't need to know — and I don't care."

## 12

**AFTER GETTING THE MONEY FROM HER ROOM, AVA LEFT** the Mandarin with Amanda at quarter to two. They walked east along Connaught Road until they reached the Hong Kong Club building, where they separated, Ava taking a right turn and Amanda continuing along Connaught.

"If things go well, I could be heading back to Shanghai tomorrow," Ava said before they parted ways.

"Then let's hope the next time I hear from you, that's where you are," Amanda said.

"If I have any cash left, I'll leave it in the tote bag and have Sonny deliver it to the office."

"That's fine," Amanda said, hugging Ava again. "You be careful."

*If one more person tells me to be careful, I'm going to scream,* Ava thought as she began the two-block uphill climb to the noodle restaurant. She had been to the restaurant many times with Uncle, but usually at night for a late meal. The couple who owned the restaurant had been middle-aged when she first went there, and if they were still operating it they would now be elderly. She had done the cooking while he served and ran the front end. Ava didn't know which job would be harder on the body.

When she reached the restaurant, there was no sign of Sonny's car. She peeked inside. Andy hadn't arrived either. There were only eight tables, and four were occupied. Luckily the largest, which was farthest from the door and could seat eight people, was available. Ava walked towards it, only to be intercepted by the man she remembered.

"Pretty lady, please take a smaller table."

"I'm being joined by five friends any minute now," she said.

He shook his head and then looked at her more closely. "You are Uncle's girl!" he blurted.

"I am."

"It's been so long."

"I haven't had much reason to visit Hong Kong since he passed."

He touched her forearm gently. "We miss him so much."

"As do I."

He nodded. "You take the big table. Do you want anything while you wait for your friends? I have tea, water and beer."

"Tea will be fine."

Ava took a seat that gave her a clear view of the doorway. She put the tote bag by her feet and took the cell from her bag to call Andy.

"We're in Central and we're walking towards the restaurant. See you in about five minutes," he shouted above the roar of traffic.

"Have you heard from Sonny?"

"He's with me. That's why we're running late. He decided to pick us up in Sha Tin. He's just parking the car."

"Why did he do that?"

"He wanted to talk to the guy personally. He wanted him to know there's zero tolerance for bullshit or games, and that he's responsible for your protection. He couldn't have been clearer."

"The fact that the guy still wants to meet with me after that is a positive sign, yes?"

"I'd be shocked if it isn't."

"Excellent. See you when you get here."

The owner put two large white pots on the table, one full of tea and the other of hot water to add to the tea when it got low. He poured her first cup and smiled. "So good to see you," he said.

Ava sipped the tea to please him, certain that, after all the tea she'd drunk at Man Wah, she'd float away if she had more than one cup. "It's possible that neither I nor my friends will actually eat while we're here," she said. "If that's the case, we will leave a very large tip. I don't want to take advantage of your hospitality."

"Uncle did that often," he said with a smile. "Don't worry, and know that you're always welcome back here."

She kicked the bag at her feet. Two million Hong Kong dollars was about three hundred thousand U.S. She had been in possession of larger cash sums before, but never in a designer tote bag — and never intended for buying information. She looked idly at the other customers. They looked like businesspeople catching a quick lunch. Then the room suddenly became darker and she saw Sonny filling the doorway.

"Hey, boss," he said, and walked towards her, with Andy, Carlo, and two men in his wake.

Ava stayed seated, her eyes fixed on the men. They were both in their forties, she guessed. One had a beard and floppy hair, the other was bald. They were both a bit taller than Andy, and more muscular, but next to Sonny they looked insignificant. They wore jeans and T-shirts that showed off the tattoos on their arms. "Have a seat," she said. "There's beer, tea or water if you want it."

"They don't need anything to drink," Sonny said, and pointed to two seats directly across from Ava. "Sit there."

When the two men had sat down, Sonny took the chair to the left of them while Andy and Carlo took the chairs to their right.

"Who am I paying for what?" Ava asked.

"He's the one who says he knows where the men are," Sonny said, indicating the bearded man sitting next to him.

"How much have we agreed to pay you?" Ava asked.

"A million dollars," the bearded man said.

"How about you?" Ava asked the other man.

"A hundred thousand."

"Before I ask you any more questions, I want to make clear that this meeting never happened. You keep your mouths shut about what is said here today, and we will as well. So, before we start sharing information, I want you to acknowledge that you'll deny you ever spoke to any of us."

"That suits us more than it does you," the bearded man said.

"Good, but I have to add that I also expect you to be straightforward. If you tell me what you know and answer my questions honestly, then we will never have a problem. Lie to me, invent things, or start telling me what you think I want to know rather than what you know for certain, and we will have a problem. Is that understood?"

"We have no reason to lie."

"Okay, tell me where the men are being held."

The bearded man hesitated. "Andy said I would get my money up front."

Ava looked at Andy.

"He told me that he definitely knows where the men are being held," Andy said.

Ava reached under the table, picked up the tote bag, and handed it to Sonny. "Give him five stacks, and one stack to the other one."

"Do you have something to put the money in?" Sonny asked them.

"No, I didn't have time to get anything," the bearded one said.

"I'm not giving you this tote," Ava said and turned towards the noodle-shop owner. "Can I get two plastic takeout bags, please?"

He shrugged, took two bags from the counter, and handed them to her. She passed them to Sonny, who opened the tote, counted out five stacks, and stuffed them into one of the takeout bags. Then he put one stack into the other bag. He handed the bags to the men.

"Those are thousand-dollar bills, one hundred in each stack. You don't have to count them here," Ava said. "They come directly from the bank, so I doubt you'll be short."

They put the plastic bags on their laps.

"I was promised a million. This is only five hundred thousand," the bearded man said.

Ava leaned towards him. "What's your name?"

"Ching."

"Well, Mr. Ching, you'll get the rest of your money once I've heard what you have to tell me. You can't blame me for that, can you. The money is right here in the bag and I'll be happy to give it to you when I'm convinced you're not stringing us along."

"Why would I do that?"

"A million dollars is a lot of money."

He shifted in his chair and Ava knew he wanted to argue with her, but Sonny nudged him and said, "Just tell her the truth and you won't have a problem."

"Okay, what do you want to know?" Ching said.

"It's simple. Where are Xu's men?" Ava said.

"They're holding them in a garage, more like a body shop actually, about five kilometres from the centre of Sha Tin," Ching said.

"How do you know that?"

"The gang has owned the repair shop for years. Sometimes it's used to fix cars; other times it's used to disguise other jobs and store things."

"Like men?"

"This isn't the first time men have been held there. The garage is in a grungy industrial area. No one pays it any mind."

"How do you know they're using it this time to hold our men?"

He looked at his friend and then at Sonny. "My cousin is Carter Wing's Red Pole. He told me."

"He told you that the men are being held at this garage? I mean, he told you precisely that?"

"Yeah."

"When?"

"Last night."

"Where?"

"At his apartment."

"Why were you there?"

"We meet twice a week for dinner."

"How did it come up?" she asked.

"I told him there's a lot of talk on the street about Carter joining with Sammy Wing to take on the guys from Shanghai. He laughed and said Carter already had them by the balls. I asked him what he meant, and he told me they'd shot Lop and were holding seven of the Shanghai men hostage."

"There are only six now. They killed one."

"I didn't know."

"No, you wouldn't," Ava said. "When did he mention the body shop?"

"After I asked where the men were being held."

"Are you swearing that you asked that specific question, and that was his reply?"

"I asked. That was his answer."

"Could he have lied to you?"

"He had no reason to. We're family."

Ava could think of many reasons, but none of them were helpful. "If you're so close, why are you prepared to tell us this? You don't think you're betraying your cousin's confidence?"

"This isn't about my cousin, it's about Carter Wing. When we were forty-niners, we had our differences. I was a few months senior to him and I might have been rough on him at first. Carter's a man who carries a grudge. Now that he's on top of the heap, he's decided to make my life miserable. I get every shit job there is. I've had enough of it."

"So this is your way of paying him back?"

"You could say that. I can also use the money."

Ava looked at Sonny across the table. He gave her a little nod as if to say, *I believe the guy.*

"Where is this body shop?" she asked.

"It's on Green Hill Lane."

"Does it have a name?"

"Phoenix Auto Repair."

"Is it clearly signed?"

"You can't miss it as long as you're on Green Hill Lane," Ching said.

"Why is that?"

"The street has a line of businesses on one side and a brick wall on the other. Phoenix is the last business before the lane dead-ends at another wall."

"What other businesses are on the lane?"

"A bunch of other auto repair shops."

"What time do they close?"

"I don't know."

"How large is the Phoenix shop?" Ava asked.

"It has three bays for working on cars, an office overhead, and a large storage room in the back."

"Where do you think they're holding the men?"

"Most probably in the storage room," said Ching.

"Is there a rear entrance?"

"Yeah, there's a narrow alley at the back that's just wide enough for a truck. Most of the businesses have delivery doors there. Phoenix has a large metal door, but it's always kept locked. As I remember, it's bolted and barred," he said.

"So trying to get into the shop through that door isn't a good idea?"

"It would be hard, maybe impossible."

"How about going in through the front?"

He frowned. "There's no good way of getting in."

"What's at the front?"

"Three bay doors and a small wooden entry door off to the side."

"That presents four possibilities."

"Except if the men are there, all those doors will be closed and probably guarded."

"*If* the men are there?" Ava said.

"I'm just saying... They could have moved them since last night. I don't think they would, but how can I be a hundred percent sure?"

"I'm paying you a million dollars to be a hundred percent sure," Ava said.

"All I can tell you is what I was told."

"You sound like you aren't completely convinced."

Ching pointed at Sonny. "I know about this guy. If I'm not completely right, if the men aren't still there, or if only two or three of them are there, I don't want him coming after me.

"And this is your way of covering your ass?" Ava said.

"Yeah, something like that... But listen, I was told they're there. I swear it."

Ava sighed. "Our problem, Ching, is that we're working with a tight deadline. We have only one kick at this can, so we have to get it right the first time. We can't make a mistake. So I don't think it's enough for you to simply tell us where you *think* the men are. We're going to need your help to confirm it," Ava said.

"How would I do that?"

"I want you to go to the garage."

"That wasn't our deal. Andy said you wanted information. He didn't mention anything else."

"No, he didn't, but I'm sure you can understand why, after hearing what you have to say, I think it's necessary," Ava said.

Ching turned to Andy. "This isn't right."

"Don't tell me, tell her," Andy said.

Ava picked up the tote bag again and gave it to Sonny. "Give him the other five hundred thousand."

Sonny took five stacks of bills from the bag and slid them across the table to Ching.

"There, we've honoured our agreement. I realize that asking you to go to the garage is more work, so I'm prepared to pay you another two hundred thousand to do it," Ava said.

Ching hesitated. "What if I say no?"

"If you've told us the truth, why would you turn down all that money?"

"What excuse can I give for going there?"

"Have you been there before?" asked Ava.

"Yeah."

"Why did you go?"

"I went a couple of times for meetings, and once to have my wife's car fixed."

"So her car needs fixing again. Tell them you're there to make an appointment for some time next week."

"It might look suspicious."

"It will only look suspicious if you act suspicious," Ava said. "You're a well-established member of the gang. Act like you have every right to be there."

"Given the money you've been paid already, plus the offer of an extra two hundred thousand, I think it's a reasonable request," Sonny said. "None of us want to think you're being reluctant because you didn't tell us the entire truth."

"The only reason I'm hesitating is because I'm scared that it will look odd," Ching said. "I don't need Carter Wing asking me questions with a knife held to my throat."

"I don't expect you to hang around there for any longer than it takes for you to make an appointment for your wife's car and then get out of there," Ava said. "All I want you to do is eyeball the place. Does it look like they're doing car repairs as usual, or is something different going on? If they are holding the men, there will be guards. Roughly how many of them, and where are they located — inside the building, outside? How are they armed? I'd like all the detail I can get, but be casual and use your common sense. There's no value to me in putting you at risk."

"I'll drive you there," Sonny said.

"What?" Ching exclaimed.

"The four of us will go with you," Sonny said, gesturing to Andy, Carlo, and the bald man. "I won't park anywhere near the garage, but I'd like to be close enough so you can walk to it. We'll wait until you're done."

Ching lowered his head, and Ava knew he wanted to say no. "Give him the extra two hundred thousand now," Ava said to Sonny. "And Ching, you can keep the money regardless of what you see in the garage. I don't doubt what you've told me, but given our time limitations. I really need certainty."

Sonny handed the money to Ching and then stood up. "Let's get going. Like the lady said, we don't have time to waste."

The other men rose to their feet and started towards the door.

"Just a minute, Andy. Can I speak to you?" Ava said. When Andy returned to the table, she whispered, "You should follow Ching to the garage. Try to see as much as you can of the building and the street. Keep a safe distance, but make sure he actually goes inside. He seems reluctant."

"He's scared. I think the only reason he's doing this is that he's more scared of Sonny than he is of Carter Wing."

"That's smart of him," she said. "Call me as soon as you have information, and don't let Ching or his friend leave until I tell you they can."

## 13

**AVA WALKED BACK TO THE MANDARIN ORIENTAL WITH** a much lighter tote bag. She knew she had overpaid Ching, and if it turned out none of Xu's men were at the garage, the money would be completely wasted. But she didn't think he had lied to her; he just wasn't on the inside, and if Carter Wing's plans had changed he wouldn't know.

She figured it would take Sonny about half an hour to get to Sha Tin, and then maybe another half-hour or so for Ching to go back and forth between the car and the body shop. That would make it three-thirty before she would know who was in the garage. It didn't leave much time to get organized. As she was thinking about calling Ko, her phone rang. It was Lam.

"Our shipment will be leaving Guangzhou at five. Barring any problems at the border, it should arrive between seven and eight o'clock tonight. We'll be going to a warehouse in Kowloon. Can Ko pick up his goods there?" he said.

"I'm sure he'll be pleased to."

"I'll get my Red Pole to phone him with the specifics."

"He'll be very thankful, as will Suen and Xu."

"Speaking of Xu, I've been thinking more about this business in Wanchai," Lam said carefully.

"Is there a message you want me to pass along?"

"Yes. Tell him that, despite the Wing family's stupidity, I think he should consider trying to do everything he can to maintain peace," Lam said. "He has my support whether he does or not, but I feel obliged to make my preference known."

"Believe me, he is trying to resolve this peacefully. I was even told to offer Sammy a larger share of the profits and a greater say in the business. He turned me down flat."

"The fool."

"There isn't much more Xu can do from his end. How this plays out is completely up to the Wings."

"Let's hope common sense prevails."

"When two parties are involved, common sense works only if it's going in both directions."

"Your point is well taken, but tell Xu what I said anyway."

"I will. Hopefully by tomorrow you can speak to him directly."

Ava was now on Connaught Road and almost at the hotel. She decided to put her cell away until she got to her suite. When she reached the room a few minutes later, the first thing she did was check the time and estimate where Sonny and the other men would be. She saw she had quite a bit of waiting ahead of her.

She went to the window and looked out onto the harbour. The clouds had lifted and the water glimmered under a clear blue sky. The colour almost startled her. After spending weeks in Beijing and Shanghai, it was easy to forget that the sky could be something other than grey, black, or brown. *As nice as it is, a blue sky isn't going to keep me in Hong Kong an hour longer than necessary,* she thought as she called Ko.

He answered with an abrupt "*Wei.*"

"It's Ava. I'm back at the hotel, and I've been busy since we met this morning."

"Good busy?"

"Lam is trucking the guns to Kowloon today. They should arrive around eight o'clock tonight. His Red Pole will call you to arrange the pickup."

"I got part of that message from Sonny. It's terrific news, because I've been having problems finding everything we need."

"Why do you think that is?"

"Most of the people I spoke to made it clear that they don't want to get involved, even indirectly, in a dispute between us and the Wings — although none of them openly took sides. It seems to me that they don't want to piss off Xu and threaten business relationships that are working very well, but on the other hand, the Wings are the local boys and there are long-standing loyalties we may not understand."

"That's what Sonny said this morning."

"I know. I kept thinking about him when I was speaking to them."

"And Lam told me that no one wants a war."

"He's right. They all wish we'd settle this with maybe a duel or an arm-wrestling match — anything except the direction we seem to be heading."

"Well, there's still hope... We think we've found where they're holding your men," Ava said.

"What did you just say?" Ko said excitedly.

"Andy, Carlo, and Sonny found a Sha Tin triad who was willing to talk for the money we were offering. We met with him and now we're trying to confirm his story and scout the location he identified."

"When will we know for sure it's the right place?"

"In about an hour, so stay close to your phone."

"Have you told Suen?"

"Not yet, he's next on my list."

"Fuck, that's good news."

"Knowing where they are and getting them out are two different things," Ava said.

"At least it would give us a shot."

"I agree, but until we hear back from the guys I think we should curb our enthusiasm," said Ava, directing that advice at herself as much as at Ko. "But I think you should make sure you have ten to twenty men ready to go into action at short notice."

"They've been ready to do something since Lop was shot and our men taken. Sitting around is making them crazy."

"I think it's better not to say anything to them until you hear back from me."

"Okay," Ko said. "I'm actually in front of the clinic in Kowloon. I came to visit Lop. I called here an hour ago and the doctor told me he's finally able to communicate. We haven't exchanged two words since he was shot."

"So he doesn't know about the men being held hostage?"

"No."

"Even if he is conscious now, don't say a word about it. There's no point in getting him riled up."

"He'll want to know what's going on. What can I tell him?"

"Does he know who shot him?"

"Not yet, although I'm sure he suspects it was the Wings."

THE MOUNTAIN MASTER OF SHA TIN     159

"That much you can tell him, but make it clear that Xu
and Suen are taking care of things."

"You know Lop. He'll want details, and he can be
insistent."

"Tell him you're out of the loop but that Suen will drop by
to see him when he gets to Hong Kong."

Ko hesitated and then said, "On second thought, maybe
I shouldn't visit him today. I don't want to lie to him — he
sees right through me. I think it's better if I wait until I have
something definite I can tell him."

"That's your choice, although I have to say it sounds like
the right one," Ava said. "Why don't you give the Red Pole
in Guangzhou a call instead, and then wait for me to get
back to you."

"I'll do that," Ko said, sounding relieved.

*That is a really solid man,* Ava thought as she ended the
call. His remark about not being able to lie to Lop had particularly struck home. What a terrific asset that was in a
second-in-command. She made a mental note to mention
it to Xu, and to Lop when he was up and about.

Suen was next on her call list. She hit his number, hoping
he would answer.

"Ava, you caught me just as I'm leaving the hospital," he
said.

"That's lucky. How's Xu?"

"They're definitely moving him out of isolation. It could
even be as soon as tonight."

"Thank goodness."

"What news do you have from your end?"

"Lam is shipping fifty automatics and semi-automatics to
Hong Kong today. Ko will have them by tonight."

"Bless Lam! Xu will be really pleased that he came through for us again. I'll start getting another fifty men ready to leave."

"And I think we may have located where they're holding your six men," she said.

"Really?" he said, his voice tinged in equal measure with doubt and excitement.

"The money worked, as it so often does," she said, and then explained what they'd been told and what Sonny and the others were doing.

"If the men are there, we have to go in after them," Suen said when she'd finished.

"Let's not rush into that decision. I want to hear the information that Ching and Andy come back with," Ava said.

"If our men are there, they will be guarded. There's no getting around that."

"True, but we need to know how many guards, and how well equipped they are. If your men are heavily guarded, that would mean a full-out assault. Men would die on both sides, and the men being held hostage would probably be the first to go. We'd also bring the Hong Kong police into the situation in a serious way, angering every other gang in Hong Kong and the Territories."

"I can't leave our men there to get slaughtered without making every effort to get them out."

"I'm not saying we shouldn't make the effort. I'm saying that whatever we do should be based on facts and thought out according to those facts," Ava said. "We'll know more soon."

"I'll come to Hong Kong tonight," Suen said suddenly. "I should have come sooner. I should have gone with you yesterday, but I was hoping you'd be able to reach an agreement with the Wings, or at least we would have another twenty-four hours of calm."

"You couldn't leave Xu until you knew how he was. As important as Hong Kong is, Shanghai is still your home and your power base. It needed to be your priority."

"I'll be in Hong Kong tonight," he said.

Ava looked at her watch and did the calculations. "It isn't for me to tell you what to do, but there are things you need to consider. Given the time, even if everything goes smoothly you still won't get here until ten o'clock at the earliest. And that doesn't leave much time for you to organize on this end. Our deadline is midnight. You shouldn't ask the men here to sit around waiting for you to get to Hong Kong."

"Are you telling me to stay in Shanghai until tomorrow?"

"Of course not. What I'd like you to do is wait for half an hour, until we have more information. When we do, you can talk to Xu, and together you can choose your best course of action."

Suen paused and then said. "If we find out for sure where our men are being held, we can't abandon them. I don't care if they're guarded by the entire fucking PLA."

Ava took a deep breath. "I know."

## 14

AVA WAS NO STRANGER TO WAITING. DURING HER years working with Uncle, she had spent countless hours waiting for phone calls, emails, and texts that would lead to meetings that would lead in turn to God-knows-what as she tracked stolen money. In those days she had occasionally called upon the services of her friend Derek Liang, the only son of a wealthy Chinese couple, who lived a privileged, idle life in Richmond Hill, a bedroom community north of Toronto with a large Chinese population. Derek didn't need to work, and his only real talent was for bak mei — the same martial art practised by Ava. She had used him on several jobs as additional muscle. On one occasion, as they waited for a meeting that they knew could turn violent, Derek had said, "What a crazy job this is: twenty-three hours and fifty-five minutes of boredom followed by five minutes of terror and mayhem."

Derek had eventually married one of Ava's best friends, Mimi, and they had a baby daughter. That eliminated Derek from Ava's list of hands-on helpers, since she couldn't risk leaving Mimi without a husband and her daughter without a father. He still helped her from time to time, though, but with his computer skills, from the safety of his home in Toronto's Leaside neighbourhood.

Ava didn't know why she was thinking of Derek as she sat in Hong Kong waiting to hear from Sonny or Andy, although it did seem that her life was becoming an ever-expanding spider's web of connections. She remembered everyone she had done business with and — taking Uncle's advice — had never closed a door, so it wasn't unusual for people to recycle through her life. Uncle referred to this act of cultivating and maintaining influential connections as *guanxi*. He had been a master of it, and there wasn't anywhere in Asia he couldn't call on someone for help. Ava wasn't his match yet, but she still had an impressive number of connections and, perhaps just as important, she was owed favours by many people who had the power to deliver on them if the need arose.

She put her cell on the arm of the chair and started to think about the challenges the garage might present. If it was heavily guarded, then a frontal attack would likely be bloody. Its position as the last building on a dead-end street gave it a line of natural defence or — depending on how it was attacked — closed an escape route. So that could be a positive or a negative. Ava sighed. She didn't like trying to predict outcomes that could be complete polar opposites.

*I wonder if I can find the garage on Google Earth?* she thought. She went to the desk and opened her laptop. A moment later she was looking at the exterior of a nondescript red-brick building with three closed single garage doors made of metal and a regular wooden door off to the right. She surveyed the rest of Green Hill Lane and saw a long line of garage doors on one side with signs advertising auto repairs. The wall Ching had mentioned was also red brick, looked to be at least four metres high, and was studded with broken glass across the top. *What's on the other side of the wall?* she thought, and then wrote the question in her notebook.

She went up and down Green Hill Lane several times without gaining any particularly useful information. To her eye, one garage looked much like any other. *What is behind Phoenix?* Ching had said there was a door. But if the door was metal and locked, it was useless to them unless they had some way of opening it, or of getting someone to open it. If it was used for deliveries, as Ching had said, then it would probably open directly into the storage room. She reached for her phone.

"Ava, Ching and Andy aren't back yet," Sonny answered.

"I didn't expect them to be, but I have something else I want checked out," she said. "Ask Carlo to go into the alley behind the garages. I want to know if the garages have any windows. If they all have doors, are they used to receive deliveries? And if he can do it without attracting attention, tell Carlo to take a photo of Phoenix's back door. Ching made it sound like an impossible nut to crack. I'd like to know what Carlo thinks."

"I'll send him right now."

"Thanks," Ava said, and put the phone down on the desk. Maybe it was wishful thinking to hope the back of the garage could offer easier access than the front, but until it was proven wrong, she had at least doubled their options.

She wandered back to the chair by the window. She gazed out onto the harbour and tried to concentrate on the ships and boats traversing it, but instead she found herself cursing Sammy Wing. He had been a thorn in her side for many years, with the two attempts on her life the most extreme examples. But he had, she admitted, a certain self-deprecating, woe-is-me charm that she had succumbed to every time his reckoning came. That charm and his continual evocation of his relationship with Uncle had softened her reaction to deeds that deserved much harsher responses. But not this time, she told herself; this time she wasn't going to let him off the hook. Her cell rang, washing Sammy out of her mind.

"This is Sonny. I'm with Andy and Ching. Do you want me to put them on speakerphone?"

"Please," she said, and then waited for a few seconds before asking, "Ching, did you get inside the garage?"

"I did," he said.

"He did," Andy confirmed.

"Are they repairing cars?"

"There are two cars sitting in bays but no one is working on them. In fact, there wasn't a mechanic in sight."

"Who was there?"

"There were four forty-niners playing mah-jong on a table near the one empty bay, two were standing inside the front door, and I thought I saw another two in the storage room. The door was only partly open, so I couldn't see right in," Ching said.

"Were the men armed?"

"I saw one gun on the table and what looked like three SKSs on the floor by their feet. The men at the door also had SKSs. I couldn't see what the men in the storage room were carrying."

"SKSs?" Ava said.

"A Russian semi-automatic rifle," Sonny said.

"Could you see any of the hostages?" asked Ava.

"No," Ching said.

"Did you hear any sounds coming from the room?"

"No, but they wouldn't have all those guys there for any other reason than guarding those men," Ching said. "And everyone was a bit skittish when they saw me. Nu, who's a lead hand for my cousin, asked me what the hell I was doing at the garage. I told him about my wife's car. I'm not sure he believed me. He told me to come back when the mechanics were working. I asked him when that might be. He told me he didn't know and said I shouldn't be there. I said, 'Sure,' and left right away."

"Ching wasn't in there very long," Andy said.

"Were there men outside?" Ava asked.

"There was a lookout sitting on a stool in front of the wall, with a clear view down the road," Ching said. "I know him. He didn't question why I was going into the garage."

"One lookout . . . That's a bit loose," Ava said.

"I don't think they're expecting visitors. That garage has been a secret stash place for a long time," Ching said.

"Maybe they're not, but given the current stakes I can't believe they'd be that casual," Ava said. "There has to be something you missed. There have to be more men on the perimeter. Andy, did you see anything else?"

"I didn't, but with all that firepower inside, they might think they don't need more than a single lookout. And he does have a complete view of the road; nothing can enter it without him seeing and giving them ample notice," Andy said.

"What do you think, Sonny?" Ava asked.

"Andy may be right, but after Carlo gets back, I'll take a slow drive around the area and see if we can identify more of Wing's men."

"Don't make it a long drive."

"I'm taking the phone off speaker and getting out of the car. Give me a minute," Sonny said. A minute later he asked, "What do you want me to do when I leave here?"

"We need to meet again. I'll ask Ko to join us."

"What about Ching and the guy from Tai Po?"

"I'm nervous about letting them out of our sight until we've finished with the garage. We can't risk Ching having a change of heart."

"That's what I was thinking too," Sonny said. "Carlo's brother lives in Kowloon. We could drop them off there and have him keep an eye on them until things are settled."

"If they try to leave?"

"Carlo's brother is a vicious little guy, and he has a gun he knows how to use."

"Then leave them with him," she said. "And since you'll be in Kowloon, why don't we meet there. Do you have any suggestions?"

"The Sheraton on that side has a big lobby with seating areas that are quite private."

Ava checked the time. "I'll be there by four-thirty. Bring Carlo and Andy with you."

"Boss, I don't want to speak out of turn and I don't want to sound like a worrywart," Sonny said, and then hesitated. "But don't you think we'd be better off letting Ko and his men handle this?"

"That's why Ko will be at the meeting," Ava said. "But I also like having our old team together again."

## 15

FOR THE SECOND TIME THAT DAY, AVA TOOK THE STAR
Ferry across Victoria Harbour, but instead of sitting at the
front, she sat in the rear so she could watch the Hong Kong
skyline receding into the distance. When she disembarked,
she got into a taxi for the short ride to the Sheraton, and
at four-twenty she walked through its massive glass doors
into a busy lobby. She had called Ko and told him to meet
her there, but there was no sign of him or Sonny. She looked
in vain for a vacant seat and then walked over to the lobby
lounge. Inside she saw a couple of unoccupied corner tables.
She pushed them together and grouped the Scandinavian-
style chairs around them.

She saw a server frowning at her, and waved him over.
"We're going to be a party of at least five," she said. "The
others will be here soon."

"Will you be eating?" he asked.

"Do we have to have food in order to sit here?"

"No, but we do have a nice snack selection."

"We'll look at the menu. I know we'll have drinks, and
maybe some of my colleagues will eat," she said. "While

I'm waiting, I'll have a glass of whatever Sauvignon Blanc you have."

When he moved off, Ava checked her phone. There weren't any messages from Sonny or Ko. She tried looking into the lobby, but her view was impeded by a wide spiral staircase that went up to the mezzanine. She began to wish Sonny had chosen a homier meeting spot. Service was prompt, though, and as she took her first sip of wine she spotted Sonny standing in the lobby, head and shoulders above everyone around him. She went to the lounge entrance and called his name. He smiled and came towards her, followed by Andy and Carlo.

"Andy, you know Ko, don't you?" she said.

"Yeah."

"Do me a favour and wait in the lobby until he arrives."

"Sure thing," Andy said.

Sonny and Carlo joined her at the table. The server appeared almost at once. He looked at Carlo, who was dressed in jeans and a polo shirt with his tattooed arms visible, and Ava half anticipated a problem. Instead the server said, "What would you gentlemen like to drink?"

"Is it okay if I have a beer?" Carlo asked Ava, recalling the no-booze policy she had imposed on jobs in the past.

"A beer is fine," she said.

"San Miguel," Carlo said.

"Same for me," Sonny added.

"Are Ching and the other guy at your brother's place?" Ava asked Carlo as soon as the server left.

"They are, and they didn't complain. I think they're happy to be as far from the garage as they can be."

"Good. And what did you find in the back alley?"

"It's narrow, with enough room for just one truck. If you believe the signs, most of the businesses take deliveries through the back. They all have doors, some double but most single. Phoenix's is single, solid metal. If it is barred and bolted like Ching says, I don't think there's any way to get through it into the storage room unless you have someone open it from the other side."

"Any windows?"

"No. Here, look," Carlo said, passing Ava his phone, which displayed a picture of a metal door and a brick wall.

"That seems to eliminate going in through the back," Ava said, and turned to Sonny. "Did you see any more of Wing's men around the neighbourhood?"

"No, and we were all looking for someone we recognized or someone who looked like a triad."

"So maybe that single lookout is exactly that — a single, solitary lookout."

"That could be a dangerous assumption," Sonny said.

"What's dangerous?" Ko asked, suddenly appearing at the table with Andy and a younger man Ava didn't recognize but who looked vaguely familiar.

"We're talking about the garage where Wing is holding your men," Ava said. "Everyone, please take a seat."

As they sat, the server arrived with the two San Miguels.

"Order whatever you want," Ava said.

"Beer is perfect for Feng and me," Ko said.

"For me too," said Andy.

"Feng?" Ava said to the young man. "Xu's White Paper Fan is named Feng. I've worked with him. My name is Ava Lee."

"He's my father, and I know who you are. You were all he would talk about when you were battling with the Tsai family. It made my mother jealous," Feng said. "It's a real honour to meet you."

"It's nice to meet you too, although the circumstances could be better."

"Where do we stand in that regard?" Ko asked.

"We were just reviewing what we know about the garage where they're holding your men. When everyone has their drink and we know we won't be interrupted, I'll summarize things for you and Feng."

"But you've definitely located the men?"

"We're as definite as we can be without physically seeing them, but let's wait before getting into that," Ava said, sensing Ko's impatience but refusing to be rushed.

It took several minutes for the additional beers to arrive, and no one spoke until they'd been placed on the table and they were alone again. Then, after a quick chug, Ko said, "Where are our men?"

"They're being held in an auto body shop near New Town Plaza in Sha Tin."

"I don't doubt you, but what makes you so sure of that?"

"We were told they were there by a Sha Tin triad who has a direct source. We sent that same triad to the garage this afternoon and he saw enough to convince me that's where the men are being held," Ava said. "The garage isn't doing any of its normal work and there are at least eight heavily armed triads inside, including a couple standing guard in a back storage room where we think the men are."

"How heavily armed?"

"SKS semi-automatic rifles."

"Those are serious weapons," Ko said.

"Well, we are dealing with serious people," Ava said.

"You said at least eight?" Feng asked.

"Eight for certain, but there could be more."

"How many men are outside?" Ko asked.

"That's what's odd. There's only a single lookout in front of the building," Ava said. "Mind you, the garage is in a short, dead-end lane and is the last building in line before a large brick wall. If the lookout is awake, he'll see anyone who enters the lane, so they must figure he's all they need."

"We drove around the whole area and didn't see any other lookouts or guards," Sonny added.

"One last thing: there's an alley behind the garage that leads to a delivery door, but that door is metal and bolted shut," Ava said. "So, in terms of getting into the building, it looks like our only option is going in through the front, where there are three metal garage doors and one regular wooden door. I think it's obvious which of those would be easiest."

"Eight men with SKSs in a confined space at close range. That could get very messy," Ko said. "Especially if they know we're coming and which door we'll have to use."

"I'm not pretending it's going to be easy," Ava said. "I'm simply telling you the facts."

"Either way, we don't have a choice. This is something we have to do," Ko said.

"Did that directive come from Suen?" Ava asked.

"We're of the same mind, and you know Lop would be as well."

"When Lop came to Hong Kong to take out Sammy Wing the first time, most of you were wearing high-grade bullet-proof vests. Do you still have them?" Sonny asked.

"Lop insisted on them — that was his military background

at work. And yes, we still have them and we'll use them," Ko said.

"I can tell you the other side won't be wearing vests of any kind," Sonny said.

"Well, that's one small advantage," Ko said.

"The other advantage we might be able to generate is the element of surprise," Ava said.

"What do you mean?"

"The lookout."

"What about him?"

"If we can eliminate him quietly, they'll have no warning. We might be able to get through that door before they know we're there."

"How do you suggest we do that?" Ko asked. "You said he can see everything that comes down the laneway."

"What if he saw someone who looked completely unthreatening?" Ava said.

"Like who?"

"A woman walking by herself."

Ko looked at Sonny and then turned back to Ava. "I think I know which woman you have in mind, but I'm not sure that's a good idea."

"Boss, you can't put yourself in that kind of situation," Sonny said.

"What else do you suggest we do? Wait until midnight and hope they don't kill those six men? Or would you prefer that we charge the garage and absorb whatever losses ensue?"

"Whatever we do, I don't want you putting yourself at risk," Ko said.

"The thing is, I don't think this is your decision to make. It's mine," Ava said, and then looked at Andy. "What do you think? Could I approach the lookout without his raising an alarm?"

"As long as he doesn't recognize you, I can't imagine why an attractive young woman would make him particularly nervous," Andy said.

"All I need to do is get close enough to get my hands on him. If I can do that, I'll put him down without much noise," Ava said. "Once that's done, you can move your men down the road to the garage and take up positions at the door. If you can break through it quickly enough we might catch them off guard."

Ko shook his head, but his expression was thoughtful rather than doubtful. "You said it's a wooden door?"

"Yes. Do you have a ram?"

"If we don't, we'll get one."

Carlo looked at Ava. "Can I make a suggestion?" he asked.

"Sure," Ava said.

"I'm thinking about the back door. Would you station some men there so they can't get out that way?"

"Yes, we would."

"Well, once the men are in place at both doors, if you hammer on the back one, you could create a real distraction. It might make it easier when the others burst in through the front."

"That's an interesting idea, Carlo. Except it might prompt some of Wing's men to pick up their weapons and it might draw more men into the storage room. I think I'd rather have them in the garage, and I prefer them not to be brandishing weapons when we come through the front door," Ava said. She looked at Ko. "What do you think?"

"The less warning we give them, the better. We'll guard the back door but not touch it."

"Well, then, it seems we have a plan coming together."

"A plan that relies almost entirely on there being only one lookout, and you taking him out without alerting the men inside the garage," Ko said.

"That's a fair summation," Ava said. "Do you have an alternative plan to suggest?"

"I do not, and I wasn't being critical of this one. I was simply pointing out where it could go wrong," Ko said.

"If something does go wrong, we'll have to improvise. The bottom line is that, one way or another. we're committed to going into the garage."

"On that we're completely agreed," Ko said. "When do you want to do it?"

"How many men can you assign, and how soon can you have them ready?"

"I'll just use our Shanghai men. I have thirty of them, and like I told you earlier, they're ready to go at a moment's notice."

"You can add me to the list," Sonny said.

"And me," Carlo added.

"Me too," said Andy.

"This isn't your fight," Ko said.

"If Ava is involved, then it becomes my fight, and I'm sure the same is true for Carlo and Andy," Sonny said.

"It is," Andy said as Carlo nodded.

"I appreciate your support," Ko said. "I assume you have your own weapons, but I'll tell my guy to bring extra vests to the meeting point."

"That just leaves the timing to be decided," Ava said. "I think we need to wait until the other businesses on the lane close for the day. We don't want civilians involved in this."

"The signs I saw said they close at six," Andy said. "Mind you, I didn't see them all."

"So let's say they'll be closed by six-thirty. But it will start getting dark around then, and that could be a problem. I want to make sure the lookout can see me and recognize that I'm a woman," Ava said.

"The garages all have outside lights," Andy said. "If you walk close enough to them, he should be able to see you."

"Okay," Ava said, and looked at her watch. "It's five o'clock now. Let's plan on meeting at eight at the first street to the left of the entrance to Green Hill Lane."

"We'll be there," Ko said.

"I don't think you should arrive in a group. That might attract the kind of attention we don't want. Can you funnel your men into the neighbourhood slowly?"

"I'll send them two or three at a time, five to ten minutes apart, and I'll spread them around so they don't look like a mob. All that matters is that by eight o'clock they're close enough so we can come together at the lane."

"I like that," Ava said.

Ko nodded and then hesitated. "We need to call Suen to tell him what we're doing. Do you want to do it or shall I?"

"They're your men. You make the call," Ava said.

## 16

**AVA LEFT THE SHERATON WITH SONNY, CARLO, AND** Andy. She hadn't wanted to voice her concerns in front of Ko and Feng, but now that they were alone, she said, "I know you all feel you have to support me, but this really isn't your fight. The danger aside, if the Wings win, all of you will be blackballed by the Hong Kong gangs. If Ko wins, you can work for him, but you'll still be treated with suspicion by the others."

"Ava, I work for you," Sonny said.

"I was referring more to Carlo and Andy."

"I don't care about the Wings and I don't need a job," Andy said. "I can always go back to working with my wife."

"And I'm sure Andy would give me a job in his restaurant if I really needed one," Carlo said with a laugh.

"I appreciate your loyalty," she said, trying to hide a surge of emotion.

"We're only returning what we've been given all these years," Andy said.

"Then let's leave it at that," Ava said, gathering herself. "Sonny, I'd appreciate it if you could drive me to the Tsim

Sha Tsui Star Ferry terminal. I'll take the boat to Central, but I would like you to pick me up at the hotel later for the drive to Sha Tin."

"Seven-thirty?"

"Better make it seven," she said. "And Andy and Carlo, I'd like you to go over to Green Hill Lane now and nose around the area. If they add more lookouts or if the Wings surround the place with more men, I want to know before Ko's crew starts to arrive."

"Okay, boss," Andy said.

They separated when they reached the car park, Andy and Carlo heading for the MTR. As Sonny drove the Mercedes out of the lot, Ava said, "I'm very lucky to have so many good friends."

"Luck has nothing to do with it," Sonny said.

"You know what I'm trying to say."

"I know…" Sonny said, his voice trailing off. "Are you going to take the Beretta with you tonight or do you want me to get you something more powerful?"

"The Beretta fits in my bag, but a silencer might be a good addition if for any reason I have to use the gun on the lookout. Can you get me one?"

"I'll try."

Ava looked out the car window as they made their way to Tsim Sha Tsui. She didn't want to fixate on what the next few hours might bring, but as she tried to focus on other things she found herself flooded with memories of a similar event. "When we were talking to Ko about the garage, it reminded me of the time we had to break into that house in Macau to rescue Simon To. Andy and Carlo were with us then as well."

"And May Ling Wong. And, as I remember, Amanda was helping," Sonny said. "We were a good team."

"Let's hope tonight works out as well."

"Ava, I hope it works better. Macau was far from perfect. We got Simon but you got shot."

"Only in the leg. It left a rather long scar that Fai says makes me intriguing."

"One scar from a bullet is one too many. I don't want to have to visit you in the Kowloon clinic."

"Speaking of the clinic, I meant to tell you that Lop seems to be on the mend. Ko told me earlier, but with everything else going on it slipped my mind."

"It would have been great to have Lop with us tonight. He gives the men confidence."

"Ko is a good man. He's solid."

"But he isn't Lop."

"Who is?" Ava asked.

Conversation stopped as they found themselves in heavy traffic. They inched forward for about ten minutes, and as Ava looked ahead she could see traffic wasn't going to improve anytime soon. She noticed the Yau Ma Tei MTR station in the distance and knew the subway would be much faster. "Sonny, I'm going to get out here. I'll take the MTR to Central. That will give both of us more time to get prepared."

"That's a good idea," he said.

She opened the car door. "If anything comes up, you can reach me on my cell. Otherwise I'll see you at the hotel at seven."

She left the car and walked to the station. As she entered and started down the stairs, a flood of people came at her from the opposite direction. It was rush hour, but thankfully she was going against the flow. She took her Octopus card from her bag and made her way to the platform. A train soon arrived, and five stops later she was walking up the stairs of the Central station and heading for her hotel.

It had been a long and emotionally draining day, the kind she liked to end with a couple of glasses of wine and a good meal. How this one would end was a mystery, she thought as she reached her suite. She looked at the room phone and saw no one had tried to reach her since she'd been gone. She went to the desk and opened her laptop. There was an email from her mother that could wait, and some spam. That was all to the good. She didn't need diversions.

She went into the bathroom and splashed cold water on her face; it was refreshing and helped her to focus. She looked into the mirror and tried to make her first decision — should she wear her hair up or down? She normally wore it up, particularly when there was potential for violence, since she didn't need flyaway hair impeding her vision or giving her opponent something easy to grab. But this was different. She had to make sure the lookout recognized that she was a woman, and an attractive, harmless-looking one at that. So she undid the ivory chignon pin, shook her hair free, and brushed it until it hung like a silky ebony frame around her face and down to her shoulders. When she was satisfied, she put on lipstick and mascara — both a little more thickly than usual. Now, what to wear?

Ava had worn black slacks and a plain white shirt to the meeting with the Wings, but they were hardly feminine enough for what she had in mind tonight. In the bedroom she opened her Shanghai Tang Double Happiness bag and took out a black skirt and a powder-blue silk blouse. The blouse was a little snug across the chest, which made it perfect. Those clothes, combined with black pumps that had a three-inch heel, shouldn't leave much doubt — even in bad light — that she was a woman.

She stripped down to her underwear and then, as she turned sideways, caught a glimpse of herself in the bedroom mirror. Her body was still toned and firm, a result of regular jogging, rigorous bak mei workouts, and her mother's remarkable genes. Ava glanced at the scar on her hip. There was a round brown mound where the bullet had entered, and emanating from it was a scar that looked like a long, fat pink worm — the handiwork of an effective but not gentle-handed surgeon. She looked at the bandage around her arm. It was holding up well, but what kind of mark would be left when it finally came off? The good news was that the wound didn't seem to have affected her ability to use the arm. It might hurt if she had to, but the pain would pass.

She put on the blouse and skirt and was adjusting the waistband when her cell rang. She sat at the desk to answer it.

"Suen, I thought Ko was going to call you," she said.

"He did. I just want you to know that I'm at the airport in Shanghai. I'm scheduled to land in Hong Kong around ten."

"How many men are you bringing with you?"

"I'm not sure exactly how many are on this flight, but by this time tomorrow I'll have about a hundred there."

"Hopefully, by the time you land the immediate crisis will be over, and by the time all of your men have arrived, we'll have reached some kind of deal with Sammy Wing."

"I wish I had your optimism," Suen said. "All I can think of are the things that can go wrong. There are a lot of them, and all it takes is one to make things worse than they are now."

"Does Xu feel the same?"

"He doesn't know what to think. He was ecstatic when I told him you'd located our men, and then worried when I told him it was going to be complicated and probably bloody to get them back," Suen said. "He's still not completely himself. He's better, but not one hundred percent."

"Did Ko tell you about our plan?"

"He did, but I was here at the airport when I spoke to him, so I haven't been able to tell Xu. Maybe that's a good thing."

"Why?"

"The last thing he said to me today was that I'm to make sure you don't put yourself in harm's way."

"I don't think I am," Ava said.

"That's not what it sounds like to me," Suen said. "According to Ko, your plan boils down to the hope that there's only one lookout. What if there are more?"

"Then we'll reconfigure our strategy. I don't have suicidal tendencies."

"I know you don't," Suen said quickly. "And I apologize for sounding so negative. It's just that Xu wouldn't accept an excuse if something happened to you."

"I will take every precaution to make sure nothing happens to me. Why don't we leave it at that."

"Okay, but one more question. Do you have to go in so early? Why don't you wait until I get there?"

"Suen, we're organized and ready to go. Having the men hanging around after they've been given a go time will only increase their stress. Besides, like I told you earlier, we can't be sure you'll be here before midnight. That's a risk I don't want to take, and I don't think you should either."

He became quiet, and Ava knew he was absorbing the reality of what she'd said.

"Good luck. I'll call you when I land," he said finally.

"Call Ko. He should be your first contact."

"Point well taken," he said.

Ava ended the call, feeling exasperated. Suen was even less nuanced than she'd thought. She knew that might make him a great Red Pole when muscle was the only thing required, but there was a broader picture that had to be looked after, including the level of trust he imparted to his own people.

She got up from the desk, putting Suen behind her, and began to think about the lookout. How was she going to eliminate him quietly and efficiently? She knew she would use bak mei, but to what degree? Bak mei wasn't a pretty martial art but it was brutally effective. There wasn't a lot of dancing about or posing; it was about concentrating all the power the body could generate through the torso, hips, and legs and transferring it to a striking point. The most famous bak mei weapon was the phoenix-eye fist, the knuckle of the first finger on the striking hand. When all the power Ava could generate was concentrated in that knuckle, it could kill, maim, or paralyze when driven into the nose, eye, ear, or various clusters of nerve endings in the upper body of the target. What she needed to do was paralyze and silence the lookout for at least a few seconds so she could get behind him and apply pressure to the carotid artery. Ava had dropped men three times larger than her to the ground that way. *I'll hit him in the ear, stun him. They always take some time to react to that and they don't usually yell or scream,* she thought.

Her cell rang, interrupting her thoughts. She wanted to ignore the call, but when she glanced at the screen, she saw it was Fai. "Hey," Ava said.

"Hi, babe. I don't want to disturb you, but I thought you'd like to know that the hospital just called Auntie Grace. They're moving Xu into a private room in the regular ward later tonight," Fai said.

"Thank goodness. She must be so relieved."

"She cried when she got the news."

"What a wonderful woman."

"I'm going to take her out to dinner. She didn't want to go, but I insisted and she finally gave in. I saw a bistro near the bakery we went to yesterday, and I figure that if she likes the bakery so much, the bistro won't disappoint."

"You'd better hope they have some Chinese food on the menu."

"If they don't, I'm sure she'll be kind enough not to complain."

"I am so happy that you two are getting along," Ava said.

"Well, we have so much in common."

"Like what?"

"Like you."

"Now who's being kind?"

"If you'd heard me fifteen minutes ago, you wouldn't have said that."

"Why?" Ava asked.

"Chen called me. He's been to see Lau Lau."

"And?"

"The son of a bitch has agreed to go into rehab."

"You don't mean that — I mean, calling him a son of a bitch — because he's agreed to go into rehab?"

"No, of course I don't. I hope he comes out clean and stays that way. I'm just nervous about your getting more involved with him. He could cost you a lot of money and a lot of heartbreak."

"It isn't just my money. May Ling and Amanda are on board too. As for my heart, he won't touch it."

Fai paused. "Well, anyway, he's agreed to go into rehab and Chen — Mister Cynical — is thrilled about it."

"Fai, let me make you a promise," Ava said. "We'll finance the rehab and, if Lau Lau comes out in one piece, we'll finance a script. But that script won't turn into a film unless you and Chen think it deserves to be one. "

"You'll let me make that decision?"

"You and Chen. I want both of you to agree. You for a whole bunch of obvious reasons, and Chen because you told me he has tremendous judgement."

"I can live with that," said Fai.

"But first we have to get Lau Lau through rehab."

"Which won't be easy."

Ava looked at the time. "Also not easy is the fact that I have to get going. I have a meeting I need to attend."

"Call me when it's over. I doubt I'll be asleep early."

"If I can, I will," Ava said. "I promise."

( 17 )

**AVA ARRIVED AT THE FRONT DOORS OF THE MANDARIN**
Oriental at five to seven, expecting to see Sonny and the
Mercedes-Benz waiting at the curb. When there was no sign
of them, she walked over to the doorman. "Have you seen
my driver?" she asked.

"No, Ms. Lee."

"I'm going to wait in the lobby. When he arrives, could
you come and get me?"

"Of course," he said, and then paused. "No need for that
now. Here he comes."

Ava looked off to one side and saw the car slowly
approaching, but to her surprise, Sonny wasn't alone. A
neatly groomed grey-haired man was sitting in the front
seat next to him. The car stopped and Sonny rushed over
to Ava. "Am I late?"

"I'm a bit early," Ava said. "But Sonny, who is that man?"

"His name is Jimmy and he's an old friend of mine. Uncle
knew him too and used his services a few times. If you have
no objections, I thought I'd bring him along with us."

"Bring him along to do what?"

"He's a sniper, an incredible shot," Sonny said softly. "He's ex-British military. I want to position him at the end of the lane. If anything strange happens, if you're in any danger, he'll be a real asset."

"Sonny, I'm not sure this is necessary."

"Maybe it isn't, but it would make me feel more comfortable. The weapons the rest of us are carrying aren't precise from any kind of distance. Jimmy can hit a dollar coin from a hundred metres away," Sonny said. "He's a precaution, some additional insurance."

She could see on his face how strongly Sonny felt. "I guess it can't hurt," she said finally. "But make sure that he doesn't freelance. If he has to shoot at anything, I want it to be because you told him to."

"I'll make that clear," Sonny said, opening the back door of the car for her.

She slid in. "Jimmy, I'm Ava. Thanks for joining us," she said.

He turned his head halfway and smiled. "Uncle told me about you. I'm glad I'm finally getting to meet you," he said.

Sonny climbed into the driver's seat, picked up something wrapped in a piece of cloth, and handed it to Ava. "Here's the addition you wanted for your Beretta," he said.

She waited until the car had pulled away from the hotel before unwrapping the cloth. The silencer was almost as long as her gun, and she wondered if she could manage to get it into her bag once it was attached. Ava took out the Beretta, held it on her lap while she screwed on the silencer, and then put it in the bag. It did fit, but only at an angle. Given where she was going, that didn't seem to matter.

Sonny drove east towards Causeway Bay and entered the

Cross-Harbour Tunnel near the Hong Kong Yacht Club. A few minutes later they exited at Hung Hom, on the Kowloon side, and started north to Sha Tin.

"Sonny explained to me what's going down tonight," Jimmy said, this time turning around completely to look at Ava. "My rifle has a range of almost two kilometres, so a hundred metres or so is child's play. Still, I'll be using a scope with night vision built in, and I won't take anything for granted."

"Jimmy, I don't want you to shoot unless I give you a direct order," Sonny said.

"That's fine. I'll have the rifle zeroed in on Ava anyway, and my reflexes are still sharp for a man my age. If you see danger, I'm sure I'll have time to react."

"How old are you?" Ava asked.

"Sixty-one."

"And what do you do when you're not assisting women in distress?"

"I'm retired. I was with the British Special Forces for twenty-five years. Now I live in Sai Kung with my daughter and her three kids. She's a widow, so I do a lot of babysitting."

"His daughter is a bank manager," Sonny said.

"She manages a small branch," Jimmy said. "She's a smart girl."

Ava sat back in her seat, now quite content to have Jimmy going with them to Green Hill Lane. His attitude, like his appearance, was neat and modest, and he exuded a sense of quiet confidence and competence.

Sonny entered Sha Tin, followed the signs for New Town Plaza for a few minutes, and then turned into a street Ava didn't recognize. He drove down it for several blocks, made a left, and pulled into a parking lot. Ava saw Carlo and Andy waiting for them at the pay station.

"Green Hill Lane is only two streets away," Sonny said as he parked.

They climbed out of the car and Sonny and Jimmy walked around to the trunk. Sonny took his gym bag and Jimmy lifted out a long leather bag. He put it on the ground, butt end first, before slinging it over his shoulder. Ava guessed he was about five foot four; the rifle bag was almost as tall.

As they walked over to the pay station, Ava saw that Carlo and Andy were carrying bags she knew contained their guns. They both wore running shoes. She hadn't told them to and suddenly felt foolish for not having made that point. She looked down at Sonny's feet and saw that he was wearing soft-soled shoes as well. *They know what they're doing,* she thought, *and I'm a bit out of practice.*

"You look really great, boss," Carlo said. "Wearing your hair long like that suits you."

Ava stared at him until he sheepishly averted his eyes.

"Hey, Jimmy," Andy said. "Glad to see you're along."

"How's it going, guys?" Jimmy said.

"Not so bad," Carlo said.

Having been told that Jimmy had done work for Uncle, Ava wasn't surprised the men knew each other. But it was another example of how Uncle, for his own, probably very good reasons, had kept her out of some loops. "Is there much activity on the lane?" she asked.

"We've walked the entire area six times, and we haven't seen anything that suggests there's more than the one lookout. There aren't many people on the street at this time of night. There are hardly any stores or restaurants around here, just factories and garages and the like," Andy said.

"I see some apartment buildings not that far away. Is it possible they could have people eyeing the neighbourhood from on high?"

"Possible, but not very likely," Andy said.

"What about Ko's men?"

"They've been moving in slowly but steadily in ones and twos. Once you know what to look for, they aren't that hard to pick out," Andy said.

"How so?"

"They are all so clean-cut, and they're nearly all wearing windbreakers or jackets," Andy said. "I guess that's to cover the bulletproof vests."

"They sound more like cops than triads," Jimmy said.

"They've been trained by a man named Lop. He's a senior triad from Shanghai, but he was a captain in the PLA's Special Operations Forces. He's imposed a structure and discipline not normally associated with triads," Ava said.

"Now I'm even happier that I came tonight," Jimmy said. "I like the idea of being part of a well-trained special forces unit again."

"We weren't good enough for you?" Carlo said.

"I would have made do, but being alongside well-trained men makes it a little better," Jimmy said with a smile.

"That's enough banter," Ava said as she checked the time. "I think we can start moving towards the lane now."

Without being asked, Carlo and Andy began to lead the way. Ava held back until they were about twenty metres ahead and then followed with Sonny and Jimmy. Carlo and Andy walked purposefully, their heads constantly swinging from side to side as they took in their surroundings. Ava noticed that Sonny and Jimmy were just as attentive.

They reached a busy intersection, crossed on a green light, and walked along the sidewalk to the next corner, where Ko was talking to several of his men. When he saw Ava, he broke away from them. "We're all here."

"So are we," Ava said.

Ko eyed Jimmy.

"He's with us. He's a sniper, ex-military. Sonny knows him, and so did Uncle," Ava said.

"Glad to have you," Ko said.

"Pleased to be here," said Jimmy.

"It isn't quite eight yet, but there's no reason we can't do this earlier. Everyone is here and ready to go," Ko said to Ava.

"Then let's do it."

"Green Hill Lane is a block away," Ko said. "We should walk in small groups until we get there. My men already know their positions."

Traffic on the street was moderate but moving at a good speed, so passing cars didn't have time to notice the large group of men congregated on the sidewalk. The area, as Andy had said, wasn't commercial and there weren't many other people on foot. The intersection where the street met the lane was dominated by a factory on the right; a neon sign advertised that it made sauces. The brick wall that ran the length of the lane was the factory's rear boundary. Ava waited until Ko's men were at the lane before walking over to it with Sonny and her men.

Half of Ko's men had crossed the lane and were standing against the front of a closed garage. The other men had stopped short of the lane and were behind part of the factory.

Ava walked across the lane by herself, glancing as discreetly as she could towards the end. As Andy had predicted, lights illuminated the fronts of most of the various automotive businesses. The lookout was only vaguely visible, as he was sitting in shadow on a stool near the middle of the lane, at the outer edge of the lights beaming from the Phoenix garage. Ava stared down the lane, trying to discern if there was possibly more than one man at the far end. When all she could see was one, she turned her attention to the route she intended to take. Nearly all of it was well lit; the lookout would have to be blind not to notice her quickly.

Sonny joined her a minute later. "Jimmy is sitting by the bottom of the wall. It's dark as hell there. The lookout won't see him."

"How about people driving by?"

"Carlo, Andy, and a couple of Ko's men are standing around him to provide cover."

"When will he be ready?"

"I'll go and ask," Sonny said.

Ko approached. "I'll be holding all my men back until you've taken care of the lookout," he said. "When that's done, we'll move as quietly and quickly as possible. We won't attempt to enter the garage until we're gathered in force. That should give you time to get back here before we attack."

"What about the back entrance?"

"There are four men there now, with guns trained on the door."

"Ava," Sonny said from across the street, and then gave her a thumbs-up.

"Looks like we're ready," she said.

"Good luck," Ko said.

"Same to you," Ava said. She took a deep breath, stepped into the lane, and started walking towards the lookout.

( 18 )

AVA FELT THE LOOKOUT'S EYES ON HER AS SOON AS she entered the lane, but she kept her attention on the garages to her left and tried not to rush or appear rushed. She stopped at the first garage, looked through its window, and knocked on the door. When no one answered, she continued down the lane and continued the performance, trying to stay in the light as much as she could. She did this two more times before she heard someone say, "What do you think you're doing?"

The lookout had left his stool and had taken a few steps towards her.

"My car broke down. I need help, a mechanic. Why do all these places close so early? Isn't anyone open?" she asked, finally looking at him.

He had moved into a better-lit area and Ava could see his face. She had been worried that he might have been at the meeting at Maxim's, but she didn't recognize him, and he didn't seem to have any idea who she was. He held a weapon cradled in his arm that was rather clumsily covered with a piece of cloth.

"None of these places will be open until tomorrow morning. Come back then," he said.

"But you're here. Why can't you help me?"

"I'm not a mechanic."

"Then what are you doing here?"

"That's none of your fucking business."

She was within five metres of him and almost alongside Phoenix. She was gauging how much closer she would need to be when the garage door opened. Ava froze. A man carrying a semi-automatic pistol stepped into the lane. She closed her eyes. He was one of the men who had been with the Wings at the restaurant that morning. *Bluff,* she thought. *My hair is different and I'm wearing different clothes. He may not recognize me.*

He blinked in surprise when he saw her, then stared. In that second she knew there was no chance she could bluff him. "What are you doing here, you fucking bitch?" he shouted, his gun pointed at her.

"My car broke down. I'm looking for a mechanic," she said, knowing he wouldn't believe her but without another option.

"That's bullshit. I know who you are," he said. He took two steps towards her and aimed his gun directly at her head. Then she heard something that sounded like a sharp gust of wind, and the man's gun arm dropped. Almost in slow motion, she saw a red hole expand in the middle of the man's forehead and his body jerk backwards before hitting the ground with a dull thud.

"Holy shit!" the lookout said, and moved towards the man. As he did, Ava took a couple of steps, closing the gap between them. As the lookout bent down to look at his colleague, the first knuckle of Ava's right hand ploughed into his ear with every ounce of power she could muster. He keeled over, his eyes rolling back in his head as his hands reached feebly for the ear. She leapt behind him, put a knee into his back, and dug her fingers into his neck. She found the carotid artery and compressed it. He was so stunned that he didn't offer much resistance, but Ava kept applying pressure until she was sure he was unconscious. Then she straightened up and looked at the garage door, half expecting more men to come barrelling through it, and then waved into the darkness at the other end of the lane.

Still anxious about someone else coming through the door, she took her gun from the Louis Vuitton bag and stepped over to the wall. She pressed her back against it and inched towards the door, stopping just short of it but close enough that, if it opened, she couldn't miss shooting whoever tried to come through.

Ko's men were in the lane now, quietly and carefully working their way towards her with their guns at the ready. Ava didn't leave the wall, her concentration focused on the noises coming from the other side of the closed door. She thought they must have heard something outside, but the voices didn't sound agitated. How long would it take before they noticed their colleague hadn't returned? She motioned to the oncoming men to move faster.

Feng was at the head of the line; Ava noticed how calm and deliberate he was. "What's going on in there?" he whispered when he reached her.

"Nothing I can hear," she whispered in return, and pointed at the door handle. "I don't think it's locked."

Ko and Sonny joined them. Ava moved away from the door to give the men more room. "I don't think we have much more time before the guys in there figure out there's a problem out here," she whispered.

"Ava says the door might not be locked," Feng said.

Ko looked at the handle, then motioned to a man carrying a steel ram. "Wait by the wall in case we need you," he whispered. He pointed to four men in the line. "Take positions by the wall. When the door opens, you're the first four through."

Ava felt a hand on her arm and saw Sonny standing by her side. "Go and join Jimmy," he whispered.

She shook her head. "I'll wait here. I'll stay out of the way."

"Don't stand in front of those garage doors. Bullets can penetrate that metal."

"I know."

Ko silently positioned the rest of his men. When he was satisfied, he nodded and held up his right hand. "One," he said quietly. "Two. Three." As his hand fell, Feng reached for the door handle, pushed down the latch, and pulled. The door swung open and the first four men hurtled through it, with the others close behind. Ava saw Sonny, Carlo, and Andy among them.

Ava had moved against the wall facing the adjacent business, but when the gunfire started, it was so loud she might as well have been in the middle of the garage. She pressed her back against the wall and held her breath. Shots were exchanged for twenty or thirty seconds that seemed like an eternity to her.

There was a pause and she started breathing again. She inched sideways, closer to the door, but then shots erupted again and she heard men screaming. When the firing stopped for the second time, she was tempted to look into the garage, but caution kicked in. She stood her ground and silently counted to sixty. When there was still no sound of gunfire, she left the wall and carefully made her way to the open door. A man wearing a windbreaker stood in the doorway, blocking her path.

"Excuse me," she said, tapping him on the shoulder. He stepped aside, and Ava looked past him to see carnage. She was no stranger to dead bodies — she'd been witness to the aftermath of multiple killings and a mass shooting in Surabaya — but she had never seen so much blood in one place. She gagged and fought back the nausea.

Ava searched the garage for Sonny, Carlo, and Andy. Andy was leaning against a far wall, clutching a blood-soaked arm. Carlo stood next to him, chatting away like mad. Sonny was having an animated conversation with Ko.

Feng approached her with a grim smile on his face. "We caught them totally by surprise. They barely had time to reach for their guns."

"Did you ask them to drop them?"

"That's not how Lop trained us. When a man is going for a gun, you don't ask questions or hesitate. You shoot to kill."

"Are they all dead?"

"They all had guns, so yes, they're all dead."

"How many?"

"Six out here and three in the storage room."

"How many of our men were injured?"

"Your friend got hit in the arm and one of our men took a bullet in the leg. Without the vests, it would have been worse," Feng said. "But we lost two of the men they were holding hostage."

"How?"

"Wing's men used them as shields when they were trying to get out the back door. When they saw that we wouldn't back off, they shot them in the head," Feng said. "It was such a stupid, pointless thing to do. If they had dropped their guns and freed our men, we wouldn't have harmed them."

"How are the other four hostages?"

"They'll be okay. They'll need medical care for the severed fingers, but other than that they haven't been abused," Feng said. "As bad as this looks, we saved four lives."

Ava stared at the bullet-riddled bodies strewn across the garage floor. "My hope was that if we surprised them with this much force they would realize it was pointless to resist," she said.

"Surprising them probably had the opposite effect," Feng said. "Things happened so quickly they didn't have time to think. They just reacted, and their natural reaction was to reach for a gun."

"Quite a mess," Ko said, finally noticing Ava.

She nodded at him and watched as Sonny made a call on his cell. He spoke, listened, and then ended the call.

"What's going on?" she asked.

"Jimmy says it's quiet at the other end of the lane. No sirens, no sign of any cops, no nosy neighbours. He said the gunfire sounded like someone in the distance setting off firecrackers. He doesn't think it will attract any attention now," said Sonny.

"That's good to know, but I still think we need to get out of here as fast as possible," Ko said. He turned to Feng. "Tell our men to start walking back to their cars. There's no point in their hanging around here."

"We have one man who's wounded, Ava's man Andy was shot in the arm, and our four men who lost fingers need some care," Feng said.

"Bring two cars down the lane to pick up the wounded men," Ko said, and then looked at Sonny. "Can we take them to Doctor Liu at the clinic in Kowloon?"

Sonny nodded. "He won't be happy, but he won't turn them away."

"What about our two dead brothers?" Feng asked.

"We have the panel van. Drive it along the alley to the rear entrance. We'll load them there," Ko said.

"What about Wing's men?" Ava asked.

"They can stay here. We should move the two men outside into the garage. Is the lookout dead?" Ko asked.

"He's unconscious," said Ava. "I don't want any harm to come to him."

"Do you really want him left alive?"

"I do."

"He'll tell the Wings it was you who came down the lane."

"He doesn't know who I am. Jimmy shot the one who did, before he mentioned my name."

"Still, the Wings may figure it out."

"That's inevitable. They'll know this was your doing and that we're working together," Ava said. "Killing that man won't prevent them from adding two and two and getting to four."

"How long will he be out?"

"It could be a while."

"Well, as much as I don't want to, we'll leave him," Ko said. "What do you plan to do now?"

"I'm not going to be doing anything until Suen arrives tonight. He and I need to talk, and it would be ideal if we can plug Xu into the conversation."

"Until then I'm going to keep all my men on war footing."

"Good. By this time tomorrow you'll have as many fully armed men available as Carter Wing does," Ava said. She looked again at the bodies on the ground and shook her head. "After this, they might decide it's time to be reasonable."

"I'll let you worry about them being reasonable. I just want to be prepared to whack them if that's what's called for."

"Do you have all the weapons you need?"

"After tonight we should. I connected with the Red Pole in Guangzhou and I have two men in Kowloon right now picking up their shipment."

The garage was now almost empty of Ko's men. Ava waved to Sonny. "We should be going as well," she said.

"I'm ready when you are," he said.

Ava walked over to Andy, stepping carefully to avoid the pools of blood that were forming on the concrete floor. "They're going to take you to the clinic in Kowloon. You'll be well looked after."

"Quite the fight, wasn't it, boss?" he said.

"Wasn't it," she said softly.

"What do you want me to do?" Carlo asked, his face pale with concern for Andy.

"You should come with Sonny and me. Ko's men will see Andy safely to the clinic."

Ava, Sonny, and Carlo left the garage and began the walk up Green Hill Lane. "That was one hell of a shot he made," she said to Sonny.

"I told you he was good," Sonny said.

"If I'd known he was that good, I might have had him shoot the lookout," she said.

"I thought of that," Sonny said. "But the light was so poor where the lookout was sitting it would have been difficult to guarantee a hit, and I didn't think you'd want us to gamble. Besides, you'd made your plans, and I've learned never to question them."

"You have that much faith in me?"

"You know I do."

Jimmy stood waiting for them, his gun bag slung over his shoulder. "Is it still peaceful around here?" Ava asked him.

"There's nothing to worry about."

"Then let's get back to Hong Kong," she said.

They walked in silence to the Mercedes.

"You'll ride with us," Ava said to Carlo when they got to the parking lot. "Where can Sonny drop you?"

"The Jordan MTR station will do fine."

Carlo sat in the front passenger seat while Jimmy sat next to Ava in the back. As the car eased out of the parking lot, Ava turned to Jimmy. "I don't know what Sonny paid you for helping us out tonight, but whatever it was, I'm going to double it," she said. "You saved my life. I won't forget that."

"You don't have to pay me extra," he said with a shy smile. "I did the job I was paid to do. Besides, I owed Uncle a favour, so maybe he and I are a bit closer to being square."

"Your shot was a remarkable thing."

"From what the Shanghai men were telling me as they left, it wasn't the only remarkable thing that happened tonight," Jimmy said. "They said they'd destroyed Wing's crew."

"They did," Sonny said.

"Are they that good?" Jimmy asked.

"When they took on Sammy a year ago, it was like men against boys. But they were led by Lop then, and I was worried that, with him out of action, they might have lost their edge," Sonny said. "I was wrong. They're a well-trained army. All you have to do is point them in the right direction."

"After tonight, will the Wings be stupid enough to keep challenging Xu?" Jimmy said.

"God knows," said Sonny.

"I hope not. I've seen enough blood to last me a lifetime," Ava said. "It was horrific."

"It *was* rough," Carlo said, his voice shaky.

"Are you okay?" Ava asked him.

"It's been a while since I was involved in anything like that," he said, and then shuddered. "In fact, I've never actually seen anything like that. Those guys were merciless."

"It was no different than a year ago," Sonny said. "Lop doesn't believe in half measures, and his men follow his lead. If Carter Wing is dumb enough to fight them, the outcome will be the same now as it was then."

"Not entirely the same," Ava said.

"What do you mean?" Sonny asked.

"If I have anything to do with it, these are the final days that Sammy Wing will be serving as Mountain Master," she said.

## 19

AFTER DROPPING OFF CARLO AT THE JORDAN MTR STA-
tion, Sonny drove Ava across the harbour to the Mandarin
Oriental. He hesitated at the car door as he opened it for
her. She sensed he wanted to talk more, but Jimmy was still
in the car and Ava had been very quiet during the last part
of their ride, a signal Sonny would have recognized as an
indication that she wasn't in the mood to chat.

"Thanks again, Jimmy," she said as she got out of the car.

"I'm available any time you need me," he said.

"I hope the need doesn't arise again, but if it does, I'm sure
Sonny knows how to reach you."

"Boss, what do you want me to do for the rest of the night?"
Sonny asked.

"I can't imagine too much will happen in the next few
hours," she said. "Check on Andy and make sure the clinic
is looking after him. After that, just stay close to your cell.
If I need you, I'll call."

Sonny nodded but didn't move.

"Is there something else?" she asked.

He looked uncomfortable, then turned his face away as

he said, "We did good tonight. Thanks to you, we saved those four guys."

*He thinks I'm upset about the men who died and he doesn't know what to say to make it better,* she thought. "Yes, we saved the four guys. Now what we have to do is try to make sure no one else needs saving," she said. "Take Jimmy home. I'll call if I need you."

It was just past nine o'clock when she entered the hotel lobby. The restaurants all served dinner until ten, and she contemplated going to either Pierre or Man Wah, but the thought of sitting in a room full of people was more than she could handle. She needed to be alone. Sonny's instincts had been correct; she was upset about the deaths. It was true they had saved four lives, but at the cost of eleven. The merits of the dead men aside, they were all just human beings trying to make a living in the way that birth, time, and circumstances had contrived for them. She didn't feel any guilt or assign blame to Ko and his men for the deaths. The Wings had been the catalyst, and if anyone bore responsibility it was them. She just wished she could have found a different way to free the hostages. But again, the Wings had imposed conditions that limited their options. *Goddamn you, Sammy,* she thought. *You and Carter sentenced your own men to death.*

When Ava arrived at her suite, she slipped off her pumps at the door, noticed there were bloodstains on both heels and toes, and felt her nausea return. She went into the bathroom, dampened a facecloth, and wiped the shoes clean. There were no visible stains on her skirt or blouse, but she took them off anyway. She found a plastic laundry bag and put the shoes and clothes into it. *Out of sight, out of mind,* she thought as she carried the bag to the bedroom and stuffed it into the bottom of her Double Happiness case. She put on a clean T-shirt and her black Adidas training pants and went into the living room.

Ava took a bottle of cognac from the mini-bar and poured it into a glass. She found the room service menu and sat down on the couch. She was hungry but wasn't sure what her stomach could handle. She was torn between nasi goreng — Indonesian fried rice with sweet soy sauce, prawns, chicken, and satay beef — and the Mandarin classic burger. Ava had been in Asia for weeks and hadn't eaten Western food since arriving. As she reached for the room phone, she reasoned that the burger would be substantial, not too spicy, and a welcome change of pace. After placing her order for that and a side of fries, she called Shanghai.

"I'm back at the hotel," she said when Fai answered.

"How was your meeting?"

"It was okay."

"Just okay?"

"It was good enough," Ava said.

"Are you going out for dinner?"

"No, I just ordered room service. I'm in for the evening."

"When do you think you can get out of Hong Kong?"

"Suen arrives later tonight, so I might be able to leave tomorrow. But I can't promise."

"Ava, do whatever you have to do and don't worry about me or Auntie Grace. We're getting along fine and she's just been told by the hospital that Xu will be moved out of isolation first thing tomorrow morning."

"I thought they were going to do it tonight."

"They need to find a private room for him, and there's none available until then."

"Still, that's good news."

"It certainly made her happy."

"What will make me happy is getting back to Shanghai for a few days and then going to Yantai," Ava said.

"Ava, are you really okay? You sound a bit down."

"It was a hard day, that's all."

"Do you want me to call you later, after you've eaten?" Fai asked.

"No, I'm too tired. I'll probably just eat and then crash."

"Then I'll talk to you tomorrow," Fai said. "Love you."

"Love you too," Ava said.

She laid her head against the back of the couch. How could things be going so well in one part of her life and be so problematic in others? When would she ever achieve total harmony? Did anyone ever? And if they did, did they become bored or find nirvana? "Shit," she said as she downed the last of the cognac.

Ava went back to the mini-bar, opened another bottle of cognac, and turned on the television while she waited for her burger. She channel-surfed, searching for something comedic. She found a rerun of a variety show starring Eric Tsang and watched for a few minutes, then gave up. Tsang was a versatile Hong Kong actor whom she had first seen and loved as the villain in *Infernal Affairs*, a film that Martin Scorsese ruinously — in her opinion — remade later as *The Departed*. Watching Tsang doing slapstick on the variety show was just as ruinous to her memory of his role in the film.

She switched to the BBC news. The United Kingdom was still intent on becoming an isolated middle power by leaving Europe, and the new American president was trying to turn back the clock to an era of white male domination.

She finished her second cognac and thought, *This is all too depressing.* Then her doorbell sounded and she was saved.

The server rolled a trolley into her room and quickly set it up in front of the couch. With its white tablecloth, first-class china and cutlery, and an array of condiments, the table setting wouldn't have been out of place in the Michelin-starred Pierre a few floors above her. Ava turned down the volume of the television so she could concentrate on her food. She had taken only two bites of her burger when her phone rang. She ignored it and then heard the beep that indicated a message. Two bites later it rang again. "Shit," she said, as the idea flashed through her head that it might be Sammy Wing. Had they found the bodies? Were they ready to negotiate? She stared at the phone and finally picked it up. "Yes."

"It's Ko."

"Did you call a minute ago?"

"Yes."

"You aren't using your own phone."

"I left mine in the car. I'm borrowing Feng's."

"What's happened? You sound upset."

"I'm at our main warehouse in Wanchai. While we were in Sha Tin trying to free our men, a group of triads helped themselves to about twenty million dollars' worth of our inventory."

Ava pushed away the trolley and walked to the window. "I don't understand," she said.

"Early this evening, they — and I'm assuming it was Carter Wing's men — raided our main warehouse. They left with two truckloads of electronic devices."

"Truckloads?"

"Yes, about sixty thousand devices in total. That's our

entire inventory for the next two months."

"Worth twenty million U.S. or Hong Kong dollars?"

"U.S. dollars."

Ava tried to absorb the number as she reverted to more basic questions. "Was the location of your warehouse well known?"

"We didn't think so, but it wouldn't take a genius to find it."

"But this had to be organized well in advance if two trucks were taken there."

"That's how I see it."

"Was the warehouse guarded?"

"Yes, but amazingly, none of the guards were injured during the robbery. They were tied up at gunpoint and evidently didn't offer any resistance."

"Do you think the warehouse guards were working in concert with the thieves?"

"I don't know," Ko said. "What I do know is that while our Shanghai men were hunting down the hostages, the warehouse and most of our other Wanchai assets were left under the protection of local men."

"Are you suggesting that those locals are still loyal to the Wings?"

"I hate to think that, but I can't dismiss it."

"Have any other assets been affected?"

"I don't know, but the night is young, and twenty million dollars is a hell of a start," he said, and then blurted, "Fuck, I can't believe this happened on my watch. I should have left some of my own men to keep an eye on Wanchai."

"You couldn't have known this was going to happen."

"True," he said, "but I should have been more cautious. I should have at least considered that the hostages were a distraction and that the Wings' real endgame was something different."

"Are you really suggesting that the hostages were simply bait? That they grabbed them to take your attention off Wanchai so they could steal sixty thousand electronic devices?"

"It's a possibility I can't dismiss."

"But we killed ten of their men. Why would they have let that happen?"

"Maybe Carter didn't think we'd find them," Ko said. "Or if we did, that they were fair exchange for the inventory he was about to steal."

"As much as I dislike the Wings, I can't imagine your last remark has any truth to it."

"I know, but it's all too fucking neat. And now I'm wondering about the Wanchai men. Who can I trust, and how much can I trust them?"

"Don't get paranoid. It would make sense for the Wings to assume, given the midnight deadline, that you and your men would be out all evening searching Sha Tin for the hostages."

"No matter how you explain it, it's still a mess. And I'm responsible for it," Ko said.

"What do you plan to do now?" she asked.

"I'm supposed to meet Suen at the airport in an hour."

"Will you still go?"

"Of course. News this bad should come directly from me."

"How will Suen react?"

"Not well. I hope the fact that we rescued four of the hostages will help moderate his response."

"For what it's worth, I think you've handled a very difficult situation about as well as anyone could have expected.

Your focus was correctly on rescuing your men. You can't be blamed for not anticipating that the Wings would scoop your inventory — assuming it was the Wings."

"Who else could it be?"

"Unfortunately, no one else comes to mind," Ava said.

"Thank God we'll have all those extra men in place by tomorrow," he said.

"What are you going to do about tonight?"

"Feng is assigning men to our more vulnerable businesses and warehouses. We would normally allocate three or four to a group, but we don't want to use the Wanchai men unless we're absolutely certain about their loyalty to us, so we're cutting back to two-man teams."

"Is there anything I can do to help?"

"Not specifically, but if something comes up and Feng can't reach me, do you mind if he calls you?"

"That's fine. I'll be available."

"And I'm sure Suen will want to talk to you tonight."

"After you've broken the news to him, ask him to phone me."

"I'm sure he will."

Ava was still at the window when she ended the conversation. She stared blankly at the harbour, for once oblivious to the panoply of lights cast by the skyscrapers into the darkness. Like Ko, she had little doubt that it was the Wings who had raided the warehouse; she just hadn't wanted to admit it so freely because it attributed to the Wings a level of intelligence and forward planning she didn't want to acknowledge. With Carter by his side, Sammy was turning into a more formidable opponent. And the scariest thing of all was Ko's belief that some of the Wanchai triads — his own men — were conspiring against him. If that was true, whatever problems Xu and Suen thought they had were going to become far more complicated.

Ava sighed, turned away from the window, and went back to the couch. Half of her hamburger and most of the french fries sat on their plates. She wiped her mouth with a cloth napkin and then placed it over the uneaten food. She pushed the trolley to the door and went back to the couch, carrying the glass that held the remainder of her cognac. As she sat down, her phone sounded again. *That was fast,* she thought. She picked it up and said, "Hi, Feng."

"You have the wrong man, but don't hang up," said Sammy Wing.

## 20

**AVA SAT BACK IN THE COUCH, NOT SURE IF SHE SHOULD** respond to him. Then she thought, *What the hell.* "Sammy, is there any particular reason you're calling me?"

"Are you in touch with Xu?" he asked.

"It isn't like you to get to the point so quickly," she said.

"I'm asking the question because I've been calling his cell for several hours and it doesn't seem to be on. It isn't like him to be so unavailable," Sammy said. "Then I called his home and his housekeeper told me he's in Vietnam on business. I'm not sure I believe her."

"Have you considered that he might not want to speak to you?"

"I've also been trying to reach Suen for the past few hours," he pressed. "I haven't been able to get him either."

"Getting to the point *and* being abrupt with me. This isn't like you at all. Has something upset you?"

"Well, I'm not the happiest of people."

"Who is happy? It's been a long, hard, miserable day."

"I blame myself for my situation. I was told this afternoon that those two clowns who used to work for Uncle were poking around in Sha Tin, offering a lot of money for information about where we were holding Lop's men," Sammy said. "I figured you'd put them up to it. The money was your idea, wasn't it."

"It was, and I'm guessing by now you know that it worked."

"Carter didn't think it would, but I warned him that you'd pay whatever it took and that there's always someone willing to rat if there's enough money in it for them. I should have been more insistent that he move the men from the garage."

"I'm glad you weren't."

"That kind of mistake won't happen again. Nothing will be taken for granted from now on," Sammy said. "And you can be sure we'll find that fucking rat. He helped you kill ten men, and I promise you, he'll die ten deaths before we finish with him."

"I couldn't care less about who you find or what you do to them," Ava said. "And, not that it matters to you, I killed no one."

"Our man — the one you didn't kill — said it was a woman who fronted the attack."

"I was an interested observer, nothing more."

"An observer. When were you ever just an observer?"

"On this occasion I was, and let me tell you what I observed," Ava said. "You assumed that shooting Lop would take the heart out of his men. It didn't. Ko is a capable leader and the men didn't forget their training. You can't fight them and win."

"There are other ways to win besides fighting."

"Like stealing a bunch of devices that can be replaced?"

Ava could hear Sammy breathing heavily and knew she was getting under his skin.

"I have a proposal for Xu," he said finally. "I want to present it to him directly. There's no need for you or anyone else to be in the middle."

"That's not your decision to make."

"Tell him to call me."

"I'll pass on your message, Sammy, but I can't promise it will be well received."

"Just tell him to call me," he said, and then the connection went dead.

*What a strange call,* she thought. *What are they up to?* Sammy had been calmer about the events at the garage than she'd expected. He also hadn't denied that they were behind the robbery at the warehouse. But what surprised her most was his criticism — however carefully couched — of his nephew. Was it possible that their relationship wasn't as one-sided as she thought? Well, whatever the intent of the call had been, it had her imagination working overtime. She called Shanghai first.

"*Wei,*" Auntie Grace answered.

"It's Ava. I'm sorry to call so late, but I need to know if a man called a short while ago asking for Xu."

"Yes. I told him that Xu wasn't home, and then he asked me where he was. When I told him it was none of his business, he apologized and told me he was a colleague from Hong Kong and was calling on a business matter," she said. "Then I told him Xu is in Vietnam. That's what Suen told me you wanted me to say if I was asked."

"You did exactly the right thing," Ava said. "Did this man give you his name?"

"No, and I didn't think to ask."

"That's fine. It isn't important that we know."

"But you know someone called here."

"I do."

"Is there a problem?" Auntie asked.

"Nothing we can't handle, and nothing you should be the least bit concerned about."

"Thank goodness for that. I'm just starting to relax, knowing that Xu will be out of the isolation ward tomorrow."

"Will you visit him?"

"I will. I'll take him some food."

"I'm sure he'll be pleased to see you, food or no food," Ava said. "Now, Auntie, excuse me but I have to go."

"Fai is sitting here in the kitchen with me. Do you want to talk to her?"

"No, I spoke to her earlier. But tell her I love her and that I'll call her in the morning," Ava said.

"Well, Sammy didn't lie to me about that," she muttered, as thoughts about what Ko had told her now crowded into her head. She phoned Sonny next.

"Boss, do you need me?" he asked.

She hesitated, not sure if what she wanted to ask of him was either appropriate or something he could manage. "I've had the strangest half-hour," she said. "First, Ko called me to say that while we were rescuing his men at the garage, the Wing gang was helping themselves to two truckloads of electronic devices, worth about twenty million U.S. dollars, from the Wanchai gang's main warehouse. Then Sammy phoned to tell me he has an offer he wants to make directly to Xu."

"Did Sammy know what happened at the garage?"

"He knew about the garage and he didn't deny that they'd robbed the warehouse. He made a bit of a fuss about the garage, but far less than I expected. He sounded — I don't know how else to say it, Sonny — he sounded *confident*. For someone who's already been beaten by Xu and has just had another taste of what Xu's men can do, I find that odd."

"Maybe he thinks the devices are better leverage than the hostages. Maybe he thinks Xu will care more about twenty million dollars than six of his men."

"That's not true, of course, and it has to be more complicated than that. The twenty million is street value, not production cost, and I'm sure Xu could replace the entire inventory within a month."

"What are you trying to say?"

"I keep thinking about what you said this morning about the loyalty of the Wanchai triads," she said. "Someone had to tell the Wings where the warehouse was and what was in it, right?"

"Right."

"And Ko told me that the guards at the warehouse offered no resistance. Is that a normal reaction?"

"No."

"It has Ko spooked. He's beginning to have doubts about who he can trust among the men he inherited from Sammy."

"That's being sensible."

"Maybe it is, but where does it leave Xu? How can he control Wanchai without Wanchai men? He'd have to leave a large group of men from Shanghai there permanently. I'm not sure he has the resources to do that over the long term."

"Even if he did, it wouldn't go over very well with the other Hong Kong gangs," Sonny said. "They might start thinking he had the same designs on them. He'd look like an invader."

"All he wants to be is a partner. The only reason he's in Wanchai in the first place is because Sammy left him no other choice."

"Ava, I'm not the person you have to convince."

She sighed. "That's why I'm struggling with this."

"What can I do to help?"

"How strong are your contacts in Wanchai?"

"I've lived in Wanchai for twenty years. Outside of Fanling and Uncle's old connections there, I'm more comfortable and better known in Wanchai than anywhere."

"I meant triad contacts."

"So did I."

"Do you know where I'm going with this?"

"I'm guessing that you want me to assess what the Wanchai triads think of Xu and their affiliation — if you can call it that — with Shanghai."

"That's exactly what I'd like you to do."

"You know better than anyone that I'm not the most subtle of men," Sonny said.

"I also know that most of the people who know you also respect and trust you. And I want you to understand that I don't want you to do anything that would destroy that trust or respect," Ava said. "I'm just looking for a sense of the feeling on the ground. I'm not asking you to be a spy."

"I'll do what I can," Sonny said without hesitation.

"Thank you, and although this may sound ungrateful, I also need you to do it as fast as you can," Ava said. "For some reason I think this entire situation is about to move quickly towards a conclusion. I'd like to have a grip on where we stand before Xu is forced to make decisions that could have a far-reaching impact."

( 21 )

**SOMETIME AFTER TEN O'CLOCK, THE COMBINATION OF**
cognac and a waning of the adrenalin that had been pumping all day took its toll on Ava. She had lain down on the
couch to watch the late evening news, and the last thing
she remembered was yawning and closing her eyes for what
seemed like only a second. When she awoke, with a dry
mouth and a need to pee, the room was already sunlit.

After leaving the bathroom, she made a coffee and checked
her cell. There were no messages and no record of any calls.
She had expected Suen to phone her when he landed. She
checked the time. It wasn't quite six, still too early to call
him. "Shit," she said. At the very least, Suen should have let
her know he had arrived safely.

She went to the window and looked out on the rarest of
things: the streets of Hong Kong not filled with cars and
people. The good weather had carried over from the afternoon before, and the stifling humidity that typified Hong
Kong summers was still a few months away. Without another
thought, Ava went into the bedroom and took her running
gear from her bag. Five minutes later she left the hotel and

jogged to the Central MTR station, where she caught a train and rode it three stops to Causeway Bay. One of the stops she passed was Wanchai; almost unconsciously, she closed her eyes at the sight of the station.

Victoria Park was one of the few green swaths in Central and a magnet for the local population, who predominantly — more than ninety percent — lived in apartments smaller than seven hundred square feet. Only forty-seven acres, it wasn't much of a park when compared to the 840 acres of Central Park in New York or the gorgeous thousand acres of Vancouver's Stanley Park, but in terms of greenery on Hong Kong Island, it was enormous.

Ava entered the park from the south side, started to run her first lap on the six-hundred-metre red rubber jogging track, and saw that she was early enough to avoid the crush of humanity that would begin to fill the park by seven o'clock. The track — the words JOGGING ONLY were painted on its rubber surface — would soon be jammed with joggers, and also with walkers blithely ignoring the restriction. As she circled the track she saw some tai chi practitioners already exercising, and there were birdcages hanging from some trees. There weren't many dogs in Central, but birds were often kept as pets; they were taken to the park for air the way that Westerners took their dogs for a walk.

Ava wanted to do at least ten laps, but as she got to eight the jogging path began to get crowded and she was forced to break stride to avoid running into walkers. Once she had to come to a complete stop behind a line of elderly men stretched across the path. Knowing it was only going to get worse, she headed back to the Causeway Bay MTR station. Fifteen minutes later she was back at the Mandarin, and ten minutes after that she walked into her suite with a double espresso from Café Causette in her hand.

The run, even though abbreviated, had helped her relax. She had rethought her conversations from the night before with Sammy Wing and Ko and had decided she might be reading too much into them. The fact that Sammy hadn't been totally belligerent and seemed intent on talking to Xu made her think he wanted to cut a deal. Maybe the annihilation of Wing's men at the garage had brought him and Carter to their senses. If they had assumed that the loss of Lop would weaken Xu's forces in Wanchai, that notion had been crushed. She also thought the looting of the warehouse had been preplanned and wasn't a reaction to events at the garage. It was a smart thing to do if their intention had been to increase the pressure on Xu to deal with them. Unfortunately, if that was true it led to the conclusion that they had never really intended to kill the hostages the night before. Well, whether they had or not, they had left Ko and his men with no choice but to act; they must have known that their threats would be taken seriously.

Her memory of the talk with Ko was a bit more problematic. Ava wasn't certain that Ko was wrong to question the loyalty of some of the men under his control, but he could be overestimating how many of them were inclined to support Sammy. Her hope was that Sonny would get a more accurate reading of the mood among the Wanchai men.

Ava took her cell from the table by the couch and carried it to the desk. There had been two texts and one voice message while she'd been gone. May Ling had simply written Hope things are going okay. Suen's text said, I'm in Hong Kong. Staying at the Kew Green Hotel. Let me know when you want to meet. The voice message was from Fai, and she'd called less than five minutes before. Ava grinned when she heard her say, "Hi. Auntie Grace just spoke to the hospital. They're definitely moving Xu into his new room this morning. They think it will be done by eight. Call me when you have a chance."

She started to phone Fai, then stopped, thinking she should get updated first. She called Suen instead.

"Good morning, Ava. You're up early," Suen answered.

"I've been out for a run already."

"Well, I've had breakfast. Does that count as exercise?"

"Only if you say so," Ava said. "What time did you get in last night?"

"Not until after eleven, and it was midnight by the time I met Ko. When he finished briefing me, I thought it might be too late to call you, especially after the day you'd had," he said. "Ava, I can't thank you enough for everything you did at the garage."

"I'm just sorry you lost two more men."

"Yes, but we saved four. And we put some hurt on the Wings and took away some of their leverage."

"Your men were terrific. Ko showed real leadership."

"He wasn't feeling so happy about his leadership abilities when I saw him last night. The warehouse robbery set him — set all of us back on our heels."

"Can I assume that nothing more dramatic has happened since the warehouse robbery?"

"That was dramatic enough, but no, nothing else has happened that we know about. And as of ten minutes ago, the situation remains the same," Suen said.

"That's good to hear."

"But we can't count on that continuing. I managed to get fifty men into Hong Kong yesterday. Fifty more will arrive today. I figure that gives us enough strength to deal with just about anything."

"I have a hunch that the Wings won't be as aggressive today," Ava said.

"What makes you say that?"

"Sammy called me last night to say he wants to talk to Xu. He said he has a proposal for him."

"That's interesting, but not entirely surprising, given our actions at the garage," Suen said. "Did he give you any idea of what he has in mind?"

"No, and I didn't press him. He had tried to contact Xu directly, obviously without any success. He even called the house; Auntie Grace told him Xu was in Vietnam on business," Ava said. "He also said he called you."

"If he tried to reach me, I have no record of it, and obviously there was no way he was going to talk to Xu."

"Speaking of Xu, Fai says he's going to be moved out of isolation this morning."

"I know. I'm waiting for his call."

Ava hesitated, unwilling to make Suen think she was usurping his role. "When you talk to Xu, tell him about Sammy Wing and ask him to give me a call when he has the time."

"Okay, I'll do that," he said. "What are your plans for the day? Do you want to meet?"

"I don't know if we need to. I was thinking about returning to Shanghai. Now that you're here, I don't see any reason for me to stay."

"I'm not so sure about that. No one knows Sammy Wing better than you."

"Sammy Wing doesn't want to deal with me. He wants to talk to Xu."

"But will Xu want to talk to him?"

Ava sipped the last of her espresso, reluctant to admit that Suen had made a good point. "I won't book a flight until you bring Xu up-to-date," she said.

She put the cell back on the desk, then headed for the bathroom. Twenty minutes later, freshly showered and wearing a clean shirt and slacks, Ava returned to the living room. She opened her laptop and checked seat availability on the Cathay Pacific afternoon flights to Shanghai. Business class looked wide open. She was thinking about holding a seat when her cell buzzed and she saw a text from Fai that read, Call me when you can.

Ava called the house phone first, but when no one answered, she tried Fai's cell.

"Hi," Fai answered. "I'm in the car with Auntie Grace. We're on our way to the hospital to see Xu."

"So he's been moved out of isolation?"

"Auntie Grace called the hospital half an hour ago. They confirmed it."

"Thank goodness."

"We're taking him food."

"Will the hospital allow that?"

"Who's going to argue with Auntie Grace?" Fai said, and then paused. "Just a second, she's asking me a question... She wants to know if there were any problems because of that man calling the house last night."

"None," Ava said, surprised again at how sensitive Auntie was to the nature of Xu's business.

"I'll tell her. She'll be pleased. I think it was bothering

her," Fai said. "When do you think you'll be coming back to Shanghai?"

Ava started to say "today" but caught herself, not wanting to create expectations until she was certain. "I'll have a better idea by this afternoon," she said, and then her cell buzzed. She looked at the screen and saw a very familiar Shanghai number. "Fai, I have a call from Xu. I should take it."

"Go ahead."

"Give him a hug for me when you see him," she said, and then switched calls. "Hey, I was just telling Fai to give you a hug. She and Auntie Grace are on their way to see you."

"It's good to be back in the real world, although I have to say it has its challenges too," Xu said in a firm, steady voice.

"You sound so much better."

"They tell me I'm out of danger but that I still need to conserve my energy, or at least not go at things full bore."

"So, a few more days in the hospital?"

"They recommend it, and as long as I have access to my cell I don't mind."

"Have you spoken to Suen?"

"I have. He told me about the garage. I'm upset that we lost the two men but I'm pleased we saved the other four. I just wish you hadn't put yourself at risk."

"What I did wasn't that risky, and I only did what I thought was necessary."

"I know there's no point in arguing with you, so I'll just say thanks."

"I was hoping it would bring the Wings to their senses, but I'm not sure it did."

"Suen told me that Sammy called you after the attack. Are you saying he was irrational?"

"No. He came close to losing it when he spoke about the snitch who led us to the garage, but on balance he was surprisingly calm."

"Suen said he wants to talk to me. I imagine the subject will be the devices they took from our warehouse."

"He didn't tell me specifically what he wants to discuss. All he said was that he has an offer he wants to make."

"He may want to make it but I don't want to listen to it. Not now, anyway," Xu said.

"Why not?" Ava asked.

"If I did, it would imply that I was treating him as an equal. I don't want to legitimatize him or what he's done," Xu said.

"What if Carter was the one who wanted to speak to you?"

"That would be more complicated, but I don't think he would ever approach me," Xu said carefully. "As long as this is about Sammy reclaiming Wanchai, the other Hong Kong Mountain Masters can justify staying neutral. If Carter comes to me directly, it will look like a territory grab, and that's something none of them want to see, because then they'd start wondering who's next. I'm sure Carter is smart enough to know he needs to keep them onside, and he can only do that by staying in the background and pretending this is about Sammy."

"But if that's the case, where can this go? How can it end?"

"I'm just beginning to grapple with that. I have some Mountain Masters I need to talk to and I need some time to get up to speed. Can you help?"

"What do you want me to do?"

"Find out what Sammy has to offer and then string him along for as long as you can."

"He wants to talk to you, not me," Ava repeated.

"Tell him that you're my conduit for any offer he wants to make," Xu said. "He can accept that or he can deal with Suen, Ko, and as many men as we can get to Hong Kong."

"Xu, I have no interest in meeting with him again."

"I'm not suggesting you do," Xu said. "Phone him. That will be enough."

"And if he keeps insisting on speaking with you?"

"You had Auntie Grace tell him I'm in Vietnam?"

"Yes."

"Tell him I'm still there and can't be reached until some time tonight," Xu said. "If you can get him to wait that long, I might be able to come up with a solution to the Wing problem."

## 22

**AVA SAT AT THE DESK THINKING ABOUT WHAT TO SAY** to Sammy Wing — assuming he would even take her call. Telling Sammy that Xu was in Vietnam and couldn't be contacted until that evening sounded weak, but if she dressed it up and threw in some promises with it, she might be able to get him to bite. She would have to lie, of course, and lie a lot. Somehow that seemed appropriate, given who she'd be dealing with.

She made some notes in her Moleskine and then went to the laptop and found a map of Vietnam. After locating what she wanted, she phoned Feng in Shanghai.

"This is Ava Lee," she said.

"Ava, I'm surprised to hear from you. Are you still in Hong Kong?"

"I am. How did you know I'm here?"

"I spoke to my son late last night. He told me about the hostage rescue. We owe you a big thanks."

"Your son did well too. He's an impressive young man."

"Unlike his father, he can do more than balance accounts."

"Everyone contributes in their own way."

"What is it you want me to contribute this time?"

"I need a favour."

"Ask for anything you want. If I can do it, you know I will."

"I want you to tell some lies," she said. "It's possible that Sammy Wing or someone else from the Sha Tin gang may contact you to ask about Xu's whereabouts. Sammy is demanding to speak directly to Xu, but Xu wants no part of any conversation with him until at least this evening. I'm trying to provide a viable excuse that won't piss off Sammy."

"What do you want me to tell them?" Feng asked.

"I want you to say that Xu is in Vietnam trying to close a deal on a new device factory. The factory is in a place called Vung Tau, on the South China Sea. Tell them he's in transit or tied up in meetings all day and won't be in touch with you until tonight, when he gets back to Ho Chi Minh City."

"When is he supposed to have gone there?"

"Yesterday, but you spoke to him late last night," Ava said. "So if any mention is made of the hostages or the robbery, you can make it clear that Xu is up-to-date."

"Do you actually think someone will call me to ask for Xu?"

"I have no idea, but if they do, our stories have to match, and the story I just told you is what I'll be telling Sammy Wing in about five minutes," Ava said. "My hunch is that Sammy won't believe me and might call you, or have Carter Wing's White Paper Fan call, to corroborate what I told him."

"I get it."

"Good. And by the way, did you know that Xu is now out of isolation?"

"Yes, Suen has been keeping me informed," Feng said. "I owe both of them a phone call, but I've been holding off until

I figure out a solution to the warehouse robbery. I've been working since early this morning trying to find inventory to ship to Hong Kong to replace the stolen goods. We can't short customers for more than a few days, or they'll start looking elsewhere."

"Like Sha Tin?"

"Why not? There's no customer loyalty in our business. All that matters is that you've got the goods and the price is right."

"Suen said the stolen goods are worth twenty million dollars. I assumed that was street price and not production cost."

"You're right. Our markup is more than a hundred percent, but whether you're looking at the cost of the goods or lost sales revenue, it's a huge hit."

"I suspect Sammy thinks that gives him a lot of leverage."

"Then he doesn't know Xu very well," Feng said. "Money doesn't factor into his decision-making when the lives of our men are at stake. When the Wings took those seven men hostage and killed one and then another two of them, they lost all their leverage."

"Xu thinks he might be able to come up with a solution, although truthfully I have no idea what he has in mind."

"Whatever it is, I can't count on having our inventory returned, so I'll keep doing what I'm doing. And if anyone calls looking for Xu, I'll tell them your Vietnam story. Do you want me to contact you if I do hear from someone?"

"Not unless you think there's a problem."

"Then here's hoping we don't have to talk to each other again today."

"Thanks, Feng," Ava said as she ended the call.

She looked at her notes again, then restructured her opening approach. When she was satisfied, she made a coffee and sat down on the couch to phone Sammy. She concealed her number in case seeing it would be reason for him not to answer. His cell rang four times and went to voicemail. She hung up. "Shit," she said. "He's not making this easy."

Ava checked the time, waited five minutes, and then called him again.

"*Wei*," he said.

"This is Ava, and it's my turn to ask you not to hang up," she said as quickly as she could.

He didn't reply but the line didn't go dead.

"This isn't what you think," she continued. "Xu will speak to you, but he can't until tonight. Can you wait until then?"

"Why?" he finally said, the word spat out.

"Why what?"

"Why do I have to wait?"

"He's in Vietnam, en route to a city called Vung Tau, where he's trying to finalize a partnership with a new factory. He'll be out of touch until he gets back to Ho Chi Minh City this evening."

"Are you trying to tell me he doesn't know what's been going on here?"

"He knows, but this trip to Vietnam has been in the works for months. He had to go."

"That's bullshit."

"Sammy, he had to go."

"That's not what I mean. There's no way he hasn't been in constant touch with Suen, Ko, and probably you."

"Feng, his White Paper Fan, spoke to him late last night. He knows about the hostages and the warehouse robbery. But no one else has spoken to him since."

"Bullshit," he said.

"Sammy —" she said, but there was no one there.

*Well, that didn't turn out to be much of a plan*, she thought. *Now what do I do?* She drank the last of the coffee as she pondered her options. Only one made any real sense, and that was to do nothing. Despite his bluster, Sammy might have believed her. Maybe he would call Feng. And even if he didn't, she had held his attention long enough to deliver the message that Xu wouldn't be available until tonight. The outcome of whatever Sammy and Carter decided to do in the interim was something Xu seemed prepared to live with, and it was obviously out of her hands. *Maybe I did enough after all*, she thought as she found Xu's number on her cell.

"Ava, your ears must have been burning. I was just talking about you with our friend Lam," Xu said.

"Did you call him or did he call you?"

"I called him to thank him for the help with the weapons, and to ask him to help me resolve this problem with Sammy."

"And Carter. Don't forget about Carter."

"Believe me, I haven't."

"Will Lam help?"

"He will, indirectly, but that's all I expected, and it's good enough," Xu said. "Did you reach Sammy?"

"We spoke. I told him you're in Vietnam and out of reach until tonight. I don't think he believed me, but at least he listened long enough for me to tell him."

"How was his attitude?"

"He swore and hung up on me, but that's a typical Sammy reaction when he doesn't get what he wants."

"I'm sorry I subjected you to more of Sammy, but your speaking to him is much appreciated."

"Xu, I have to tell you I've had enough of Sammy, and I've had enough of Hong Kong," Ava said. "Unless you have some urgent reason why I need to spend another day here, I intend to fly back to Shanghai this afternoon."

"Yes, do that. Suen can manage things on the ground while I try to work out some kind of accommodation with the Wings."

"Accommodation?"

"It's either that or we go to war in Sha Tin. It's a war we could win, but the political cost with my fellow Mountain Masters would be enormous. Keeping those friendships and alliances intact is more important to me than punishing the Wings — although that doesn't mean there won't be some retribution," Xu said. "That's why I was talking to Lam. He's trying to gauge for me how far I can go with the Wings before I start to alienate the Hong Kong Mountain Masters."

"So you have no intention of giving up control of Wanchai?"

"No intention whatsoever."

A long string of questions popped into Ava's head as she thought about what Sonny had said about the loyalty of the Wanchai triads. "Are you sure Ko and thirty men will be able to maintain control?" she said.

"If I resolve the Wing issue, why wouldn't they?"

"Sammy has claimed — more than once — that there are many men in the Wanchai gang whose primary loyalty is to him. Unless you completely remove him from the scene, don't you run the risk of Sammy becoming a recurring problem, aided and abetted by men you think are loyal to you?"

"Removing Sammy is what I'm discussing with Lam and the others, but even so, I think Sammy is exaggerating the extent of his support. I don't doubt that there are men who resent our presence there, but as long as they are respected and well paid, they shouldn't become a problem. I mean, they haven't exactly flocked to Sammy's side in the past few days."

"Perhaps I shouldn't have said anything. I'm oversensitive where Sammy is concerned."

"No, I'm glad you spoke up."

"I did a bit more than that," Ava said. "I asked Sonny to poke around to see how much truth there is to Sammy's claim."

"What did he find?"

"I don't know yet. He's just started talking to people."

"Let me know what he thinks. I have a lot of trust in Sonny's judgement."

"I will," Ava said, and then she saw she had an incoming call. "I should go."

"Call me after you've booked your flight; I'll send Wen to the airport to meet you. Auntie Grace and Fai will be glad to have you back in Shanghai, and of course so will I."

"I will," she said, switching calls. "Hello."

"Ava, this is Sonny. I'm with Andy."

She knew it was Sonny, but his voice sounded nothing like him. It was a dull monotone that was completely out of character. "What's happened?" she asked.

"We're standing outside the apartment building where Carlo's brother lives."

"What's happened?" she demanded again.

"There are three bodies on the sidewalk in front of the building."

She felt a cold shiver run down her back, and her hand trembled. "Carlo?" she asked, dreading the answer.

"Carlo and Ching and the triad from Tai Po."

"How were they killed?" she managed to ask through a jumble of emotions.

"You don't want to know," Sonny said.

"Tell me," she said.

"Ava —"

"Sonny, tell me."

"Their throats have been slashed and their bodies cut to ribbons. Ching has a rat stuffed in his mouth," he blurted.

She took a deep breath. "Are the police there?"

"They arrived a few minutes ago. The intention was for me and Andy to see the bodies first."

Ava closed her eyes as she tried to make sense of what Sonny was trying to tell her. "I don't understand," she said finally.

"Carlo's brother phoned Andy half an hour ago to tell him Carlo wanted to see us. The brother said Carlo would meet us in front of the apartment building and we should get there as fast as possible. When we arrived, there wasn't any sign of him. A moment later a panel truck stopped in front of the building, four guys leapt out and opened the back door, and before we knew what was happening, they'd dumped the bodies onto the sidewalk."

"Did you recognize any of the guys in the van?"

"No, and we didn't get the licence plate number either. We were both stunned."

"Did you talk to Carlo's brother?"

"Not yet, but I'm sure he'll tell us someone was holding a gun to his head when he called."

"Oh God, I feel so terrible."

"Ava, I'm sorry, but there's more," Sonny said. "There was a note pinned to Carlo's shirt."

"Do you have it?"

"It's in my hand."

"Read it to me."

He hesitated, then uttered a sound that was somewhere between a groan and sigh.

"Read it," Ava said.

"This is what happens to rats and people who pay for rats. We aren't finished with those who did the paying."

## 23

**AVA DIDN'T RESPOND IMMEDIATELY TO THE NOTE** Sonny had read to her. She repeated its words under her breath, slowly absorbing their full meaning. Then she said, "Sonny, I'm worried about you and Andy."

"They could have shot us here on the sidewalk if they'd wanted to," Sonny said. "I think they want to drag this out. They want to make us sweat. Even if they never come after us, the fuckers will be pleased with themselves because they've planted seeds of doubt and fear in our heads."

"Did Andy read the note?"

"Yeah."

"How is he reacting?"

"He's nervous. He's afraid of what might happen if they come after him when his wife is around," Sonny said. "He's also afraid for you. As am I."

"Could Andy stay with you for a little while?" she asked, not wanting to discuss the reference to her.

"Sure."

"And tell him his wife should move out of their apartment for a few days."

"I'll do that," Sonny said, and then paused. "Just a moment, Ava. I see a cop I know coming out of the apartment building. I'm going to talk to him."

Ava was grateful to have a few moments to cope with her surging emotions. Carlo and the other men dead? Threats to Sonny, Andy, and her? The Wings had changed the scenario once again. This wasn't about hostages or stolen smartphones anymore. It was about living under a cloud of fear — or, even more to the point, about living or dying. *Fuck the Wings,* she thought. *They aren't going to do this to me.*

"Ava, are you still there?" Sonny asked.

"I'm listening."

"Carlo's brother is dead. The cops found him in the apartment with his brains blown out."

"I guess that shouldn't come as a surprise," she said. "Don't let Andy out of your sight, and make sure his wife moves in with friends or family."

"Okay, boss."

"When the wife is in a safe place, call me."

"I will, but what about you? Should you change hotels?"

"I'm staying put," Ava said, her brain starting to function again as the shock receded. "Sonny, how did they find out about Ching?"

"The only possible source would be the lookout. I'm guessing he told them that Ching showed up at the garage in the afternoon. Someone put two and two together, grabbed Ching, probably tortured him, and one thing led to another," Sonny said. "We should have killed that lookout. I thought about it at the time, but in our hurry to get away from the garage it slipped my mind."

"I told Ko not to harm him," she said. "That was my

decision, and it was obviously the wrong one."

"It might not have been the lookout," Sonny said quickly. "Maybe someone from inside Ko's organization, one of the Wanchai men, leaked the information to the Wings."

"I don't think that's how it happened."

"Don't be so sure."

"What do you mean by that?"

"I've been talking to people, like you asked. A lot of Wanchai brothers are happy that Sammy is making a move. They may have kept their feelings to themselves while Lop had everything tightly controlled, but now that they see there's a chance for Sammy to come back, they're not so quietly rooting for him," Sonny said. "Ava, Wanchai is a nest of snakes. Even if Suen wins this battle, I don't think it will be the end of the dissatisfaction. I'm not sure how many Wanchai men he could really trust if he had to call on them to help."

"Dissatisfaction with what, with whom?" she said. "From everything I've been told, everyone has been treated well and paid fairly."

"I know it sounds stupid, but there's a lot of prejudice in Hong Kong towards mainlanders, and the brothers aren't any different from the average Hong Konger in their attitudes. They call Xu's men 'the China people,' and they almost sneer when they do," Sonny said. "And I've also been told that the negative feelings about Xu's control of Wanchai go well beyond the triads on the street. Evidently there are Mountain Masters who aren't happy about it either. They may respect Xu, but he's still an outsider in Hong Kong."

"Who mentioned the Mountain Masters?"

"Some old friends of Uncle's, senior people. They won't say anything to Xu's face, but they talk among themselves.

Their fear, irrational as it might be, is that one of them could be his next takeover target."

"That *is* irrational."

"I agree, but I don't think it can be ignored," he said.

"That's true, and if the feelings among the Wanchai triads are as deeply rooted as you think, Xu has a bigger mess on his hands than he imagines."

"Boss, it isn't your mess," Sonny said. "I've been thinking that maybe you should leave Hong Kong. If you stay we'll protect you as best as we can, but who knows what the Wings have planned."

"You're right that what goes on in Wanchai shouldn't concern me, but what happened to Carlo does," Ava said.

"He knew the risks. He would never expect you to feel any responsibility for what happened to him."

"That may be true, but it doesn't lessen my sense of obligation. You know I don't take my obligations lightly, and this is one that's crying out to be met. I don't know how I can leave things as they are."

Sonny sighed. "I'm not going to be able to convince you to leave, am I."

"No, because even if Carlo were alive there's still the matter of — "

"Then tell me what we're going to do, because whatever it is, I'm in this with you, and I know Andy will feel the same way."

"I don't know what I want to do, and that's the truth," she said. "I need some time to think. In the meantime, why don't you and Andy make sure his wife is safe. I'll call you later, after I've sorted things out."

"Boss, please don't try anything without us."

"You have my word on that," she said.

Ava was still sitting on the couch, and that was a good thing, because she wasn't sure her legs could have supported her during the early parts of her conversation with Sonny. Now she pushed herself to her feet, walked to the window, and looked out at the harbour and the streets below. Thousands of people were going about their daily business, oblivious to what had just happened in Kowloon. Four lives had come to an abrupt and ugly end, and it didn't stop there. How many more people — children, wives, siblings, parents, lovers, friends — would their deaths impact? Ava was struck again by the transience of life, how easily it was lost and how difficult it was to measure the repercussions. *What was it Uncle used to say?* she thought. "*Huo zai dang xia* — live in the moment." He had said it a lot, both before and after his diagnosis of terminal cancer.

She thought about Carlo. In many ways he had been silly — trying so hard to be a ladies' man but finding success mainly in the brothels of Macau, or pretending to be tough when he was actually timid. Her last memory of Carlo was of him standing next to Andy in the garage, his voice full of concern as he looked at his partner's wounded arm. A tear ran down her cheek. *Carlo didn't deserve to die like that*, she thought, and the tears began to flow more freely.

Her phone rang but Ava ignored it. Five minutes later it rang again. She looked at it as if it were something she'd never seen before. *I should have asked Andy about his arm*, she suddenly thought. *It has to be okay if he was on the streets with Sonny, but it was inconsiderate of me not to have asked.*

The tears had gradually stopped and she was beginning to reconnect with her surroundings. Ava turned away from the harbour, walked to the couch, and picked up her smartphone. Suen had called, and a number she didn't recognize. Two messages. She accessed the first.

"This is Suen. I heard what happened. Call me."

She opened the second. "You should know by now that I found the rat and the rat's helpers. I needed to send a message: there's no room for rats in my world," said Carter Wing, his voice grating. "I haven't decided yet what to do about the other clown who helped the rat, or your goon, Sonny. That decision may depend on you. Sammy asked me to leave you out of this, and I've agreed for now. But I want you to get out of Hong Kong today. Just go the fuck back to wherever you came from. You don't belong here."

Ava listened to Carter's message twice more. He spoke deliberately, but that didn't disguise the underlying anger and hatred. If she hadn't been his enemy before, she certainly was now. What she was less sure about was his assertion that she would be left alone. Could she trust what he said? She shook her head. It would be foolish to believe him. It was safer to assume he wanted her dead. *Wanting me dead,* she thought with a grim smile, *is almost becoming a Wing family tradition.*

Ava made a quick mental list of the people she needed to talk to. Sonny was first. She called him from the room phone.

"Boss, is everything okay?" he answered. "I didn't expect to hear from you so soon."

"I heard from Carter Wing. He left me a voice message. I'm going to play it for you," she said, holding her cell next to the phone.

"That son of a bitch," Sonny said when the message had ended.

"At least it makes things very clear," she said.

"You can't trust him," Sonny said.

"I don't. And I think it's obvious that this has gone well beyond any question of trust."

"What do you mean?"

"I was thinking about Lok. Do you remember him?"

"The Red Pole in Macau? He's a hard man to forget."

"Yes, the one I shot in the head."

"You had no choice," Sonny said.

"That's what Uncle told me at the time. He knew I was upset afterwards, but that doesn't mean what he told me was any less true," she said. "He said he had known men like Lok his entire life. They are the kind of people who never forget a slight; they have a passion for revenge that never goes away. Somewhere, sometime, he told me, the timing and circumstances would be perfect for that passion to turn into action. He said, knowing Lok as he did, it would have been foolish of me not to get rid of him, because sooner or later he would have come after me."

"And I agreed with Uncle."

"I know. I also know that he ordered you to kill Lok if I didn't," Ava said.

"It was the right thing to do."

"Tell me, Sonny, how are the circumstances with Carter and Sammy Wing any different than they were with Lok? You, Andy, and me — we're all at risk."

There was a long silence on the other end of the line, and then Sonny said, "Boss, what are you thinking?"

"I'm thinking that Uncle always gave sound advice, and that it would be foolish of me not to follow it now."

## 24

**TALKING TO SONNY HAD HELPED DULL THE PAIN OF** Carlo's death for Ava — mainly because it had brought clarity to the situation in which she now found herself. Carter and Sammy Wing wanted her dead, maybe not that day or the next day, but she was an irritating itch, and eventually the need to scratch it would overwhelm them.

She sat at the desk with her Moleskine open. As she saw it, she had two options. The first was to leave Hong Kong. The problem with that was that it didn't resolve anything. Sonny and Andy would still be at risk, and every time she returned to Hong Kong she would have to worry that Wing thugs would be waiting for her. She was also concerned that they might target members of her family or her business partners.

Her second option was simpler and would bring closure: she could kill Sammy and Carter.

She searched for some middle ground between what she knew were two extremes, but nothing stuck. As hard as she tried, she couldn't get past the fact that she didn't trust them and they weren't predictable — except in their desire for revenge.

Complicating matters was Xu's relationship with the Wings. She wasn't sure exactly where he stood. She didn't doubt his support for her, but would it extend to standing by, or even helping, if she told him she wanted to eliminate the threat posed by Carter and Sammy? She realized it could cause a falling-out with other Mountain Masters and a disruption in business that could cost Xu tens if not hundreds of millions of dollars. She had to talk to him, and she had to do it soon. But first she returned Suen's call.

"Ava, did you get my message?" he said.

"I did."

"I'm sorry about Carlo."

"I'm sorry about all the men. It sounds like they were brutalized before they died."

"You spoke to Sonny?"

"Yes, and Andy was with him."

"Are they safe?"

"For now. I received a phone message from Carter saying he has no immediate plans to go after them or me, but I'm not sure I believe him," Ava said. "He also, not so nicely, told me to leave Hong Kong today."

"Will you?"

"No."

"What are you going to do?"

"I want to talk to Xu before I make a final decision."

"I tried to reach him a short while ago. They're running some tests on him right now. He should be back in his room in about half an hour."

"Does he know about Carlo and the others?"

"Not yet. If he did, he would have called you."

"What are your plans for the day?" she asked.

"I'm trying to locate two truckloads of stolen devices and I'm making sure our warehouses and businesses are protected," he said. "Other than that, I'm waiting for orders from Xu and I'm about to make a trip to Kowloon to check on Lop."

"Please give him my regards. I'm sorry I haven't gone to the clinic yet."

"There wasn't any point. The doctor told me he wasn't sufficiently recovered to have visitors until this morning."

"He'll want to know what's going on."

"I'll tell him."

"Knowing Lop, he'll want you to attack Sha Tin."

"Well, that is one of our options," Suen said.

"I'd prefer that you didn't."

"That's a strange thing for you to say."

"Why?" she asked.

"I would have thought that, after what happened to Carlo, you'd have blood in your eye."

"I have Sonny, Andy, and Andy's family to worry about. A negotiated agreement is probably best for them," Ava said. "And Suen, I keep hearing that you shouldn't count on the loyalty of the men who served under Sammy for all those years. I would hate for you to attack Sha Tin and find yourself having to fend off men coming at you from behind your back. Do you have enough manpower to fight on two fronts?"

"Who's saying that about the men in Wanchai?"

"Ko had some reservations, especially after the warehouse robbery, and I asked Sonny to poke around. Sonny confirmed that there are men who would welcome Sammy back in his full capacity. These are men who have no respect for Lop and his Shanghai ways."

"Have you told any of this to Xu?"

"Yes, but only as a suspicion, before Sonny reported back to me. Now I'm beginning to believe that what was a suspicion is a reality."

"I can't fight on two fronts."

"I know."

"And we can't hold Wanchai without local men."

"I can understand how that would be difficult," Ava said.

"But it might be just as difficult to reach an agreement with the Wings that satisfies everyone. Xu can't be seen to be caving in to them, and what they're demanding would mean just that," Suen said. "Maybe they need to be softened up a little."

"Spoken like a true Red Pole."

"Do you have any other suggestions?"

"Actually, I might, but I need more time to think them through. Perhaps by the time I talk to Xu I'll have something specific in mind," she said. "In the meantime, I think keeping your men on the alert and in a holding pattern is probably the best strategy for you."

"I wouldn't do anything more aggressive without clearance from Xu."

"That's good," she said. "Suen, I know the status quo isn't to anyone's liking, but maybe there's a way to tip the balance in our favour without going into full war mode."

"I'll wait to hear from Xu," he said. "Whatever he decides, my men and I are ready."

"I'm sure you are. I'll talk to you later, after things are clearer," she said, ending the conversation.

Ava left the desk, made a coffee, and walked back to the window for what felt like the tenth time that day. She stared at the harbour but was so preoccupied that she took in nothing she looked at. She turned, walked across the room to the door, stopped, turned, and retraced her steps to the window. She stood there briefly, then turned and repeated the walk to the door. For the next twenty minutes she paced back and forth between the window and the door. Her steps were measured but her mind was going a hundred miles an hour as she tried to construct a plan for dealing with the Wings that wouldn't create havoc. She was so focused that when her phone rang, it startled her. She picked it up and rather absent-mindedly said, "*Wei.*"

"Are you okay?" Xu asked.

"I'm as good as can be expected," she said, the sound of his voice bringing her back to the present.

"Fai and Auntie Grace are here at the hospital, but I told them I had to make some phone calls that required privacy, so they've gone downstairs to the cafeteria," he said. "I wasn't sure what we're going to discuss, but I want to be candid and I don't want to alarm them."

"That was the right thing to do. We don't want those two worrying more than is necessary."

"I like this Fai. She is gentler and sweeter than the woman I saw with Tsai."

"She can be herself now."

"And it sounds like Sammy and Carter are being themselves now as well."

"Yes, and they are the furthest thing from gentle or sweet," she said. "They're fucking animals."

"I'm sorry about Carlo and the other men, but I can't do anything about them now," Xu said. "I'm more concerned about you and the phone call Suen just told me you got from Carter. Did he threaten you?"

"He made it clear that when it comes to me, Sonny, and

Andy, he's only giving us a temporary pass. He implied that he's reserving the right to kill any one of us whenever he sees fit," she said. "Then he told me he wants me out of Hong Kong today."

"And if you don't go?"

"He didn't say. I guess he figured he didn't have to, that I'm smart enough to understand the possible consequences."

"Suen told me you're not leaving."

"That's right."

"Is that wise?"

"No one is going to tell me when I can come and go from Hong Kong, or anywhere else."

"Of course not. I was only suggesting that you get out of harm's way until I can resolve these issues with the Wings."

"Do you have a plan for doing that?"

"I'm working on one," said Xu.

"Did Suen also tell you that Sonny thinks your hold on Wanchai is less secure than you might have believed?" she asked. "Or that he was told that some of the Hong Kong Mountain Masters aren't thrilled that a Shanghai gang has taken possession of a local operation?"

"Suen and I discussed Wanchai. It is a concern, but it can't be my primary one right now," he said. "And none of the Mountain Masters have expressed reservations to me about our presence there."

"Maybe the Mountain Masters are reluctant to ruffle your feathers, in case they become your next target. Before you say anything, I know that isn't how you would react, but, according to Sonny, that's what some of them expressed privately," she said. "As for Wanchai, I can understand why it isn't a priority, but I think it should be."

"Let's put the Mountain Masters to one side for a moment. Tell me why you think Wanchai should be a priority."

"Because I think you can take what is a potential problem and turn it to your advantage."

"Ava, you're going to have to explain yourself."

She took a deep breath. "Before I do, let me ask you a couple of basic questions," she said. "What does Wanchai mean to you, and why do you want to hold on to it?"

"It's one of our biggest markets for a wide range of products, and it's now our major distribution centre in Asia for our devices and software."

"Could you maintain it as a market and a distribution centre without having complete control?" she asked. "As I remember, it was one of your biggest markets when Sammy ran things there."

"That's true, but now we've added the distribution capacity."

"But that's just a business like any other. What if someone like Lam were running Wanchai? Could you work out an arrangement with him to operate your distribution system in a territory he controlled?"

"Sure I could, but I trust Lam."

"Then what we need to do is find someone to take over Wanchai whom you can trust equally," she said. "And, while we're at it, to find someone to replace Carter Wing in Sha Tin."

"Ava, slow down for just a second," Xu said.

She waited for him to speak again. When he didn't, after a minute she asked, "Did Fai and Auntie Grace come back into your room?"

"No, I was thinking. I'm not up to speed yet, so it's a slower process," he said. "And what I was thinking about — aside from the obvious complexities of removing Carter from his position in Sha Tin — was how to explain the contradiction in that comment you made about the Mountain Masters. If, as Sonny claims, some of them are unhappy about my control of Wanchai, surely by making a move on Sha Tin we'd only make them more paranoid and unhappy."

"Sonny also told me that Carter has been leaning on neighbouring gangs and cutting into their action. He's the new bully on the block. They might be pleased to see the end of him," she said. "If Carter were eliminated and the Sha Tin gang taken over by someone local who everyone is more comfortable with, I'm sure the Mountain Masters would thank you rather than be pissed off with you."

"Ava, you used the word *eliminate*. What did you mean by that?"

"I have to deal with Carter Wing — and Sammy too, while I'm at it," she said. "I'd like your help, but if I have to go it alone, I will."

Xu became quiet again. Then he said, "Auntie Grace and Fai have come back. Would you like to talk to them?"

"I'd love to."

"You and I need to talk more about your suggestions."

"I'm not going anywhere."

"I'll call you when I can."

## 25

**IT WAS STRANGE TO SWITCH TOPICS SO COMPLETELY,** but after a few minutes on the phone with Auntie Grace and Fai, Ava felt her emotions returning to something resembling normalcy. The two women were going to spend the rest of the morning at the hospital and then explore more of the French Concession. As they spoke about their plans, Ava felt a touch of loneliness. "I wish I could be with you."

"When will you be?" Fai asked for the second time that day.

"I'm aiming for tomorrow night."

"It can't be soon enough."

"For me too," Ava said. "Now I have to go. Enjoy the Concession. I'll talk to you later."

As she ended the call, Ava noticed her battery was low. She took the charger from her bag, plugged the cell into an outlet near the desk, and then sat down. She opened her Moleskine, read the notes she'd made earlier, and then took a pen and underlined the words *find a way to isolate them*. Further down the page she underlined *make their loss acceptable*. To her mind, those two points were the key elements in the plan that was forming.

Isolating the Wings was crucial. She needed the two of them together with as few other men as possible, and she needed them to be in a place that wasn't public, or at least one with limited public access. It would also have to be somewhere they felt comfortable.

Making their loss acceptable wasn't that important to her on a gut level, but she knew it would be a high priority for Xu. The last thing he'd want would be to start a full-scale war with Sha Tin, and maybe parts of Wanchai. And he would be keen to avoid any blowback from fellow Mountain Masters. The biggest challenge she could see to making it work was the timing. Ava wanted to move quickly. Sammy's demand that Xu speak with him directly provided a window of opportunity for what she wanted to do, but she knew Sammy wouldn't wait too long for a response. If her plan was to succeed, Xu would have to act quickly and persuasively.

Would Xu be willing to do what she needed him to do? It was a question that kept entering her head. Part of her couldn't imagine him saying no, but this was a big ask — the biggest since she'd known him. In essence, she was asking him to choose her over the lives of two Mountain Masters, and at the risk of alienating other Mountain Masters. Despite that, she couldn't imagine him not supporting her. But if he didn't? The question wouldn't leave her in peace. "I'll go it alone if I have to," she muttered. "I'll find a way to get it done."

Her cell rang and she saw Sonny's number. "Hi," she said.

"Are we making any progress?" he asked.

"I'm waiting to finish my discussion with Xu. I started it and then we were interrupted."

"How was it going until then?"

"Well enough that I think we should start making some preliminary preparations."

"Like what?"

"Ask Jimmy to make himself available tomorrow."

"I'll do that."

"And can you find two other men you trust completely? Men who won't object to taking part in our project?"

"I can find more than two if we need them."

"Two good men should be sufficient," she said.

"Anything else?"

"Yes. I'd like Andy to go with you to New Town Plaza and show you where Sammy and Carter parked their car last time. Also ask him how many cars accompanied them, and see if he remembers their makes and colours. Then scout the entire area. How many entrances to the parking garage? How is the garage laid out? Can we access it by foot down a ramp or do we have to use an elevator? Which is the quickest way out? Are there security cameras in the garage? Are there security guards nearby?"

"Two black Land Rovers," Sonny said.

"What?"

"Andy told me that Carter and Sammy left the garage in a black Land Rover with a driver and one bodyguard. The other men had their own black Land Rover."

"That's a good start. Now we need the other information."

"We'll go today," Sonny said, and then paused. "Will Suen or Ko be involved?"

"My preference is to use them as spotters and maybe as backup. I'd like for us to be able to handle the dirty work ourselves."

"I feel the same way, and so will Andy."

"Sonny," Ava said carefully, "I'm assuming Xu is going to help us, but if for any reason he can't or won't, are you okay with us doing this on our own?"

"I'm more than okay with that."

"There could be repercussions."

"I don't give a shit."

"How about Andy and the others?" she asked.

"They won't give a shit either."

"Good. So, one way or another, we'll be busy tomorrow."

"I'll call Jimmy and my friends and have them on standby."

Ava thought about asking him to do one more thing but decided he had enough on his plate. "I'll be here at the Mandarin. Call me when you and Andy are finished at the plaza."

"Talk to you then," Sonny said.

Ava looked at her notes; she'd covered everything she had wanted to say to Sonny. Now it was all about waiting for Xu. Was there nothing she could do in the interim? There was, she decided, and phoned Suen.

"Ava," he answered quietly. "I'm with Lop."

"How is he?"

"He wants to get out of bed and head to Sha Tin, but common sense and three bullet holes are holding him back."

"Have you heard from Xu in the past hour?"

"No."

"I have. We talked about a new way of dealing with Carter and Sammy."

"Do you want to tell me?"

"No, I think it will be more appropriate coming from Xu," she said. "But there's something you could ask Lop that might contribute to a resolution."

"What?"

"Ask him if there's a natural leader among the Wanchai triads."

"What do you mean?"

"I mean if Sammy was removed and Xu decided to pull your men out of Hong Kong, is there someone among the current senior people in Wanchai who could function as a competent Mountain Master?"

"That's an odd question."

"I'd still like you to ask him."

"Okay, give me a minute," Suen said.

*I shouldn't have done that. It was up to Xu to ask that question,* she thought. *But it's too late now.* She could hear voices in the background and wondered if she'd upset Lop. A moment later, Suen returned.

"Lop says Fok, the Vanguard, is a solid guy," he said.

"Is he loyal to Sammy?"

"That's the second question I asked, and no, according to Lop, Fok couldn't care less about Sammy. All he cares about is the health of the gang."

"Does he have a mind for business?"

"How would I know?"

"Ask Lop."

"Why don't you ask him yourself," Suen said. "I'll pass my phone to him."

"Ava," Lop whispered a few seconds later.

"My dear Lop. I can't tell you how happy I am that you're going to be with us for many more years to come."

"You're no happier than I am. But why are you asking all these questions?"

"I intend to remove Carter and Sammy Wing from their

positions tomorrow, and I don't want to leave chaos in my wake. If there's someone capable of running Wanchai who's local, it will be beneficial. Would this man Fok be business-like enough to partner with Xu and maintain the market and distribution centre under some kind of negotiated new deal?"

"Remove Carter and Sammy?"

"I don't want to elaborate on that. Let's focus on Fok."

"Ava, remove Carter and Sammy? Are you crazy?"

"That aside, is Fok smart enough to understand that doing a deal with Xu would be completely in his gang's interest?"

Lop muttered something that Ava couldn't hear clearly, then said, "Yes, I think so."

"Thank you," she said. "I'm not sure I'll be able to see you on this trip, but please know that my thoughts are with you."

"Ava, be careful," Lop said.

*There's that word again,* she thought.

## 26

AVA WAITED FOR XU'S CALL. AN HOUR PASSED, AND then another. She was hungry, impatient, and anxious, and none of those conditions would be resolved until she spoke to him. She tried watching television, but she had no attention span. Finally Ava opened her laptop and sent long, chatty emails to May Ling, her mother, and her sister, Marian, who lived in Ottawa. When that was done, she checked flight schedules from Shanghai to Yantai and then from Yantai to Toronto. She knew planning those trips was premature, but she'd fallen into the idea of taking Fai to Toronto after Yantai.

*How will Mummy react to Fai?* she wondered. Thus far Ava hadn't said a word about Fai to her mother, but if Amanda was correct about Marcus Lee knowing, then certainly Jennie knew as well. That she might know and hadn't mentioned it wasn't unusual, given their relationship. Ava's sexuality was a subject they had never discussed directly. It was enough for Ava that Jennie knew and accepted it; the details weren't important. There had been times, though, when there was awkwardness.

Jennie had met Ava's previous girlfriend, Maria Gonzalez, on many occasions. She had always been kind to her, although their conversation was limited to generalities. But one summer Ava had rented a cottage for an extended period. Jennie had stayed with her and Maria travelled north for the weekends. Whenever Maria moved in, Jennie had moved out. When Ava told her mother that wasn't necessary, Jennie had said, "I think you girls would be more comfortable doing your own thing if I wasn't around." Ava knew her mother was probably more concerned about her own comfort, but she had to smile at the phrase "doing your own thing." She wondered if her mother had any idea what that "own thing" could be.

The thought of going to Toronto with Fai made Ava a little nervous. That was strange, because Ava had never felt anxious about introducing other women to her mother and friends. Maybe that highlighted just how special Fai had become to her. She had no doubt that her mother would adore Fai; her real concern was that Jennie would go overboard because of her love of movies. When Ava was a child, every few months Jennie would bundle Marian and her into the car and make the forty-minute drive south from their home in Richmond Hill to the old Chinatown in downtown Toronto. Their destination was a dingy movie house in a mall at the corner of Dundas and Spadina that showed the latest Chinese films. Ava swore that her mother had seen every film starring Gong Li and Chow Yun Fat at least five times, and she wondered where Fai fit into her mother's pantheon of Chinese film stars. *I should ask her,* she thought, and started a new email.

Mummy, I forgot to tell you that I've developed a very close friendship with Pang Fai. I know I told you she's the face of the PÖ fashion line, but she has become more than that to me. I'm thinking about inviting her to join me in Toronto for a holiday, and I'd like you to meet her. Are you okay with that? Love, Ava.

She stared at the message, debating whether she should actually send it. *What the hell,* she thought, and hit the Send button.

Her phone rang, tearing her away from any thoughts about her mother. She looked at the screen and saw Xu's number. It had been nearly three hours since she'd last talked to him.

"Hey," she said.

"I'm sorry it took so long for me to get back to you," Xu said. "I've been involved in some quite complicated discussions."

"I understand why that might be the case."

"It seems that you were as well," Xu said. "Suen tells me you've confused Lop no end."

"I apologize," Ava said quickly. "I realize I had no business asking him those questions about Wanchai. I was out of line."

"It's okay. The questions were going to be asked in any event, and you prepared him to have answers for me."

"Still, I should have waited for you or Suen to raise the subject with him."

"We don't have to talk about that anymore," Xu said. "What we do have to talk about is when, where, and how you think you can take out Carter and Sammy Wing."

*He's backing me,* she thought, almost embarrassed that she had doubted for even a second that he would. "The when is tomorrow. The where is New Town Plaza in Sha Tin. And the how is with Sonny, Andy, and three other men who have no connection with Shanghai," she said.

"How can I help?"

"I don't want this to backfire on you."

"Ava, I've spent the last few hours talking to Lam and the Mountain Masters in Tai Po, Fanling, and Kowloon. None of them will be unhappy to see the last of Carter Wing."

"They actually said that?"

"Not in those exact words, but their sentiment was clear, especially when I told them I'm thinking about pulling my men out of Wanchai and returning control to local triads," Xu said. "Lam has been acting as a middleman in all of this. He has tremendous credibility with the Hong Kong Mountain Masters."

"I'm going to owe him more favours than I can ever repay."

"He'll find a way that you can, but in the meantime we seem to have found a way out of this mess."

"And you're really prepared to pull out of Wanchai?"

"That depends on how the meeting goes between Lop, Suen, and Fok," Xu said. "They're going to make Fok a proposition. We'll see if he accepts, though he'd be stupid not to. We're prepared to turn control of Wanchai over to him during the next three months. What we want in return is his commitment to keep buying from us and his agreement that we continue to manage the distribution centre on his turf."

"And if he agrees?"

"Then we'll let Lam and the others know we'll be vacating Wanchai."

"What do you get in return, aside from maintaining a business relationship?"

"The Mountain Masters will turn a blind eye to whatever happens to Sammy and Carter Wing. And Chan — he runs Tai Po — will reach out to his friend Sung, the deputy

Mountain Master in Sha Tin, and urge him to make peace," Xu said. "Chan is confident that Sung will take his advice, because evidently he's not a warrior and he's been uncomfortable with the way Carter has been operating."

"What about the stolen inventory?"

"Chan expects he can convince Sung to return it as a goodwill gesture."

"Xu, what if Fok or Sung don't go along with these arrangements?"

"I guess Carter and Sammy Wing will be dead and I'll have a whole new set of problems to deal with."

"You don't sound like that would bother you," Ava said.

"I'm optimistic that we've laid the groundwork for an agreement, and I don't expect Fok or Sung to be difficult," he said. "We're being fair, and besides, Suen and a hundred or more of our men are still in Hong Kong, ready to fight."

"When will Fok be meeting with Lop and Suen?"

"Tonight."

"Do we have to wait that long?"

"Wait to do what?"

"For you to call Sammy. I know you might not want to until you have a finalized agreement, but I feel pressed for time. So I'd appreciate it very much if you would talk to him as soon as you can."

"And what is it specifically that you want me to discuss with him?"

"He said he wants to make you an offer. Could you tell him you're flying to Hong Kong tomorrow morning and will be pleased to meet with him and Carter to discuss it in person?"

"Is that how you want to set them up?"

"We want to isolate them, and the prospect of a meeting with you is the only enticement we have. So, yes, that's the plan, unless you can come up with something better."

"If Sammy agrees to a meeting, he'll want it to be in a place of his choosing, and probably quite public."

"That's what I'm hoping for," Ava said. "When we met him and Carter, it was in Maxim's Palace restaurant, on the eighth floor of New Town Plaza. The restaurant, which is very large and public, was their choice."

"You aren't concerned about civilians getting caught up in this?"

"I have no intention of it getting that far. When they arrived for the last meeting, they parked their cars in the parking garage at the mall. We'll ambush them there."

"How do you know about their cars?"

"Andy and Carlo trailed them after the meeting. They saw them get into two black Land Rovers. Carter, Sammy, and two bodyguards were together in one and two bodyguards were in the second."

"How will you know where they're going to park?"

"That's where I might need some help from Ko and his men," she said. "I have Sonny and Andy scouting the parking garage now. We'll need to post men at all the entrances and on various levels to spot the Land Rovers when they arrive."

"What if they come in something other than black Land Rovers?"

"Then we have a problem. But why would they switch vehicles?"

"I don't know, and that's leaping ahead in any case. The first priority is for me to get them to agree to a meeting."

"Sammy sounded anxious to talk to you," Ava said. "I can't imagine they'll say no."

"And you think they'll agree to meet at Maxim's in New Town Plaza?"

"If it was good enough for them yesterday, why not tomorrow?"

"That's a point I will make if there are any objections," he said. "Do you have any preference when it comes to time?"

"We met in the late morning last time. The plaza wasn't too crowded then and there was lots of parking available."

"I'll tell Sammy I'll be there around eleven."

"Depending on what Sonny and Andy find out at the plaza, we'll need Ko's men there earlier."

"You can work that out with Ko and Suen. I'll tell them to give you as many men as you need, and any other assistance you want," Xu said, and then paused. "But Ava, I have to say I wish you'd let them carry out the entire plan. There's no reason for you to put yourself in danger. Our men can handle the Wings."

"Sammy Wing has tried to kill me twice, Xu, and I'm convinced he'd try again if given the chance," she said. "And Carter mutilated and killed my friend Carlo, plus three other men whose only crime was helping us find the hostages. When he told me to leave Hong Kong, the implication was that he'd kill me if I came back. I'm not giving him that chance."

"I don't disagree that Hong Kong would be a better place without Sammy and Carter, but why do you have to get rid of them personally?"

"Carlo was my man, and his loyalty to me was what led to his death. I owe him. That obligation doesn't belong to

Suen or Ko; it rests with me," she said. "Besides, Uncle often told me that I should never ask someone to do something I'm not prepared to do myself. And Xu, I've been down this road before, with Sonny and Andy by my side. We made it work then and we'll make it work now."

"I wish I could persuade you not to do this," Xu said. "But since it seems I can't, all I can do is promise you all the support it's possible for me to provide."

## 27

**WITH XU ONSIDE, AVA HAD NOTHING TO DO UNTIL SHE** heard from Sonny, and that gave free rein to an appetite that was already screaming to be fed. She thought about Man Wah and then realized it was late in the afternoon, past the time when they served dim sum. She groaned as the fleeting anticipation of Man Wah's har gow disappeared. *There has to be a good dim sum restaurant nearby,* she thought, and went to the laptop to search. A minute later she found Ding Dim 1968, which was on nearby Wyndham Street, no more than a fifteen-minute walk from the hotel.

Ava went to the window to check the weather. The sky had darkened and it looked like it might rain. She decided she'd better wear her Adidas jacket, and went to the bedroom to retrieve it. When she took it from her bag, she had another reason to groan. She had forgotten that the front of the jacket had been slashed by a knife during the altercation in Beijing. She returned to her laptop. There was an Adidas store on Queen's Road West in Central, only a few minutes' walk from the restaurant.

Ava left the hotel in her Adidas jacket, training pants, and runners. The air was damp and heavy, but the rain had held off. She headed for the Adidas store first. It had been a while since she'd made her last purchases, which were usually basic traditional running gear. The Central store carried far more than basic lines, and Ava found herself admiring a soft grey wool knit jacket. It fit like a glove and seemed warm enough for both autumn and spring days in Canada. She was carrying it to the cash register when she passed a display of stylish hoodies. She picked one up and examined it. Aside from the hood, which could prove useful the next day, the garment had zipped side pockets large enough for her gun. She chose one in black.

A few minutes later Ava left the store wearing the new jacket and carrying a bag containing her old one and the hoodie. It started to rain lightly, and she hurried to reach Ding Dim before it got worse. As she stepped inside the restaurant there was a clap of thunder and the sky opened.

The restaurant was busy but Ava got a table near the door and settled in. A server brought her a pot of tea and a menu. As he filled her cup, she started to fill out the dim sum slip. "Don't leave. I'm almost finished," she said as she ticked off chicken feet in black bean sauce to go along with stuffed chili peppers, siu mai, and har gow.

Ava was placing her cell on the table when, almost on cue, a call came in. "Sonny, where are you?" she asked.

"Sitting in my car with Andy outside the entrance to the parking garage."

"What did you find?"

"Ava, I'm sorry, but I think you're going to have to forget trying anything inside the garage."

She was taken aback. Sonny wasn't typically so abrupt or negative. "Is it that problematic?" she asked.

"There are closed-circuit cameras everywhere. I doubt there's a square metre that's not being monitored. On top of that, there's a security office on the main level and security guards patrolling the area in golf carts," he said. "They would have eyes on us from the moment we arrived. I doubt we'd even have a chance to set up before they'd be heading our way."

"Did you go to the spot where Andy saw their cars?"

"We did, and like I said, there a lot of cameras and security guards."

"Is there anything we can do about the cameras?"

"There are too many of them, and anyway, the guards would be all over you the instant you started messing with the cameras," he said. "But Ava, it isn't all bad news. Andy and I are in agreement about not going after Carter and Sammy in the garage, but we think the outside has possibilities."

"How so?"

"There's only one entrance from the street. If they want to park at the mall it's the only way in. We've been watching it for the past fifteen minutes. Even if there isn't another car in front of you, you can't enter it at any speed. At the very least you have to slow down to a crawl, because not far down the ramp is the ticket dispenser and a raised-arm gate. The cars have to wait for the gate to go up, so we could go after them there. There is a CCTV problem again, but we haven't seen any guards."

"Could we get to them outside the entrance, before they start down the ramp?"

"We've been talking about that, and we think it is possible. We would need to use our own cars and have lookouts,"

Sonny said. "They have to approach the garage from Sha Tin Centre Street. It's one-way, and from where they would turn onto it to the entrance is about half a kilometre."

"So we could see them coming?"

"Yeah, and with enough notice we could put one of our cars in front of them and lead them to the entrance."

"And stop there?"

"We'd have to go partway down the ramp before we stopped, so they'd be blocked."

"Couldn't they back up?"

"We could have a second car follow them and stop behind," Sonny said. "Our men and you would be in the cars."

"And the CCTV cameras?"

"I could see at least two of them. Jimmy could shoot them out."

"The other option is simply to wear masks, like the balaclavas we had in Macau. We could put them on at the last minute so we wouldn't attract any attention beforehand," said Ava.

"I still have mine."

"Do you know where you can buy more?"

"I'll find out who sells them and pick some up tonight."

"What about our licence plates?"

"We'd get fake ones," Sonny said. "I also wouldn't use my own car."

Ava's mind turned over as she tried to find a weakness in the plan. "What if the cars are bulletproof?" she blurted.

"That was one of the first questions I raised when Andy and I began discussing this idea, so he made some phone calls. There are three Land Rover dealers in Hong Kong. The closest to Sha Tin is in Aberdeen. Andy told them he thought his friend Carter Wing had purchased several cars from them. When they confirmed that Carter had actually bought four, Andy said he really liked the cars and asked if all their features were standard. They confirmed that they were standard factory models, so no bulletproofing, unless it was added later."

"That was very clever of Andy."

"I've never known him to want anything as badly as he wants to put a bullet into Carter Wing's head. He's doing everything he can to make sure he gets the chance."

"Sonny, do you think this will work?"

"Will Ko and Suen help?"

"What do you need from them?"

"Two unmarked cars, fake plates, and lookouts."

"They've been told to give us all the help we need. Why don't you call Ko directly and tell him what you want. I'm sure he can supply it all. If there's an issue with him, let me know and I'll talk to Xu."

"If they've been told to help, they will," he said.

"I agree. Given that, how certain are you that this plan will work?"

"It will work."

"Well, then, it sounds like we're still on for tomorrow morning."

"Andy will be pleased."

The server brought the chili peppers to Ava's table. It was the fourth dish to arrive, but Ava had been so engrossed in her conversation with Sonny that she hadn't noticed. "Look, I'm about to have something to eat. I'll head directly back to the hotel when I'm finished. Call me there after you finalize things with Ko."

She ate slowly, not letting her appetite get ahead of her enjoyment. As she did, she thought of Uncle. One of his quirks was his propensity to bolt down food. It had surprised Ava at first, because she had never met anyone who was so calm and collected on the outside; the way he ate indicated that perhaps there was something raging on the inside. When he was ill with cancer, he had begun to reminisce about his early life, and that finally provided a clue as to why he ate so quickly. Ava already knew that as a young man Uncle had swum from China to Hong Kong to escape the Communist regime. What she didn't know was that his entire family had died of starvation, brought on by Mao Zedong's Great Leap Forward — an economic policy that resulted in a widespread famine that killed millions in China. "When you have gone without food and you have watched people die slowly from starvation, you never take it for granted again. I still have irrational fears that my food will be taken from me," Uncle had said.

It was dark outside by the time Ava left Ding Dim. Thankfully the rain had stopped, and she took her time walking back to the hotel, oblivious to her surroundings as her mind focused on the intricacies of what might transpire at New Town Plaza the following morning. A few hundred metres from Connaught Road, Ava was brought back to the present when her phone rang.

"Is this a good time to talk?" Xu asked.

"I'm walking back to my hotel, but it's fine."

"I just finished talking to Sammy Wing. What a chore that was."

"Did he agree to meet tomorrow morning?"

"He did, but it took some persuasion."

"Why?"

"He didn't see any need. He said he has a proposal he's prepared to discuss over the phone. I told him that after what's gone down in the past few days, I thought it was more appropriate to meet face-to-face. He kept saying that wasn't necessary, and we went back and forth for several minutes before I said I had to insist on a proper resolution," Xu said. "He began to bend at that point. Then I added that, in line with a proper resolution, I wanted Lam to attend the meeting as an observer. He asked me why, and I told him I didn't want there to be any disagreement in the future about what we had discussed."

"He bought that idea?"

"He said he had no objection to Lam attending, as long as Carter was included as well. I told him that was fine, and then asked him where he thought we should meet," Xu said. "When he said he didn't know, I asked him where he met with you. He said Maxim's Palace in New Town Plaza. I told him that would work for me, and he went along with it. So there we are."

"The meeting is scheduled for tomorrow?"

"Yes, at eleven, exactly as you wanted."

"But what about Lam? They might call to confirm he's going to be there."

"Lam will back us up."

"Thank you."

"Save your thanks until everything is concluded and you are safe."

"In that case I'll thank you in person, when I get back to Shanghai tomorrow night," Ava said, and ended the call. She called Sonny as she walked into the hotel lobby.

"*Wei*," he said.

"I just spoke to Xu. We're on for tomorrow at eleven at Maxim's. How are you doing with Ko?"

"He's doing everything we asked. He'll have three cars for us. Andy will pick up one of them tonight. He's also bought the balaclavas. We agreed to meet in the morning at the Sha Tin parking lot we used the other night, when we went to the garage. Ko is bringing the other cars there to meet up with us."

"Ko is coming himself?"

"He made that clear, and it wasn't for me to tell him no."

"I understand."

"He also said he's bringing four men with him and bulletproof vests for all of us."

"I'm pleased about the vests, but I'm not sure we need that many lookouts."

"Truthfully, I don't think it can hurt."

"Okay. What time did you tell them to be at the parking lot?"

"I was waiting until I spoke to you," Sonny said.

"What time does the plaza open for business?"

"Ten, but I'm sure staff and some customers start arriving before that."

"We need to get there early to make sure we're positioned properly. I want to get a feel for the place, and we shouldn't take it for granted that the Wings won't show up well before eleven. We have one chance to do this right, so let's get everyone there by eight."

"I'll let them know."

"Will you pick me up?"

"I'll be at your hotel by seven."

"See you then."

"Ava..." Sonny began hesitantly.

"Yes?"

"You're doing the right thing. You can't spend the rest of your life looking over your shoulder, wondering if this is the day the Wings come after you."

"And then there's the matter of Carlo."

"Yeah, but Carlo is gone and you're still here. You're the one I worry about."

Ava heard the emotion in his voice and felt a surge of her own. "I'll see you in the morning, Sonny," she said.

## 28

AVA WENT DIRECTLY TO HER HOTEL ROOM. IT HAD BEEN
a long, drawn-out day, and the evening promised more of
the same, she thought as she closed the door behind her.
Normally the prospect of what they had planned for the
next morning would have her completely energized, but
this time it left her feeling cold. Maybe that was because it
had been a while since she'd undertaken a job like this. Or
maybe it was because the job's purpose was so completely
different from anything she'd done in the past. This wasn't
Ava throwing her body and mind into saving clients, their
money, and sometimes their lives; this time the objective
was to kill two men.

*Why did the Wings force this confrontation? Why did
they leave me with no other options?* Her motivation, she
told herself, was to preserve her life, and those of Andy and
Sonny. But even that fact didn't bring any sense of rightness;
it was just something that had to be done. As Uncle had said,
it was something that would be irresponsible not to do. But
could she do it? That question hung around on the edges
of her thought process. She had done it once before, when

she deliberately put a bullet into Lok's head and brought closure to their Macau raid. But she had hesitated under similar circumstances in Surabaya, when common sense had demanded that she kill a Scottish banker. He had died, but from a heart attack, and she often wondered what she would have done if serendipity hadn't intervened. *Shit, why am I doing this to myself?* she thought. *There are no other options. Think about something else.*

Ava brushed her teeth, checked the bandage on her arm, and walked back to the bedroom. There she put on a clean T-shirt and then returned to the living area, sitting down in front of the computer. She needed a distraction, so she opened her email, hoping to find one. She wasn't disappointed.

There had been a late-day flurry of business activity and she'd been copied on a series of emails between May Ling, Amanda, and Chi-Tze, a young woman who worked for them in Shanghai and represented their interests at PÖ.

Chi-Tze wrote that Clark Po wanted to move beyond their basic clothing line. He had started to design bags and shoes and was anxious to put them into production. It would involve a major investment up front without any guarantee there would be a market for the finished goods. Chi-Tze supported Clark. May Ling was more skeptical and wanted some assurance that the bags and shoes would be marketable. She was also concerned that if they weren't well received, they might downgrade the strong image they'd built for PÖ clothing. Amanda hadn't taken sides, other than to acknowledge that shoe and bag lines could be enormously profitable, and in her last email she suggested a compromise. She proposed that they finance a small sample run and then organize meetings with major customers in Europe and North America to gauge their reactions. Ava sent a message supporting Amanda's position and then rather idly wondered if there would be room on the marketing team for her and Fai.

Two other emails caught her eye. One was from Chen, confirming that Lau Lau had agreed to go into rehab and would be heading to a clinic in Singapore the following week. She thanked Chen for his efforts and asked him to give Lau Lau her best wishes. The other was from her mother, in response to the one she'd sent about Pang Fai. It read: For some reason I thought there was more to your relationship with her than just business. I hope it is making you happy. As for me, I would be thrilled to meet her if she comes to Toronto with you. Would it be too much if I organized a party while she was here?

*A party? She's starstruck,* Ava thought. She replied: I'm pleased you're okay with Fai and me. She's a wonderful, warm person, but a party might be a bit much. If you want to invite a few of your friends to dim sum or dinner, that's okay. No more than that though.

Ava sat back in the chair and thought again about how well things were going in most parts of her life. The Wings aside, she had so much to be thankful for. And if all went well, by tomorrow the Wings would be only a memory. *Could be only a memory,* she corrected. *Don't jinx yourself. Take nothing for granted.*

She checked the time. With Sonny coming to get her at seven, she calculated when she needed to wake up. A bak mei workout could take up to an hour, but it would get her adrenalin flowing and her body into gear. Then she had to shower, dress, down some coffee, and take some time to get her head in the right place. She decided she'd better get up at five, so she set the alarm on her smartphone and called the hotel operator to ask for a wakeup call.

She went to the mini-bar and poured herself a double cognac. She set the drink on the bedside table and then climbed into bed with her phone. She hit Fai's number.

"Hi, baby," Fai answered. "What are you doing?"

"I'm in bed. I have a meeting tomorrow and it will be an early start."

"We just got back from the hospital. Auntie Grace is finally starting to relax. She says Xu is starting to look and sound like his old self."

"That's such a relief."

"Now all we need to make things perfect is to have you back in Shanghai."

"If the meeting goes as planned — and I'm hopeful it will — I'll be there tomorrow night. One way or another, I should know by noon."

"When do you think we can leave for Yantai?" Fai asked.

"We should stay in Shanghai until Xu is home and has really settled in. So that should be, what, five or six days from now?"

"My mother is really excited. I haven't been home very often in recent years."

"Does she know I'm coming with you?" Ava asked.

"She does."

"How did she react?"

"She was surprised, then curious, and then worried when I mentioned that we'd be staying at the house — it isn't very big. I told her not to worry, that we'd be sharing a room, and if that made her or my father uncomfortable, we'd stay in a hotel."

"She didn't find that odd?"

"If she did, she didn't say anything," Fai said. "Besides, I thought it was best to drop a little hint about us ahead of time. They'll have time to talk things over before we get there."

"I told my mother about us today," Ava said.

"What did she say?"

"She wants to throw a party in your honour when we go to Toronto," Ava said.

"You mean in *our* honour."

"No, you're the star. I'm just the daughter," Ava said, laughing.

"I don't believe that."

"I'm not saying she doesn't love me, but she can be a bit of a snob, and she and her friends do get competitive when it comes to their husbands and children. My mother is at a clear disadvantage when it comes to the husband. My sister did graduate from law school, but she's a stay-at-home mom, so there's no credit given there. And until recently she couldn't explain what I did for a living. So my having you as a 'friend' is quite a coup for her, and she wants to take maximum advantage of it. But truthfully, I also know she's a big Pang Fai fan, and I'm sure most of her friends are as well. So, with or without me, just meeting you would be special for them."

"Ava, as pleased as I'd be to boost your mother's image with her friends, you know I'm not a person for parties."

"Don't worry, I already told her there won't be a party but you might meet some of the friends."

"I'm okay with that if you are."

"We'll deal with Toronto when we have to," Ava said. "For now, all I want is to get this meeting out of the way, get back to Shanghai, and then go with you to Yantai."

"I'm assuming this meeting is about the problem with Sammy Wing that took you to Hong Kong in the first place."

"It is."

"You haven't said much about it since you got there."

"There hasn't been much to say," Ava said. "Anyway, my expectation is that after tomorrow morning the problem will have disappeared entirely and we'll have no reason to discuss it ever again."

"If you say so," Fai said, sounding slightly doubtful.

Ava took a sip of cognac and said, "Listen, I do have a very early start tomorrow and I should get as much sleep as possible, so I'm going to call it a night. I'll phone you as soon as the meeting is over."

"I hope it goes well."

"I'm sure it will."

"Then sleep tight," Fai said.

Ava put down the phone. *At least she didn't tell me to be careful,* she thought.

## 29

AT FIVE MINUTES TO SEVEN AVA WALKED THROUGH THE lobby of the Mandarin Oriental towards the hotel entrance. She had slept fitfully and awoken at five, done an hour of bak mei, showered, and drunk three coffees while she mentally prepared herself for the day. Then she very deliberately lowered herself to her knees at the side of the bed and prayed for the second time in less than a week to Saint Jude. She did not mention the Wings in her prayer; instead she invoked the names of Sonny, Andy, Jimmy, and Ko and mentioned the unnamed other men who would be standing with them. She asked only that no harm come to any of them and that they all safely return to their families and friends.

When the prayer was over, Ava finished dressing. She already had on training pants, a black T-shirt, and running shoes. Now she slipped the new black hoodie over her head and walked to the room safe. She took out the Beretta and unscrewed the silencer and put it back in the safe. The gun fit snugly into one of the hoodie's zippered side pockets. Her phone and room access card went into the other pocket. She took one last look at the room as if trying to memorize it.

Sonny stood just inside the hotel entrance waiting for her. He wore black jeans and a black T-shirt that strained across his massive chest and shoulders; a plain black cap was jammed onto his head.

"Morning, boss," he said. "I like the hoodie."

"I like your cap."

"I thought it might make me harder to recognize until I put on the balaclava."

Ava followed him from the hotel towards the Mercedes. As they neared it he said, "I've already heard from Ko this morning. He's really up for this."

"It's our thing, not his."

"Then you'd better talk to him, because he thinks he's a big part of it."

"I will," Ava said, and then saw Jimmy waving at her from the front passenger seat. He wore a black windbreaker. "Did he bring his rifle?" she asked.

"It's in the trunk if he needs it, but he has a semi-automatic with him as well. He's a good man with any type of gun."

"Good morning, Jimmy," she said as she slid into the back seat.

"Morning, boss. I didn't expect to see you again quite so soon."

"Me neither."

"I can't complain, though. It gets me out of the house."

"You do know what we're planning on doing this morning?" she asked, surprised by his casual tone.

"Sonny explained it. That's why I brought the semi-automatic. The rifle doesn't work as well at close range."

Ava nodded and then asked Sonny, "Where's Andy?"

"He'll meet us at the parking lot with Machi and Wai, the

two other men I recruited. Ko, Feng, and their four men will meet us there as well."

Ava shook her head. "Feng is coming? Ko keeps adding men. Let's get going — I do need to talk to him."

Sonny drove east towards Causeway Bay into a sun that had barely cleared the horizon. Ava blinked as she looked into it, her mind starting to lock on to what lay ahead. *Our plan is solid enough,* she thought, *but there are always glitches and it's hard to anticipate all of them.* It was good that they were getting there early; it would give them time to review things in detail, try to identify what could go wrong, and how to react if it did.

"Sonny, last night you said it took about two minutes to drive from the parking garage entrance back to Tsing Sha Highway," she said.

"That's right."

"Were you speeding? Were there traffic lights along the route?"

"We didn't speed and there weren't any lights."

"Good. That's one less thing to worry about," she said as the car entered the Cross-Harbour Tunnel.

Sonny took what was becoming a familiar route to Sha Tin. Traffic was light, and it had just turned seven-thirty when signs began to appear along the Tsing Sha Highway for New Town Plaza.

"Is this the route the Land Rovers will take?" she asked.

"The only access to the plaza by car is Sha Tin Centre Street, and the only way to get to that street from any direction is this highway."

"Turn onto the street when we get there. Then take me past the plaza and stop at the parking ramp," she said. "I'd like to see it for myself."

A moment later Sonny turned left at Sha Tin Centre Street, drove down it slowly, and came to a halt at the parking garage entrance. Ava saw that it was exactly as Sonny had described: a single downward ramp leading into the parking garage and a single lane coming out.

"We can go now," she said.

The car drove past the plaza, rounded the corner, and headed back towards the highway along the other side of the complex.

"Do you want to do that again?" Sonny asked.

"No. Let's go meet Andy and Ko."

Five minutes later Sonny turned the Mercedes into the public parking lot they'd been in two days before and drove to the far end. As they approached a fence, she saw Andy, wearing a bulky black sweater and blue jeans, standing in front of a red Toyota HiAce van. Sonny parked the Mercedes several spots away. As Ava got out of the back seat, she saw Andy walking towards them.

"How is your arm?" she asked.

"I've got it wrapped tightly and I'm on painkillers. I'll be able to use it."

"Excellent," she said. "Did you get the balaclavas?"

"I've got a dozen of them in the back seat."

"With all the men Ko is bringing, we may need that many."

"I thought we were doing this without them," Andy said.

"They're here as lookouts and to help with the getaway, but having a few extra guns might not be a bad thing. I'll sort it out with Ko when he gets here."

"Speak of the devil . . ." Andy said and pointed to the parking lot entrance.

Ava turned and saw Feng behind the wheel of a black BMW

with Ko sitting next to him. A white BMW, a black Honda Freed, a red Nissan Serena, and a grey panel van were in a line behind Feng. The cars entered the lot and drove towards them.

As the cars emptied out, Ava counted six men, so at least Ko hadn't added more since his last conversation with Sonny. Still, there were more vehicles than she'd imagined.

"Good morning," Ko said, his voice animated.

"Thanks for coming," Ava said.

"This is something I didn't want to miss," he said.

Ava nodded in the direction of the cars. "I thought we were going to use three vehicles. How many do you have in mind?"

"The BMWs are ours; they'll stay here until we're done. The other three we'll use for the job, along with Andy's Toyota, so we'll have four in total. Sonny explained the plan to me last night. While I think it will work just fine, I began to worry about what we'd do if more than one of our cars was disabled. I thought having a van would be useful backup."

"And the cars are all untraceable?"

"We stole them all last night, including the van."

"That's good," Ava said, but then she leaned closer to Ko. "I want to speak to you alone. Let's move away from the others."

She waited until they were out of earshot before she spoke, and even then she lowered her voice. "Ko, I really appreciate everything you've done for us, but this is our show. And by that I mean Sonny, Andy, and I have scores to settle. I don't want you or your men getting in the way of that."

"We're here to help, that's all."

"Making decisions for us isn't helping; it's taking over. Bringing the van was probably the right decision, but you should have cleared it with Sonny or me first."

Ko looked uncomfortable. "I'm sorry, you're right. It is just that the boss — Xu — talked to me last night and again this morning. He made it clear that he wants nothing to happen to you. He's made me, in his words, responsible for your safety."

"Given what we're trying to accomplish, I think that's a completely unreasonable request. I don't expect you to be responsible for anyone but yourself and your men."

"Maybe it is unreasonable, but I'm not about to say that to the boss, and he's still going to hold me accountable," Ko said. "Can we work out a compromise?"

"What do you have in mind?"

"I know that you, Sonny, and the others want to take out Sammy and Carter personally. I'll make sure none of my men get in the way of that. What we will do is provide close cover. If any of Carter's gang so much as looks at you the wrong way, we'll take care of them."

"What do you mean by 'close cover'?"

"Well, how do you intend to deploy your men?"

"I thought that Sonny, Andy, Jimmy, and I would ride in the first car — the one that blocks their path into the parkade. My expectation is that Carter and Sammy will be in the first Land Rover with at least two bodyguards, and the rest of their security team will be in the second. I don't want to have to walk past two cars to get to them. If we're in the first car they'll be directly behind us."

"I think you're probably correct that Sammy and Carter will ride in the first car, which makes it crucial that we cover their second car."

"We'll have our two men, Machi and Wai, in a car right behind it."

"As good as those two men might be, they could be out-numbered," Ko said. "With your permission, I'd like Feng and me to ride in the car with them."

Ava hesitated, looked at Ko, and saw nothing but sincerity. "Okay, we'll do it your way."

"Thank you."

"Now let's go talk to the other men and get organized. I still want to drive the route a few more times and really understand what we're going to be contending with on the parking ramp."

Ava and Ko returned to the other men and called them together. "This is how we're going to manage this," she said. "First, we'll need a lookout parked as close to the Tsing Sha Highway exit as possible. Ko, who do you suggest?"

"I think the van should be there, with Harry and Max. They can text me and Sonny the second they see the Rovers."

"Good. We'll park the other three cars as far apart from each other as we can manage on Sha Tin Centre Street. We can't afford to look conspicuous. My car will be closest to the parking garage, with Ko's next in line and the two backup cars farther back. When the targets turn off the highway and onto the street, we'll have to ease on to Sha Tin Centre Street. It's crucial that there be nothing between my car and the first Land Rover and nothing between Ko and the second. We need to sandwich them."

"If there are other vehicles on the road that could be a problem," Ko said.

"I know, that's why I'm stressing it. Because other vehicles or not, we can't let them get between us and the Land Rovers. It will be up to our drivers to make sure that doesn't happen."

"What about the backup car and van?" Feng asked.

"They should stay out of the action but be close enough to pick us up quickly if one of our cars gets put out of commission," Ava said. "After it identifies the Land Rovers, the van should move into position close to the other backup car."

"Who's riding in each car?" Andy asked.

"You, me, Jimmy, and Sonny are in the first car. Ko, Feng, Wai, and Machi are in the second. That leaves two men in the van and two in the backup car," Ava said.

"You aren't afraid they'll recognize one of us in our car? Those Land Rovers ride high," Andy said.

Ava turned to Jimmy. "Do any of Wing's men know you?"

"I don't think so."

"Can you drive?"

"Of course."

"Then you drive the lead car," she said. "Andy, did you wear gloves when you were driving it?"

"I did. There will be no fingerprints."

"Then give your gloves to Jimmy," she said. "As for the rest of us, we'll have to stay as completely out of sight as we can. We'll have to duck down or lie on the floor or back seat. We brought balaclavas to wear, and I believe Ko brought bulletproof vests, but you shouldn't put them on until the very last minute. It's one thing for the CCTV cameras to see you wearing them but another for Wing's men when they follow us or drive past."

"What if they have more than two cars?" The question came from Feng.

Ava shot him a glance. "It will be the same drill. As long as we have them blocked in front and behind, they aren't going anywhere. It might mean they have more men, but if they do, we'll just have to deal with them," Ava said.

"My experience with Sammy is that he's a creature of habit, and I only hope Carter has inherited that family trait. I expect to see the two of them with a total of four bodyguards in two black Land Rovers."

"Do you expect that Carter and Sammy will be armed?" Ko asked.

"I've never known Sammy to carry a gun. I don't know about Carter," Ava said. "We should assume the bodyguards will be armed to the teeth."

"The instant they see us, they'll start firing," Sonny said.

"That's why we have to fire first. We can't wait to find out how they're going to react," Ava said. "I'm afraid this is a take-no-prisoners exercise."

"Better to be safe than sorry," Ko said.

Ava looked at the men. None of them seemed uncomfortable with the prospect of a gunfight. "Any more questions?" she asked. When no one answered, she continued. "We need to stay connected by phone. If any questions come up, don't hesitate to ask. We also don't want any surprises, so if you see anything odd, let us know right away."

"I want my men to route their communications through me and Feng. We'll contact Ava or Sonny if the need arises. Remember, better safe than sorry," Ko said. "And speaking of safety, I'll ask Feng to hand out the vests now."

"When you have the vests, Andy will distribute the balaclavas and we can move to our positions," Ava said.

## 30

**WHEN THEY REACHED NEW TOWN PLAZA, AVA ASKED** Andy to drive the Toyota past the garage entrance and around the plaza several times before finally telling him to park it roughly a hundred metres from the entrance. Ko's car, which had been following her, drove past and, when it next appeared, stopped a hundred metres behind them. She looked out the rear window and saw that the backup car was another fifty metres behind Ko. The van was stationed at the very top of the street. She phoned Ko. "It's looking good, but contact the men in the van and ask them about their sightlines."

He called back a few minutes later. "They can see well in both directions. One of them will fix on the eastbound exit and the other on the westbound."

Ava was sitting in the back seat with Sonny, the gym bag containing his Cobray at his feet. Jimmy and Andy had their guns on the seats next to them. "We're set," she said to Sonny.

"We haven't talked yet about how we're going to handle the first Land Rover," he said.

"I have been thinking about it," she said. "Am I wrong to

assume that Carter and Sammy will be sitting in the back seat?"

"I'll be surprised if they aren't."

"Which means there'll be a driver and a bodyguard in the front."

"Also most likely."

"Then the men in the front are our first targets. If we're out of this car fast enough, we should be able to hit them before they have time to react," she said. "But we don't all need to be part of that first assault. In fact, if four of us try to get out of this car at the same time, we'll probably get in each other's way. What I suggest is that Andy bail out on the left-hand side and you on the right, so you have them in crossfire. After the first round of shots you should start moving towards the Land Rover, and then Jimmy and I can follow."

"I like that," Sonny said.

"Andy, are you okay with it as well?" she asked.

"I'm looking forward to it, although I have to say I hope we don't hit Carter and Sammy with that first burst. I want to be close to those sons of bitches so I can watch them squirm before we put bullets into them."

"If you hit them, you hit them," Ava said. "Don't try to be too fine with your shots. We've got to take out the men in the front seat before we can even think about the Wings."

"I know, but I can't help feeling the way I do."

"I understand," Ava said.

They all lapsed into an uncomfortable silence, and the next few minutes seemed to stretch much longer than that. Like Ava, Sonny had always been good at waiting, but she saw that both Jimmy and Andy were looking antsy. "Jimmy, tell me about your military service," she said. "Where did you serve, and how did you become a sniper?"

Jimmy began to talk and Ava kept prompting him with more questions. At one point Andy joined in and spoke about his two-year stint in the army. Ava hadn't heard about that before, and she quizzed him until she'd wrung the subject dry. As they were talking, they forgot about the time, and both men seemed to relax.

Around nine o'clock other cars began appearing on the street and making their way into the parking garage. Ava assumed they were store employees. At nine-thirty the traffic picked up noticeably. *More store employees*, she thought, *and maybe some early-bird shoppers.* By ten there was a steady stream of cars and time began to move more quickly.

"Andy, remind me. How early did the Wings arrive for our last meeting?"

"They got there about fifteen minutes before you."

"We were on time for that meeting and it took us close to ten minutes to get from the parking garage to the restaurant, so for them to get to the restaurant fifteen minutes before us, they must have arrived at the plaza around ten-thirty," she said. "If they stay true to form, we should expect them around then."

Andy looked at his watch. "That's close."

"We'll have about a one-minute warning from the van. When we get it, you and Sonny should put on your balaclavas and get low. I'm just going to pull down my hood. Jimmy, they'll see you driving, so you can't put on a balaclava until the action starts."

"I'm not bothered by that. No one's going to recognize me."

"Wear my cap just in case," Sonny said, handing it to him.

"We should put the vests on now as well," she said. "Jimmy, you'll have to wear yours under your windbreaker."

"*Momentai*," he said, taking off the jacket.

Ava's phone rang. She looked at the screen, expecting to see Ko's number. It was Xu.

"Has something happened?" she asked.

"I just got a call from Sammy. He wanted to know where I am. I told him I've landed in Hong Kong and am on my way to Sha Tin."

"How did he sound?"

"Cautious," Xu said. "He also called Lam last night and asked him how he was getting to Hong Kong. Lam said he'd be driving and would be there early this morning."

"Are you worried he might be trying something underhanded?"

"I wouldn't put it past him."

"Well, we're here and we're in position. If he comes, we're ready for him; if he doesn't, we'll find another plan."

"I might be reading more into his phone calls than I should," Xu said. "Logically, I can't think of a good reason for him not to attend the meeting. I hinted strongly enough that we're prepared to offer them a good deal and an olive branch. If that isn't enough for him and his nephew, that's one more reason why getting rid of them is an excellent idea."

"Ava," Sonny said, putting a hand on her arm. "I have a text. The Land Rovers have arrived."

"I have to go. They're here. I'll call you when this is over," she said to Xu and abruptly ended the call.

Sonny and Andy, already wearing their vests, were pulling on the balaclavas.

Ava pulled the hood over her head and tied it tightly under her chin. She took the Beretta from her pocket, looked at her vest, and decided to forego it. "I'll lie on the floor and you take the seat," she said to Sonny, who was taking his Cobray from the gym bag. "Jimmy, you should be able to see them in your rear-view mirror any second now. When you do, pull onto the street slowly and make sure you're in front of them."

She slid onto the floor and waited for what seemed like an eternity.

Above her, Sonny was looking at his phone. "Shit, I just got a text. There are three Land Rovers," he said.

"And there are a couple of civilian cars in front of them," Jimmy said.

"You'll have to cut in," she said. "I don't care how you do it, but it has to be done.

Jimmy eased the car forward. A few seconds later he said, "I'm alongside the second civilian car. I've put on my turn signal and I'm trying to tuck in behind it. The fucking Land Rover doesn't want to let me in."

"Just do it, Jimmy," she said.

"Yep," he said.

Their van lurched to the left and Ava held her breath, half expecting to hear the sound of metal hitting metal. Instead, all she heard was the blare of the Land Rover's horn.

"The driver is pissed at me, but I'm waving at him and he's backing off a little."

"How close are we to the parking garage?" she asked.

"Maybe thirty metres. The two civilian cars are going into it. We'll have to wait for them," Jimmy said.

"Three Land Rovers means more bodyguards, and we can't be sure Sammy and Carter are in the first one," Sonny said.

"I know, but the lead vehicle still has to be our first target," Ava said. "Jimmy, while Sonny and Andy are going after it, we should focus our attention on the second vehicle. If we can get our shots off fast enough, we might be able to keep whoever is in it pinned inside. It's going to be much harder for them to shoot out than it will be for us to shoot in."

"I'm with you, Ava," Jimmy said, and then added. "The first civilian car has gone into the parking lot. The second one is going down the ramp to the ticket dispenser. We're at the top of the ramp now."

The seconds multiplied as they waited, not moving. "Is there a problem?" Ava asked.

"The driver can't seem to work the ticket dispenser," Jimmy said. "She's waving at me. I think she wants me to help her."

"You'd better go before one of the guys in the Land Rover decides to," Ava said.

Above her head Ava could hear Sonny's heavy breathing. Her eyes were closed, an irrational reaction to the fear of being seen.

Jimmy's door opened and he stepped outside. She heard him say something to the woman she couldn't quite make out and then his footsteps as he walked down the ramp. A moment later he returned, slamming his door shut. "Wing's bodyguards were looking at me but they didn't leave the Land Rover," he said.

"Could you see if Sammy and Carter are in that one?" Ava asked.

"No, I was trying not to look too nosy," Jimmy said. "Ah, there goes the woman's car and now here we go."

The Toyota rolled a few metres and came to a stop. Ava noticed Sonny wasn't breathing.

"Get ready. Starting to open my door," Jimmy said. "Three, two, one. *Now!*"

Sonny's hand had already been on the door handle, and in almost one motion he pushed the door open and swung his legs past Ava's head. As she struggled to her feet she heard the distinctive *burp, burp, burp* of the Cobray and, from the other side of the car, Andy's semi-automatic spitting out bullets. There was a wall of noise as glass shattered, bullets bit into metal, and other guns joined the fray.

Ava threw herself from the car and ran past Sonny with her gun aimed at the second Land Rover. On the opposite side, Jimmy was ahead of her, his semi-automatic already splintering windshield glass. She heard a shout from behind and froze for a second, fearing that one of Wing's men had somehow escaped the first car and was aiming at her back. As she turned, she saw Sonny pointing his gun through broken glass into the front seat of the first car. He fired twice.

Andy had joined Jimmy and both of them were firing indiscriminately at the second Land Rover. Glass flew in all directions, and Ava was wondering how anyone could survive that firestorm when a rear door opened. A bodyguard she recognized from their Maxim's meeting jumped out. He looked stunned, and when he looked in Ava's direction, she wondered if he was actually seeing her. Just as she was thinking that, he raised his gun in her direction. She dropped onto one knee, aimed, and squeezed the trigger. Her first bullet hit him in the upper chest. He reeled backwards but didn't drop his gun. She shot him again in the chest, and this time he fell, pitching forward onto his face.

Ava got to her feet and moved forward. Ahead of her, at the third Land Rover, a battle was being waged. Perhaps because they had to approach the vehicle from the rear and had been forced to wait for Sonny and Andy to launch the first attack, Ko, Feng, Machi, and Wai hadn't had the first-strike advantage. Their own car was shot up and Wai lay on the ground in a pool of blood. Feng was shooting from a sitting position, his left leg ripped by a bullet.

"Stay there," Jimmy shouted to her. He bent over close to the ground and edged his way to the front of the third Land Rover. The windshield was still mostly intact. Jimmy stood up and unleashed a torrent of bullets through it. She heard cries of pain and then saw Ko at the left side of the vehicle. He aimed his gun and fired. She couldn't imagine anyone surviving the crossfire that Ko and Jimmy were generating.

Then for a few seconds, there was quiet.

Ko looked into the third vehicle. "They're all dead," he said loudly.

Andy stood by the second Land Rover. "Same here."

"Is Sammy or Carter among them?" Ava asked.

"No, they're here," Sonny said, standing at the rear window of the first vehicle.

Ava walked down the ramp towards the Rover. "Both of them?" Ava asked. As she reached the car, the rear door opposite Sonny flew open and almost threw her back. She stumbled and nearly fell. As she tried to regain her footing, Carter Wing ran past her and down the ramp.

She didn't react, not sure in that instant if she should chase him. Before she could make that decision she heard the *burp burp burp* of Sonny's Cobray once more. Carter was almost lifted off the ground as the bullets thudded into his back. His body catapulted forward and he landed face down on the ramp. He didn't move, not even a twitch.

She stared at him, trying to process what had just happened. As she did, Andy ran past her. He stood over Wing, kicked him in the side, then aimed his gun and fired. "That's for Carlo!" he shouted as the back of Carter Wing's head exploded.

"I still have Sammy," Sonny said.

Ava turned away from the ramp and walked towards Sonny. He was pointing his gun through the rear window. She looked inside and saw Sammy cowering in the corner. He slowly raised his hands above his head.

"We came here in good faith," he said.

"You wouldn't know good faith if it spit in your face," she said.

"We had a deal with Xu."

"*This* is your deal, and it's the only one you're going to get."

"What are you going to do?"

"I'm going to kill you."

Sammy shook his head. "No, you're not."

Ava raised her gun.

"Uncle would never have approved of this."

She looked at Sammy and suddenly saw a fat, old, useless man. He was staring up at her with an almost pathetic smile on his face. She kept pointing the Beretta, but her trigger finger seemed to be frozen.

"I know you can't do this," Sammy said.

Three shots rang out, ripping Sammy's face apart. Sonny brushed past Ava, his gun still pointed at Sammy. "Sorry, boss, but I've been wanting to do that for a long time."

## 31

AVA TURNED AWAY FROM WHAT WAS LEFT OF SAMMY
Wing and ran towards Ko, with Sonny right behind her. Ko
was standing over Feng.

"We need to get out of here. He'll need a doctor," Ko said.

"How about Wai?" she asked.

"He's dead," Ko said. "Caught a bullet in the head."

"We still have to take him with us. We can't leave him."

"I know," Ko said, and then waved in the direction of the
backup car and van.

Both vehicles had been blocking the road as the battle
took place. Behind them a long line of cars stretched towards
Tsing Sha Highway. Some of the occupants had left their
vehicles to see what was going on and now formed a fright-
ened mass on the outskirts of the action.

"Your car is shot to pieces," Ava said. "Thank goodness for
the van. That was great thinking on your part."

Ko looked at Sonny. "Are the Wings dead?"

"Yeah."

"Then let's not waste any more time here."

The Nissan and the van pulled up behind Ko's car.

"Sonny, please help Ko get Feng and Wai into the back of the van," Ava said. "The rest of you get into the Nissan and head back to our meeting point. Andy, remind the driver not to speed, and take off your balaclavas as soon as you leave the property."

"Okay, boss," Andy said.

Sonny opened the back doors of the van and helped Ko lift Feng off the ground and carry him. They sat him in the back seat and then came back for Wai's body. When it had been laid in the rear of the van, Ava, Sonny, and Ko climbed in. Ava sat in the front with the driver while Ko sat next to Feng, clutching his arm to help him stay erect. Sonny sat behind them on the floor.

The van drove away slowly. Ava looked back. The Land Rovers and their own cars looked like they belonged in a junkyard. "No sign of security or any police yet," she said.

Ko looked at his watch. "I know it seemed like a long time, but it's been only ten minutes since the shooting started. Even the Hong Kong police can't move that fast."

"It was a good operation," Feng said through clenched teeth.

"They were like sitting ducks. They had no time to react," Sonny said.

Ko took off Feng's balaclava and then his own, shaking his head as if traces of wool still clung to it. "Xu wanted you to call him as soon as we were finished here," he said to Ava.

"I'll wait until we're on the highway," she said.

The van continued unimpeded along Sha Tin Centre Street, and when they saw the first sign for the Tsing Sha Highway, Ava felt her tension begin to ease. As the van reached the highway entrance she reached for her phone.

"Ava, are you all right?" Xu answered after half a ring.

She imagined him sitting in his hospital bed with the phone in his hand. "I'm fine, but Feng was shot in the leg and one of the men Sonny brought with him is dead," she said. "We've left the plaza and are on the highway, going back to the rendezvous point. So far we haven't seen any police."

"What happened with Carter and Sammy?"

"They're both dead, and so are about ten men they had with them. It was a bloodbath."

Xu paused. For a second Ava wondered if he was going to ask who had actually pulled the trigger that killed the Wings, but he said, "Will you take Feng to the clinic in Kowloon?"

"I imagine that's where we'll go."

"We're giving that doctor so much business we should become partners in his clinic," he said.

Despite the gory reality that underpinned his comment, Ava smiled. "I don't think he'd take us up on that kind of offer," she said.

"No, I don't imagine he would," Xu said. "Now, as for our dead man, did he have a family?"

"I don't know. I'll ask Sonny later."

"If he does we'll look after them, of course, and we'll cover the costs related to his funeral."

"I'm sure that will be appreciated."

He hesitated again. "Ava, I know this has been hard — "

"It was necessary," she interrupted. "It was the responsible thing to do for many reasons. But I have to say I hope you can find a way to prevent any of us having to go through that again."

"As soon as I end this call, I'll be contacting Lam. Between us we'll be reaching out to every Mountain Master in Hong

Kong, Kowloon, and the New Territories. We want them to hear the news directly from us. We also want them to know we have a plan that will bring peace to Sha Tin and Wanchai and allow me to bring my men back to Shanghai."

"And you're sure they'll accept your plan?"

"The groundwork has already been laid, but now we're in a position to finalize things. Lam's first call will be to Chan, the Mountain Master in Tai Po. Chan will call his friend Sung in Sha Tin and tell him he's just lost Carter Wing as his boss, and that we will all support him as Carter's replacement."

"What about Wanchai?"

"Fok visited Lop at the clinic this morning. Our proposal was put to him and he accepted, with one condition."

"Which is?"

"Instead of a three-month transition, he wants to make it six. He told Lop he has a lot to learn from him and doesn't want to be rushed," Xu said. "Lop was really pleased. He doesn't get many compliments from people other than you and me."

"And the other Mountain Masters are okay with Fok taking over Wanchai?"

"Most definitely, and they also have no objections to us maintaining our distribution centre in co-operation with him."

"Letting go of control in Wanchai is the smart thing to do."

"I just wish it hadn't taken this war to make me realize it."

"You would have figured it out — you always do," she said. "Besides, you have enough going on in Shanghai and in all those factories elsewhere to keep you busy. You don't need all this aggravation in Hong Kong."

"When are you going to be leaving?"

"As soon as I can pack and get to the airport."

"Will you stay long in Shanghai?"

"I'll be there until you're settled at home."

"Thanks for that," he said. "Thanks for everything."

"I only do what any *mei mei* would do."

"You're a *mei mei* unlike any other."

The car came to a stop. Ava looked out the window and saw they had arrived back at the parking lot. "I have to go," she said. "I'll call Fai when I've booked a flight. She can pass along the information to Auntie Grace and Wen. I'll see you tomorrow."

The van entered the lot and drove to the far end, where the BMWs and Mercedes were parked. Ko jumped out and opened the back door. Sonny slid out onto the tarmac. "Help me with Feng," Ko said.

The two men walked back to where Feng was sitting, his eyes closed and his jaws clenched.

"How are you feeling?" Ko asked him

"It hurts like hell."

"We'll have you at the clinic in half an hour," Sonny said.

"Let's move him to my BMW," Ko said.

Feng wrapped his arms around the necks of both men and Sonny put a hand under his good leg. Together he and Ko picked up Feng and carried him to the BMW. They lay him on the rear seat, his back against the door and his legs stretched out in front of him. "We'll be out of here in a few minutes," Ko said.

"Do whatever you have to do," said Feng. "Don't worry about me."

Ava joined Ko and Sonny. "The men are ready to put away their gear," she said.

"I'll open the trunk of my car," Sonny said.

"Before you do, we have to decide what to do about Wai," she said. "Xu has committed to taking care of the funeral expenses and looking after his family, but that doesn't resolve the immediate problem of what to do with the body."

"There's a funeral home in Fanling that's accustomed to dealing with triads," Sonny said. "Let me call them. If they're prepared to take Wai, Andy can give them the body and ditch the van."

"Who will notify his family?" Ava asked.

"He didn't have any that I'm aware of."

"That makes it a bit easier," Ko said.

"Not for Wai," Ava said, and then quickly added, "Sorry, Ko, I wasn't being critical of your remark. I'm just upset about losing him."

"No problem," Ko said.

"What about the other car? Will you just leave it here?"

"That was always our plan."

"Then I guess we should get moving," she said. "Sonny, will you please call the funeral home and then speak to Andy?"

"Sure, boss."

When Sonny had left, Ava moved closer to Ko and said softly, "Thank you for your help. This was a nasty business, and we wouldn't have come through it without you."

"From what I heard of your conversation with Xu, I think I should be thanking you," Ko said. "Has he really resolved the problems with Wanchai and Sha Tin? Can we actually start thinking about going home to Shanghai?"

"It certainly seems that way, although you won't be leaving immediately. It will take a few months to get things properly organized."

"Still, we're in a much better place than we were a few days ago," Ko said. "Those Wings were so stupid."

"Stupid and cruel."

Ko nodded but his attention was drawn to the street behind Ava. She turned and saw a police car drive by at breakneck speed.

"We should get going. We can't assume the cops won't be able to track us to here."

Ava walked over to the Mercedes, where Sonny was talking to Andy and Jimmy. "Are we ready to go?"

"The funeral home will take Wai with no questions asked," Sonny said. "Andy will drive him there and Jimmy is going to keep him company."

"That's very good of you, Jimmy," she said.

"It's only a short train ride home from there," he said.

"All the same, it is good of you," she said, and turned to Andy. "And you too, Andy. Thanks for doing this."

"It's the least I can do for Wai. I've known him for years."

Ava stepped towards him and placed her hands gently on his shoulders. "My dear friend, whatever you want, whenever you want it, all you have to do is ask."

Andy nodded, his embarrassment apparent.

"It's time for us to go now, boss," Sonny said.

"Yes. After all the work we've done and all the luck we had this morning, it would be ridiculous to let the cops catch us here."

## 32

**AVA THOUGHT ABOUT SITTING IN THE FRONT OF THE** car with Sonny, but he opened the back door with such alacrity that she decided it wasn't the time to upset the status quo. Neither of them spoke during the drive until they reached Kowloon. It was Ava who had started to say something when her phone rang. She excused herself and took the call, from a number with a Beijing area code.

"Chen?" she said.

"This is Lau Lau," he said in a smoky, trembling voice.

"How are you?" she asked, slightly taken aback at hearing from him.

"I'm grateful, as long as you aren't fucking with me about this rehab thing."

"I'm not fucking with you."

"Good, because I want to get better. I want to work again."

"And we want to help you in any way we can."

"I have this film idea..." he said, his voice trailing off.

"I know you have film ideas. That's why I suggested rehab."

"This idea will make me more enemies that any one person should have."

"I'm listening," Ava said, not sure where the conversation was headed.

"It's about Tiananmen Square in 1989 — the protest, the massacre."

"Yes…"

"The boy, the young man who stood in front of the tanks and defied them to run over him," Lau Lau said. "I keep thinking about him. I can't get him out of my head."

"You want to make a film about him?"

"No."

"Lau Lau, you're confusing me."

"I want to make a film about his mother. I want to tell the story of Tiananmen through her eyes," he said. "The protest went on for weeks, and every morning her son left his apartment and went to the square. And every morning she begged him not to go, because she had lived through the Cultural Revolution — she knew what the government was capable of doing to their own. She had fears based in reality; he had hopes rooted in pipe dreams."

"I still don't understand the basis for the film," she said.

"The night the protest ended, the night the PLA used tanks and guns to kill twenty thousand, fifty thousand — perhaps even a hundred thousand — unarmed people in the square, her son didn't come home," he said. "The film is about her search for him, for any scrap of him that was left after the tanks ran over him."

"You do know that this film could never be made in China."

"I know."

"And could never be distributed in China."

"I know that too."

"So why are you telling me this now?" she asked.

"Because it's the only film I really want to make before I die," he said. "It's the only film worth the pain of going through rehab."

Ava drew a deep breath. "Lau Lau, go to rehab. While you're there, write that script. If Chen and Pang Fai tell me it will make a great film, then I won't care about the politics. I'll put up the money to have it made."

"Chen is a good judge of a script."

"So I've been told."

"Fai isn't so bad either."

"And both of them want you to succeed."

"With a film that will never be shown in China?"

"Your work is universal. We'll find a market that will appreciate it."

He became quiet and then blurted, "I'm going into rehab."

"I couldn't be more pleased."

"And when I come out, I'm going to make a film that's so good the government will want to put me in jail, or worse."

"Yes, Lau Lau, I believe you're still capable of making a film that's that good. And trust me, we'll stand by you when you do."

"Then I'll talk to you again soon," he said, ending the conversation.

Ava saw Sonny eyeing her through the rear-view mirror. "That was Lau Lau, the film director. We're thinking of backing him."

"Making movies? That's something new for you," Sonny said.

"Not just me. May Ling and Amanda and Pang Fai are all prepared to participate," Ava said. "Besides, we wouldn't actually be making movies, we'd just be making it possible for movies to be made."

"Still, it's a different kind of business for all of you."

"Uncle always encouraged me to try new things. I remember him telling me that people who don't welcome change are condemned to live in the past."

"Like Sammy Wing."

"What do you mean?"

"He couldn't let go, could he. His best days were behind him, and even though Xu offered him a way to live out the rest of his life with respect and in comfort, he couldn't adapt."

"I know. I still regret that it had to end the way it did," she said.

Ava saw Sonny eyeing her again, and she could sense that he was uncomfortable. "Is something bothering you?" she asked.

"Yes. I should never have taken it upon myself to shoot Sammy. That was your right. In fact, when I think about everything you went through with him, it was almost destined," Sonny said. "I'm sorry I got between the two of you."

"Is that your way of trying to make me feel better?"

"I don't get what you're trying to say."

"You know I might not have shot him. You know I might not have been able to pull the trigger," she said. "Even though he tried to kill me twice and he couldn't let go, you knew it was possible I couldn't bring myself to do it. So you did it for me."

"Ava —"

"Sonny, I'm not upset. I'm grateful. It was the right thing to do."

He nodded and his shoulders seemed to settle. "He just couldn't let go."

"Unlike Uncle."

"It wasn't that easy for Uncle either for the first few years after he left the Fanling gang."

"How so?"

Sonny shrugged. "Maybe I shouldn't be talking about this."

"No, you started it and now I want you to finish."

"Well, when you're a triad, you're in or you're out. When Uncle left, a lot of people stopped having anything to do with him. It wasn't that they didn't respect him; it was that he wasn't a part of their daily life anymore. That bothered him, because the gang was the only family he had," Sonny said. "What was strange was that while he was Mountain Master, he had a reputation for being a loner. Outside of Uncle Fong and, before him, Xu's father, not many people could say they knew him well. What no one guessed was how much they all meant to him and how intensely loyal he was to each of them."

"How did he get past that?"

"He started the debt-collection business. He brought me, Carlo, and Andy into it and we became a new family. Then he cared about every client as if they were family, and he would go to any length to help them. When you came along, you filled the biggest void in his life — or however you want to express it."

"The biggest void?"

"He said he'd loved four women in his life. The first three — his mother, his sister, and his fiancée — had all died years ago. You were the only one alive, and he worried about you constantly. In fact, there were many times when he thought about closing down the business, but he was afraid that if he did, he wouldn't see you again."

"Of course I would have seen him."

"I think he knew that, but maintaining the business kept you close — although there was a cost," Sonny said. "He knew you would do anything for him, for us, and for the clients. He watched you take risk after risk, and every time a job ended it was like fifty pounds had been lifted from his shoulders."

"He never once mentioned anything like that to me."

"That's because he knew you would be respectful enough to listen but then you'd go off and do what you thought had to be done anyway," Sonny said. "He said you reminded him of himself as a young man, and that scared him, because he'd always been willing to do what he thought was the right thing, regardless of the personal cost."

"I think he saw more in me than there is."

"No, he didn't," Sonny said. "He thought you were special. And those of us who know you agree with him."

"I can accept different, but I have trouble with special."

"Uncle wouldn't agree."

A rebuttal and then a question formed in her mind. She put them both aside. Uncle had often told her that she should learn to take compliments. This time she would.

**COMING SOON**
From House of Anansi Press
in July 2020

Read on for a preview of the next thrilling
Ava Lee novel, *The Diamond Queen of Singapore*

**AVA LEE WAS NERVOUS. IT WAS AN UNUSUAL STATE FOR** her, especially given the circumstances. She was in her car, an Audi A6, driving north on the Don Valley Parkway, in the centre of Toronto, towards the northern suburb of Richmond Hill, where her mother, Jennie Lee, lived. Normally, visiting her mother was something Ava looked forward to, but this time was different, because sitting next to her was Pang Fai, one of China's leading film actresses — and Ava's lover. Fai was about to meet Jennie for the first time, and to complicate matters, Jennie had invited some of her friends to join them.

Toronto was Ava's home, but ever since graduating from Babson College in Massachusetts with a degree in forensic accounting, she had spent almost as much time travelling as she had in the city of her birth. The travel was part of her job as a partner in a debt-collection business run out of Hong Kong by an elderly man called Uncle — a man Ava treated like the grandfather she never had. Uncle had a web of international contacts, and the collection jobs they took on — all of them large, usually involving millions of dollars — had allowed Ava to see almost all of Asia, much of Europe, and even parts of the Americas. When Uncle died, Ava gave up the business and started an investment firm with her good friend May Ling Wong and her sister-in-law Amanda Yee. Amanda was married to Ava's half-brother Michael — one of her father's four sons from his first marriage, and part of a complicated family structure comprised of three wives and eight children spread across three continents.

The investment firm now had ownership or part owner-ship of a furniture manufacturing company in Borneo, a trading company in Hong Kong, logistics and warehousing operations in Shanghai and Beijing, and PÖ, a dynamic fashion design business based in Shanghai that sold into the international market. Ava's responsibilities related to those businesses kept her on the move, and had brought her into contact with people who were becoming as impor-tant to her as Uncle had been. One such person was a man named Xu, the head of the triad organization in Shanghai, Uncle's godson, and someone — unknown to Ava — whom Uncle had mentored. It was only after Uncle's death that Ava and Xu connected, but now they were extremely close, referring to each other as *mei mei* ("little sister") and *ge ge* ("big brother").

It was also through her new business associations that Ava had met Fai. Fai was hired to be the spokesperson for PÖ, but Ava's relationship with her quickly developed beyond any business ties. The two women had now been lovers for almost a year, and they were still intensely happy even as they struggled to find time to be together. Their work com-mitments had been one impediment, and the fact that Fai's home was in Beijing was another. But they were now in a position where Fai had no scheduled film work, and Ava had no business issues that required her physical presence. The result was that they had spent the previous month together in Beijing, in Shanghai, and in Fai's home city of Yantai. When they were in Shanghai, Ava had to go to Hong Kong for several days to handle a problem for Xu, but other than that, they'd been inseparable.

The trip to Yantai had been particularly memorable. Fai's sexual identity was something she'd kept secret, certain it would ruin her career if it became public. On a private basis she had engaged in mostly clandestine one-night stands until she met Ava. Fai's secrecy had extended to her immediate family until she and Ava visited Yantai. Fai had dropped some hints to her mother before they arrived, but her mother obviously hadn't picked up on them because she spent their first hour together trying to sort out separate sleeping arrangements for Fai and Ava. Finally, Fai said, "Mum, Ava and I are going to sleep together. We're in love. I know you would have preferred me to bring home a man, but that's not how it is, and that's not how it is going to be."

It had been awkward for a few days, but eventually everyone began to relax, and at one point, Fai's father had said to her, "I never liked your taste in men. None of them were worthy of you, especially that Lau Lau. It is nice to see you being so comfortable with someone."

The mention of Lau Lau caused Ava and Fai to exchange glances. He had been China's finest film director until liquor, drugs, and the pressure of concealing his true sexuality destroyed his career. Ava — a huge fan of his work — met Lau Lau while she was in Beijing visiting Fai. She had paid for him to go into rehab, and over Fai's objections had decided to finance his writing a new film script. Fai thought nothing good would come from it. Ava agreed that was possible, but was willing to take the chance.

After Yantai, Ava and Fai went back to Beijing for a few days, and then decided to fly to Toronto so Fai could meet Ava's family and friends. Ava's sexuality wasn't a secret to her closest friends and immediate family, but it wasn't something she talked about openly, especially with Jennie. Culturally, even in liberal Canada, the Chinese community was generally averse to the idea of same-sex couples. Ava's mother didn't share those views, but neither was she loudly supportive. She loved her daughter and was accepting of whatever Ava wanted to do with her life, but that didn't mean she wanted to discuss it with Ava or anyone else. That suited Ava just fine, and she and her mother had happily co-existed knowing what the reality was, but not needing to talk about it. Fai's visit would likely change that, and that made Ava nervous.

Ava and Fai had arrived in Toronto three days ago and had spent their time quietly getting adjusted to the time change. Ava owned a condo in Yorkville, a trendy district in the heart of the city, just steps away from a myriad of high-end shops, first-class restaurants and museums, and Queen's Park, the seat of the provincial government. If she wanted to take Fai further afield, the subway line was almost at Ava's front door, and sights like Niagara Falls were just a few hours away. But the drive to Richmond Hill was the first time they had gotten into a car.

Ava contacted her mother on their second day in town to tell her they had arrived. Ava had already told her that Fai was a "special friend" and that she would be bringing her to Toronto. Jennie's first reaction was to organize a party for them. To be fair, Ava knew that her mother was an avid fan of

Chinese cinema, so her wanting to meet Pang Fai the movie actress should have been expected. But a party was too much.

"How about you just invite a few of your friends and perhaps some of mine for a few drinks and appetizers?" Ava had suggested.

"What about husbands?" Jennie asked.

"No men."

"Good thinking," Jennie said. "What time?"

Ava knew that if Jennie and her friends weren't out playing baccarat at the nearby casino, then they would be playing mah-jong at one of their homes until the early hours. "Would four o'clock work?"

"That's perfect."

"And Mummy, not too many people, please."

"I'll try to restrain myself," Jennie said.


"I can't believe how green everything is," Fai said, interrupting Ava's train of thought.

Ava smiled. Their drive took them through the Don Valley, a long strip of inner-city wilderness, but Fai had voiced the same sentiment several times during their walks through more urban parts of the city that were interlaced with parks and trees. She had also marvelled at the city's air quality and the brightly-coloured sky, which wasn't a surprising reaction from someone who lived in Beijing, where the smog-laden sky was various shades of gray and black, and where on many days the air was so foul that residents wore masks over their noses and mouths. "When you live here, you don't think twice about it," Ava said.

They approached Highway 7, the southern boundary of

Richmond Hill, and Ava exited the parkway. She drove west past a nearly continuous line of strip malls filled with stores and restaurants signed in Chinese. Ava noticed that they caught Fai's interest and said, "There are more than half a million Chinese living in and around Toronto. This is one of the most popular neighbourhoods for them."

"And this is where you were raised?"

"Yes, but I went to school in the city, at Havergal College, which isn't that far from my condo," Ava said. "You'll meet my best Canadian friend, Mimi, today. She and I met at Havergal, so you can grill her about what I was like as a teenager."

"When you say 'best friend,' do you mean she was a girl-friend, a gay girlfriend?"

"No," Ava said. "She's straight. In fact, she married my friend Derek Chiang. I wasn't crazy about the idea at the time, but it has worked out very well; I'm the godmother to their daughter."

Ava turned right onto Leslie Street and started north. After three kilometres the landscape began to change from office and retail buildings to houses, and when Ava turned left onto 16th Avenue and then took the next right, they were in a completely residential community of two-storey brick homes of mostly similar design. When Ava's father, Marcus, bought the house for Jennie, it had just been built; the driveway had been gravel and the front yard a sea of mud. Ava had never liked the uniformity of the neighbourhood, but her mother loved the house, especially the front yard, which she kept neatly trimmed, and the back yard, where she maintained an herb garden. The house was now worth at least a million dollars and was her mother's largest asset.

"The houses are so large," Fai said. In Beijing, Fai lived in a small row house that shared a common courtyard with about ten others, in a compound located in a hutong that was several hundred years old. Her entire living space was no more than 200 square metres. Her parents' home in Yantai was only marginally larger.

"They are more than most people need, but that was the style when these houses were built, partially because land was so cheap. That isn't the case anymore, so building lots have shrunk in size and so have the houses."

Ava turned onto her mother's street. Jennie's house was the third on the left, and the first thing Ava noticed was how many cars were parked on the driveway and along the street out front. She hoped they all didn't belong to people her mother had invited, but she had a sinking feeling that they did.

She found a parking spot three houses down from her mother's. She and Fai stepped out of the car and into the bright sunshine of an early summer day, the heat moderated by a slight breeze. Wearing black linen slacks, black pumps, and a pink, long-sleeved Brooks Brothers' button-down shirt, Ava was dressed far more formally than was typical for a visit to her mother's, but she knew this was an occasion when her mother would have been disappointed by anything less. Fai wore a loose-fitting light blue sleeveless cotton dress that ended just above her knees. Even in something so plain, in flat shoes, without make-up, and with her hair hanging loosely around her face, Ava thought she looked incredible — and said so.

"I'm trying to look as professional as you, but we do have different styles."

"You're a movie star. No one expects you to look professional," Ava said, and then caught herself. "That didn't come out the way I intended."

Fai laughed. "Is your mother as direct as you?"

"Only with me, Marian, and my father," Ava said as they started up the driveway.

The front door opened before they reached it. "Welcome, girls," Jennie Lee said, her voice filled with excitement.

Ava didn't know her mother's exact age because Jennie had always waved off any questions. "Why does it matter what age I am? All that matters is the age I feel, and I feel as young as I've ever felt," she'd say.

At five feet four inches, Jennie was an inch taller than Ava and just as slim and fine-boned. She parted her hair — dyed jet black every few months — down the middle and had it stylishly curved to mid-ear. She spent several thousand dollars a year on skin creams. Ava didn't know if the creams were the reason her mother's skin was still unlined and wrinkle-free, but Jennie was convinced they were, and would have gone without food before forgoing them.

"Hi Mummy," Ava said.

Jennie stepped out of the house and walked towards them. It was normal for them to hug when they met, but this time Jennie's attention was fixed on Fai. She held out her right hand, palm down, inviting Fai to take it. When Fai did, Jennie said, "It is such an honour to have you here. And my goodness, you are even more beautiful in person than on the screen. How is it possible?"

"And now I can see where Ava gets her looks," Fai said. "Are you sure you are her mother and not her older sister?"

Unlike Ava, Jennie was never bashful about accepting

compliments, and she responded to Fai with a smile and a slight nod of her head. "Let's go inside. Everyone is so eager to meet you."

Ava had hoped that her mother would restrict her invitation list to her mah-jong and casino friends, but when they entered the house they found themselves facing several clusters of women, maybe twenty in all.

"Most of you know my daughter, Ava, and this — of course — is her friend Pang Fai."

"I think I'm going to faint," one of them said, which generated a wave of nervous laughter.

"Ava, when your mother said you were bringing Pang Fai to visit, I didn't believe her," said a woman who Ava recognized as one of Jennie's long-time mah-jong partners.

"Why didn't you believe me?" asked Jennie.

"Because it was too fantastic to be true, or so I thought," the woman said. "I apologize to you, Jennie."

"How are you enjoying Canada?" another woman asked Fai.

"Well, I've only just arrived, but so far I really like it. Everything is so clean here — especially the air."

Someone else started to say something, but Jennie cut her off, "Ladies, that's enough questions for now. Let me get Ava and Pang Fai a drink, and maybe something to eat. They're not rushing off, so you'll have time to talk to them."

"Ava," a voice said from the entrance to the kitchen.

Ava turned and saw her sister Marian. She rushed towards her and the two sisters hugged. "When did you get here?" Ava asked.

"I flew in this morning."

"And when do you go back?"

"Early tomorrow morning."

"Can't you stay a bit longer?"

"My regular sitter wasn't available, and Bruce is in the middle of a federal-provincial government negotiation. Getting him to stay home with the girls today was enough of a feat."

Bruce was Marian's husband and a senior public servant in Ottawa. Marian was trained as a lawyer, but after the birth of the first of her two daughters she became a stay-at-home mom. It wasn't a life that Ava would have chosen, and although Jennie had stayed home with Ava and Marian, she still complained from time to time about Marian wasting her education.

"How are Bruce and Mummy getting along these days?" Ava asked.

"Same as usual — they're not," Marian said with a tight smile. "I've given up hoping they ever will."

"What are you two talking about?" Jennie asked as she guided Fai towards the kitchen.

"Bruce," Ava said.

"My daughter married a *gweilo*," Jennie said to Fai. "He's a nice person, but we don't get along all the time — although he is very kind to my daughter and he did give me two beautiful granddaughters."

Ava started to say something but stopped. There was no point in discussing Bruce with her mother. They were oil and water, and their different approaches to life were never going to be reconciled. "What do you have to drink?" she asked.

"Just about anything you can name, but most of the women are drinking wine," Jennie said. "And since you are driving, you should probably stick to one glass."

"There's also lots to eat — dumplings, spring rolls, cha siu bao," Marian said.

"I'll eat later. For now I'll have a glass of Chardonnay," Ava said.

"That will suit me as well," Fai said.

"I'll get them for you," Jennie said.

When Jennie left, Marian said to Fai, "You have caused quite a sensation. Mummy's friends were here early with their smart phones fully charged. Fair warning about that, they'll want to take selfies and film themselves with you. I'm surprised how tech savvy they all are."

"I am rather accustomed to dealing with fans," Fai said.

"Of course you must be, it is just that I find this particular group of women rather overpowering at times. Some of them are really smart, but given their situations they don't have many ways of expressing it."

"What do you mean by 'their situations'?" Fai asked.

Ava turned to Fai. "Marian means that many of them are second or third wives like our mother. Their husbands support them but spend most of their time in Hong Kong with their first wives, so these women have a lot of free time on their hands."

"Which they fill with mah-jong, long dinners, and casino outings," Marian said.

"That's true to a point, if still a little unfair," Ava said. "I know most of them like to gamble, but I think socializing is a large part of that experience for them."

"Bruce doesn't see it that way."

"He's also not Chinese, and he's not dependent on a small circle of friends like Mummy."

Marian lowered her head. "Sorry, you are right, I shouldn't

be so judgmental. It is just that when you live as far away as I do and have such a different life, it's easy to forget what Mummy went through."

Ava reached for her sister and pulled her close. Disagreements about their mother and her behaviour had characterized their relationship for years, and Bruce's attitude towards Jennie had only intensified things. Ava had resolved several years ago not to engage, and felt badly every time she did. "I'm sorry too. I know it is difficult to understand her sometimes."

"Ah, how nice to see my daughters so close," Jennie said as she returned with two glasses of wine. She watched Fai take a sip, then added, "Can we leave the kitchen and mingle a little?"

Fai took another sip and smiled at Jennie. "Mrs. Lee, I'll be happy to mingle, and I don't mind people taking a few pictures, but I'm really here to meet you, Marian . . . and Ava mentioned her friend Mimi?"

"Yes, please keep everything in moderation," Ava said to her mother. "And speaking of Mimi, where is she? Did you invite her?"

"Of course I did. She called me last night to confirm my address," Jennie said. "I'm surprised she isn't here yet. She was always a punctual girl."

Ava reached into her bag and took out her phone. She called Mimi's number. When it went directly to voicemail, Ava ended the call and sent a text that read, Where are you? Anxious to see you.

"Shall we go into the living room?" Jennie asked.

"Sure," Ava said, and then looped her arm through Fai's. "I'll stay close."

For the next hour Fai circulated among the guests, posing for pictures and chatting, with Ava by her side and Jennie hovering nearby. Twice, Jennie left to refill Fai's glass, and Ava and Fai took just five minutes to eat a small plate of food that Marian brought to them. "When everyone leaves we can have a proper meal just the four of us," Jennie said.

By five o'clock there was still no sign of Mimi. Ava checked her phone frequently to see if she had replied to the text. She hadn't, and Ava began to worry. Mimi was conscientious as well as punctual, the kind of person who would let them know she was going to be late. Ava tried her phone again with no success, and then sent another text. As the guests began to leave and things calmed, Ava found a quiet corner and phoned Derek.

His phone rang four times and Ava was readying to leave a message when he answered. "Yes."

Even in that one word Ava sensed distress. "Derek, its Ava, has something happened to Mimi? I'm at my mother's. She was supposed to join us."

"She's okay. I mean, nothing has happened to her," he said, the distress even more evident.

"But something has happened or she would be here."

"Yes, it's her father," Derek said.

"Is he ill?"

There was a long silence, and then Derek said, "He's dead."

Ava struggled to respond and finally found the words to say, "When, how?"

"This morning..." he began, and then went strangely silent again.

"What about this morning?" she asked, and then added almost impatiently. "Derek, don't make me guess."

"Mrs. Gregory found him in the garden shed around lunchtime. He had spent the morning trimming bushes and cutting the grass," he said. "She watched him go into the shed with his tools when he was finished, and then she heard a gunshot... He had put a gun into his mouth and pulled the trigger."

## ACKNOWLEDGEMENTS

It never ceases to amaze me how engaged many of my readers are with Ava and the people in her life. Every book seems to generate more emails than the one before. *The Goddess of Yantai* was no exception, and that makes me quite anxious to see what kind of reaction *The Mountain Master* generates, since it is — in many ways — more reflective of the earlier books. So, if you are reading this after you've read the novel, email me or get in touch any way you wish, and let me know what you think of it.

As always, I had help and input from a great many people, and I wish to thank them. Their contributions were invaluable.

First, the team at House of Anansi, led by my editor, Doug Richmond, and the managing editor, Maria Golikova. Between them, they make the book-writing process as smooth and as stress-free as I imagine it probably can be.

Then there is my publicist, Laura Meyer, who does a thankless job in a difficult age with as much grace and enthusiasm and professionalism as anyone could muster.

My agents — Bruce Westwood and Carolyn Forde — were again completely supportive. Carolyn left the agency before this book was published, and I wish her well in her future endeavours. Bruce soldiers on, and he is a fine man to have on your side.

My first readers are a special group, and I owe them so much. Thanks to my wife, Lorraine, Kristine Wookey, and Robin Spano. My list of readers of the Advanced Reading Copies keeps expanding, and their input and influence does as well. Thank you, Catherine Rosebrugh, John Kruithof, Carol Shetler, Ashok Ramchandani, Christina Sit, and Carleena Chiang for your comments and eagle eyes.

**IAN HAMILTON** is the author of thirteen novels in the Ava Lee series. His books have been shortlisted for numerous prizes, including the Arthur Ellis Award, the Barry Award, and the Lambda Literary Prize, and are national bestsellers. BBC Culture named Hamilton one of the ten mystery/crime writers from the past thirty years who should be on your bookshelf. The Ava Lee series is being adapted for television.

# NOW AVAILABLE
## from House of Anansi Press

### The Ava Lee series

**Prequel and Book 1**

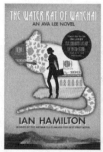

**Book 2**

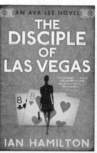

**Book 3**

**Book 4**

**Book 5**

**Book 6**

**Book 7**

**Book 8**

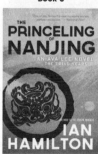

**Book 9**

**Book 10**

**Book 11**

www.houseofanansi.com • www.facebook.com/avaleenovels
www.ianhamiltonbooks.com • www.twitter.com/avaleebooks

## ALSO AVAILABLE
## from House of Anansi Press

Uncle returns in...
The Lost Decades of Uncle Chow Tung

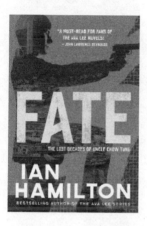

## COMING SOON

January 2020

January 2021